HEARING HIDDEN VOICES

THE ERASEHER SERIES BOOK THREE

SARA NICHOL QUINCY

First published by Milcann Hunnee 2022

This novel is entirely a work of fiction. The names, characters and incidents portrayed in it are the work of the author's imagination. Any resemblance to actual persons, living or dead, events or localities is entirely coincidental.

Sara Nichol Quincy asserts the moral right to be identified as the author of this work.

Sara Nichol Quincy has no responsibility for the persistence or accuracy of URLs for external or third-party Internet Websites referred to in this publication and does not guarantee that any content on such Websites is, or will remain, accurate or appropriate.

ISBN: 978-1-957719-04-7 (Epub)

ISBN: 978-1-957719–05-4 (Paperback)

ISBN: 978-1-957719-12-2 (Hardcover)

SaraNicholQuincy.com

Milcann Hunnee
PUBLISHING COMPANY

For Phoenix

The scared little girl that I locked up in a dark place in my mind for so many years because I thought I hated you and that you would never be good enough. I was wrong; you've achieved more than I could have ever imagined and I'm sorry. You are enough; you have always been. This is for you beautiful, be free. I'm proud of you!

CONTENTS

I

THE VOICE

"Jump!"

didn't understand why I felt like I did. I knew the voice was in my head, not some external person speaking to me. Not only that, but I was beginning to hear it all the time after we got to New York. I don't know where it came from or why it was there, but it had gotten stronger, and I had no idea how to make it stop.

I should have stopped listening to it, but I couldn't. So often I felt like I had no choice but to listen. It was like something inside myself, trying to protect me from feeling pain—emotional pain. I wanted to fight it, but I felt powerless like I had no control, no choice but to relent to it, hoping if I obeyed it would stop the pain.

"Just jump, that way it will all be over!"

I couldn't help but question it this time as I looked down. I was high, very high… *Why am I this high?* I didn't want to listen to it or do what it said. *Why am I even here? Think about Jake.* I tried everything I could to change my mind. *What will this do to Jake?*

"You're replaceable."

It was right; I was nothing but a Gypsyin. Jake could surely find someone else just as easily as he'd found me. I didn't have a child with him yet. I didn't even know if I could anymore. Just like his mom said, I wasn't good for him; he could do better. I didn't want my thoughts to go there, to agree with the voice, but I couldn't help it. They concurred with each other so well. They were giving me no choice. I had to do it. He couldn't love me. I was holding him back. I couldn't let him love me. I wasn't good for him, and it would be selfish of me to hold on... I couldn't hold on.

I looked down one more time, secretly stalling, rebelling against the voice, just hoping for more time to think. Maybe there was some way I was wrong. If I were, there would be no way back. I could only make the choice once. I needed to know if it was the right one. It was so far down. I hesitated... *What am I doing?...*

I heard the roof's door open behind me. I froze for a moment, trying to think about what it meant. *Have I been caught? Will I have to tell whoever it is what I'm doing?*

"You should feel ashamed of yourself. You had your chance, and you didn't take it. Now you look stupid!"

Before I thought much further, I couldn't help but turn to see who it was. "Lane?"

"Kaleah, what are you doing up here?" He didn't sound mad. He asked calmly like he already knew the answer, as he gently shut the door behind him and cautiously walked closer to me.

I didn't respond. I was still frozen, and I knew I was caught. Now I felt horrible and ashamed just like the voice told me I should. I didn't want to answer him. I didn't want to admit anything to him. I didn't want him to tell Jake.

"It's okay, it doesn't matter why you're here... but... Miles is gonna be here soon. So... if you don't want him to read my note saying you ran away, then we should hurry and get back down there before he does."

"If he finds out I left you he's going to be really mad at me. I hate it when he's mad at me."

He slowly moved closer as we talked, trying not to make any quick movements. He swallowed as he hesitated to respond. "No, he won't be mad. He'll just be happy I found you… Why don't you come here? You're too close to the edge. Just walk over to me, okay?"

"You're lying!" I couldn't help but call him out. I knew Jake would be upset with me.

"Kaleah… *please*… Can we talk about this on our way back?" He cautiously toed the ground like he wanted to come closer, but didn't feel comfortable near the edge like I had.

"I don't want to talk about it on the way back. I don't want him mad at me again. Please don't tell him. I don't want him to yell at me again like he did this morning."

"Kaleah… This morning was a misunderstanding. Give him time and he'll see it. Please… just get away from the edge. If you fall or if anything happens to you, and I didn't stop it… he'll kill me! Do you want that? You don't want him upset with me either do you?"

I shook my head. He was right. I didn't want Jake mad at him, either.

"Good girl… Just come over here then, and we can put this all behind us, all right?"

I began to nod, agreeing to walk over to him when a thought popped into my head, stopping me. "Wait… How did you find me up here?"

Much Much Earlier…

"Lane, I know you think it's still safe to go sixty miles an hour down the freeway, but it's not, so slow down."

"Oh… Sorry, Miles. Am I waking her up?"

"No, she's still out, but I can't put a seat belt on her back here when she's laying down like this, so be more careful and don't drive so fast."

"Sorry, man. I can… it's just hard when I've hit an area without all the abandoned cars. It's not every day that I get to drive out of the state. I bet that was a nice perk when you were still working, right?"

"No… it was boring. I'm glad to be done with it."

"Boring? What, are you serious? I would have loved the agency to put me in Track and Capture."

"I had to do a lot of things I'm not all that proud of, especially while I was still in the unit in New York. So no, just be happy that the only position you ever took was being a Recon Scout."

"Nah, talk about boring. All it feels like I ever do is watch people. I can't even go in and do anything to them, like at least make me a spy or something… I didn't know it was hard for you in New York. I thought you just got transferred. What things are you talking about? What did you have to do, if you don't mind me asking?"

"*After* I made T and C, most of my captures in New York weren't Gypsyins. The problem was before that. The ones I caught and brought in… especially the women… it bothered me not knowing what they did with them after I turned 'em in. I mean, I know what the protocol was, but it just never felt right. I think they were using them for other things after they erased them, you know… The protocol in Nashville is to release them though, so I asked to be transferred. I didn't want that on my conscience."

"Wow, man, you never told me all that… Is that how you wound up with her? Like, I mean… I heard the story you told her about how you met and all but why would your commanding officer send you that far south for a random Gypsyin? I know you told me some stuff already on the way to get her, but the whole thing is still a little odd."

"No, you're right. There're things I haven't told you about her yet… I'm not trying to keep anything from ya, man, I just… I'll tell you when I know it's safe to do so."

"You know I was listening this morning when you were back there talking to her… You said you were telling her everything you still hadn't told her yet… So does that mean—"

"Shhh… yeah there's more… I'll let her know when she's ready."

"Ok… I just know you said you were telling her everyth—"

"Lane!"

"Sorry… I thought you said she was asleep… I just—"

"She is… but I don't know how much she can hear while she's asleep. She's got some unique talents. I still don't think I've discovered them all."

"Ah, talents like… uh, is she uh—"

"Stop… I didn't mean sexually if that's what you're thinking. I'm not talking to you about that part of our relationship. You know that's not what I meant, anyway."

"Dude, you never had an issue telling me about that part of you and Kat's relationship… Speaking of which, you haven't mentioned or even asked about her once this whole trip. Aren't you even a little curious how she's doing?"

"No, she made it clear we were done, so her life is her business, not mine. Besides, that was over a year ago. It's obvious I've moved on. I don't need to ask about her."

"Good, I'm glad you say it like that. To be honest, I never liked her. I just never told you 'cause I didn't want to hurt your feelings, but I'm glad she broke it off before the wedding. Man, that would have sucked if you got trapped with her as your wife."

"Are you serious? How did you hide that for four years?"

"Uh, yeah that's a good question. I don't know… She was just too prissy for you. I like Kaleah, though. She's really sweet. You should keep her!"

"That's the plan… You know when me and Kat split I was upset at first but then after a while I was kind of shocked when I realized I didn't really care. I thought there was something wrong with me, like

Kat might have been right. After I got promoted, maybe I did change… Maybe I was too hard… too calloused, you know? When you spend so many years with someone you're planning the rest of your life with, you'd think it would have torn me up not having her anymore, but it didn't… Kaleah showed me something… I hadn't even known her for a full two weeks when I felt something for her I hadn't ever felt for another woman before… Tell me, Lane, how does that make any sense? How can I love her so much, and I haven't even spent that much time with her?"

"Ah… good question… I don't think I'm the one you should ask for advice about love, though. I still can't get myself to talk to a woman I like without blanking, let alone make her fall in love with me."

"True…"

"Have you thought about how you're going to tell your mom she's a Gypsyin?"

"I'm not."

"Okay?… Dude, your mom is like wicked scary, though. You never keep secrets from aunt Liz, she'll tan your hide!"

"You know you're an adult now right, Lane? You don't have to be afraid of my mom anymore."

"Whatever, you know what I meant. If she finds out Kaleah is a Gypsyin and you weren't the one to tell her—"

"She'll get over it, just like she got over the fact that I wasn't going to marry Katherine. It might hurt her feelings to think so, but she isn't in charge of my life anymore. I'll be with whatever woman I want to be with, Gypsyin… Sicari… it doesn't matter."

"Dude, Gypsyin is one thing, but don't even talk about being with a Sicari, that's heresy… Let's just say you and Kaleah stay together forever… yeah that sounds good… If not, you sound like you're willing to go past taboo into the realm of stupidity, and we can't have that. I won't stand by and let you do something that dumb. You'll get yourself killed doing that shit… naw, man… naw."

"I get it, Lane, chill!"

"Okay, sorry. It's just been a rough couple days of driving. It won't be long until we're there, though. Where were you taking her first, your parents? Too bad you sold your house when you went to Nashville... We can take her to mine if you wanna stay there for a while with her. My guest room never gets used, so you're welcome to it."

"Thanks, I appreciate it, but I don't think your place would be as safe as my parents'. To anyone from the outside she'll just blend in with the other Gypsyins they have working for them."

"Yeah, that's probably true. I hope that goes over well when you tell her."

"Tell her what?"

"That people in New York use Gypsyins as sla... uh... indentured servants... And your parents have three. But not to worry, she'll fit right in. That might get a little warped in the bedroom department... but hey, whatever floats your boat."

"Lane, shut the hell up!"

"Okay, it was a joke, but for real... What are you going to do about her papers?"

"She's not getting any freakin' papers, Lane. She's not a damn dog."

"Shh, you tryin' to wake her up? I'm just saying... I know you don't want to treat her like she's something you own, I get it. But if she ever gets caught, and she doesn't have her papers saying she's yours... well... You know they'll take her and eras—"

"Shut up, I know... Dude... just shut up. Do you not think I've already thought of all that?"

"Well... I would have thought so since you're normally good about that kind of thing, but you don't act like you have a plan this time, so I just thought—"

"I do... so stop thinking, it doesn't suit you."

"Ha... funny... you're so funny, Miles... not!"

. . .

The car ride was beyond soothing. I don't know how long I was asleep, but waking up with my head in Jake's lap felt like heaven considering what I had been used to the previous three weeks dealing with Luca. I loved the way it felt being with Jake again, the way he cared for me. It was different from the way Luca cared for me. Jake was more sincere like his love was real, not just what a physical lust would drive him to do.

I also felt better after he finished telling me everything else he knew about me. There were so many things he said he didn't want to tell me while I was around Luca, for obvious reasons. He explained everything about how we met and why. How he captured me, but then we fell in love. The story sounded so romantic I felt a little sad that I couldn't remember any of it myself. I trusted him now, though. The things he told me, they all made sense, so much so that I began to feel bad that I would have ever believed anything Luca said in the first place.

I told Jake that while I was with Luca I had had a few flashbacks that helped me see Luca wasn't telling me the whole truth and that's why I felt more confident trying to escape. He seemed more interested in that than anything else, like it wasn't usual after being erased. Thankfully, he explained the other man in my vision was someone who wasn't a problem to me anymore. He seemed quite uncomfortable with my description of him and didn't want to give me many details but just knowing he was out of the picture was enough. I didn't need to know more than that.

"Here, baby, you wanna sit up and look out the window? You've never seen New York before, you might enjoy it."

I was enjoying my head being in his lap, but he was right. How could I deny the lure of seeing a sight I'd never seen before? I sat up to look around, for whatever reason expecting to see large buildings and lots of people, but in contrast that was the opposite of what we were passing. "This doesn't look like New York," I said, looking back at him as he leaned over, reaching for my seat belt to fasten it for me.

"No, not the city, but the state, yes," he smiled, unaware that I felt like he just tricked me out of my cozy place.

"Aren't we going into the city?"

"Well, yeah… it'll be the city. You have to realize though, when the war happened, as everyone migrated there, the actual city itself expanded quite a bit so the areas we're going into are just gonna look like normal suburbs. The inner city itself—probably what you're thinking of with all the skyscrapers—that would be too dangerous to take you into, for right now anyway." He said it so sweetly; I wanted to feel disappointment, but I couldn't. I didn't want to hold that against him.

"You will take me there someday though, right?"

"Someday…" He said, in a way that didn't instill in me much confidence as he looked away, out the window.

"Don't worry, Kaleah. He has to eventually…" Lane now spoke up seeing that Jake wasn't giving me the response I'd hoped for, "that's the only place he can get—"

"Lane, I swear man, sometimes your mouth is a lot less than helpful." Jake cut him off before Lane could divulge the info.

I looked at Lane's face through the rear-view mirror. It looked like he was smiling and not too concerned with Jake's rebuke of his mouth.

"Someday… okay," I said, looking back at Jake, agreeing that I would wait until he felt like I was ready.

He smiled, then wrapped his arm around me and pulled me in to rest against his side as he reached to take a hold of my hand. "Someday, baby, I promise." He said, then kissed me on top of the head.

"You shouldn't make promises unless you plan on keeping them," Lane said like he was joking, while still trying to jab at Jake.

"Think you're funny huh, Lane?" Jake was gearing up to jab back. "Kaleah, would you like to hear about how Lane can't get a serious girlfriend 'cause he chokes on his words anytime a woman tries to talk to him?"

I was about to respond with an absolute yes, wanting to hear what good gossip Jake was about to hit me with when Lane cut him off.

"Miles! Shut your freakin' mouth! I've had plenty of girlfriends! Don't make me… I'll pull this car over, drag you out, and whoop your ass."

I couldn't help but laugh hysterically at the image that put in my head. I could feel Jake chuckling as well. I don't remember if we laughed much together before, but it felt good. At that moment, despite everything that had happened the past three weeks, all that I'd been through, and how I was physically feeling—I was happy.

2

MEET THE GYPSYINS

We never drove through anything I thought would have been close to the actual City of New York. Most of the things we drove past didn't look like a city at all, actually. Just as Jake said, it looked like a bunch of small towns chained together, like they were holding on to one another, keeping themselves and each other as connected to the real city as possible. I did start to see more people though, just as I had expected. I didn't really have any memory of what being in a city looked like, so I knew any of my expectations weren't probably very realistic to begin with.

It didn't take long after I woke up before we finally arrived at his parents' house. As we pulled up to the large black gate at the entrance to the drive, I instantly became overwhelmed by a strong nervous tension that felt like it took over my whole body. It might not have been so bad, but I could tell Jake seemed to have his own case of nerves. Maybe it had been a while since he'd seen or spoken with them. I didn't know, but assumed it was probably from something like that.

Set back from a short drive inside the gate was what I thought must have been considered a mansion. The house, at first glance, took my breath away. It was magnificent looking, not like anything I had been exposed to in the grotto lands. The elaborate stone exterior was obviously being well maintained by someone unlike the inn Jake had saved me from, with its abundance of vines seeping from its many cracks.

Lane pulled the car around the drive and parked it directly in front of a grand front entrance that sat under a large overhang with a balcony extending from the second story. Jake didn't say anything, he just opened the door and stepped out, then reached his hand in to help me out.

Sensing my hesitancy, he bent down to reassure me. "Don't worry, my parents won't be home until later." He smiled warmly, knowing I was nervous about meeting them.

"I'll carry your bags to your room for ya, Miles, if you want to just help her in." Lane spoke from the trunk as he began to pull Jake's bags out of it.

Jake extended his hand even further, gesturing for me to take it. "It's okay, baby. I'll help you get all cleaned up and settled in… No one else has to see you like this."

I didn't know why I was hesitating, but realized he was probably spot on. If I looked as bad as I still felt, my fear was likely from not wanting anyone else to see me in that condition the first time I was to meet them. I grabbed his hand finally and allowed him to help me.

Lane having already picked up a couple of Jake's bags, walked in, leaving the door open for us to follow him. As we passed through the grand glass entryway, I was taken aback even more by the inside than I had been by the outside. My eyes quickly jumped around from one wall of ornate woodwork to another. Then to a delicate array of what looked like fine crystals hanging from a row of chandeliers that adorned a long brightly lit hallway leading into what I assumed was a living room.

Jake, still holding my hand trying to guide me, turned around to face me, seeing my pace had slowed significantly. He didn't say anything at first, he just watched as I let my eyes slowly wander from one thing to the next.

"Mr. Miles, I'm sorry… I hadn't expected you." An older man

spoke after he quickly rounded the corner now seeing me and Jake standing in the entryway.

Jake turned back to address him, "Steven! No… it's no problem… Here, let me introduce you to my girlfriend." Jake turned, motioning toward me, "Steven, this is Kaleah… Kaleah, this is Steven, a Gypsyin that my parents have working for them."

There were too many things all at once trying to run around my mind for me to really pay attention to what he was saying. I wasn't sure why, but I had expected him to call me Bria. Then, after I quickly realized why I initially thought that, I was taken aback a little by the thought of just being his girlfriend. That was the first time I hadn't been introduced as someone's wife, and even though I knew I wasn't, I felt the loss of the title, like I had been demoted. I also heard him say the man was a Gypsyin… *I was a Gypsyin…* I couldn't help but wonder what the significance was in Jake sharing that with me.

"Nice to meet you," the man said now staring at me like he was waiting for me to say the same.

"Oh… yes, sorry… you too!" I said finally suppressing the distracting thoughts just long enough to respond.

As we made it to Jake's room, I caught myself feeling overwhelmed by all the thoughts on top of all the new shiny things my eyes couldn't help but feel compelled to stare at.

"How many of them work here?" I asked as I started to sit down on the bed, but stopped myself, knowing I might have bled through the rag again that I had shoved down in my pants.

"Three, I will introduce you to them all later if you would like," Jake replied quickly like he wanted to answer my question but had other things on his mind as well, "You need more rags, don't you?"

"Um… yes," I said, realizing he was much more observant than I had internally given him credit for.

Before he had a chance to turn around, Lane came back into the room with the rest of the bags.

"Oh good, you're back," Jake said now talking to him. "Will you go get Bethany and tell her to come here? Kaleah needs things that she'll know how to help me find."

"Sure," Lane sounded as chipper as ever as he turned to leave again.

"Another Gypsyin?" I asked, trying to puzzle all the pieces together. I thought I remembered Jake saying he had a sister, but I didn't think she lived with their parents still, and I didn't remember her name being Bethany.

He nodded. "Is that going to bother you?"

"No, I think I'm only scared of other Gypsyins, you know, wild ones," I said, thinking about the inn and what I had been through.

Jake began to laugh, then seeing I hadn't intended it as a joke, quickly stopped. "I'm sorry," he said as he bent down to grab his bags, one at a time. He then placed them neatly in a row on top of a long dresser sitting against a wall across from the bed.

"This doesn't look like your room," I said, looking around again while I waited for Bethany to get there. The room was large and bright, with a massive bed that looked like it was for a couple, not just one man. One wall was nothing but a row of giant windows, each with neatly drawn sheer curtains. Then, halfway down another wall, there was a small alcove that looked like it probably led to another room, but I couldn't tell for sure.

"They just call it my room for when I want to visit. This isn't the house I grew up in. We didn't live this close to the city when I was a kid. We lived in upstate New York. They only moved here when the war started."

"Oh…" I started to sit down against the bed again out of instinct, but thankfully caught myself before I actually let my butt touch it. "Where is your cat?" I asked as I moved away from the bed towards the windows, making sure I wouldn't do it again by removing the temptation.

Jake stopped pulling things from his bags and turned to look at me like he was dumbfounded by such an innocent question. "We don't have a cat… Is there a reason you think we do?"

I stopped to think about what he said and why I asked, "Um, well… I don't know." I didn't, and now I was trying to ask myself the same question, but I couldn't come up with an answer.

Before I took too much time to think about it, I was distracted by a soft voice that I heard coming down the hall toward the room. "Jacob Miles? Are you back?" No sooner had I heard it than I saw a short, petite figure move into the room with effortless grace.

"Bethany!" Jake said as she quickly went over to give him a welcoming hug. I couldn't tell, but she looked young like she was probably in her late teens.

"Bethany, this is my girlfriend, Kaleah," Jake said after she let go of him and stepped back. She didn't initially turn, though. She acted like she was happy to see him and wanted to stare to make sure she wasn't imagining things. When she did finally turn to look at me, she acted surprised, like she didn't know there was anyone else in the room so she wasn't sure who he was talking about.

"Your girlfriend? Oh... why hello there," she said finally. I couldn't help but be drawn to her. There was something about her that made me want to stare.

"Hello..." I said, feeling a bit shy and awkward. She was pretty, too pretty to be a Gypsyin, I thought initially. Then I realized she wasn't a wild one like I was used to so maybe she wasn't too pretty. Maybe that was the standard for what they looked like in New York.

"Is she staying here with you, Jake?" She turned back to him to ask.

"Yes! I need to talk to you about something if you don't mind, though," he said as he moved over to shut the door behind her.

"Uh... Okay?" She pooched her lips in confusion.

"What I'm going to tell you, I don't want anyone knowing about. It's none of their business. It's only mine and Kaleah's, am I clear?"

"Sure, Sir." Her mannerisms quickly changed to stay in alignment with how Jake was now addressing her.

"We were expecting a child... and well... she's miscarried, so she needs some things."

Before he could continue, she turned her head toward me with a sorrow in her eyes and interrupted, "Oh my gosh, of course... How can I help?"

Jake went on, "Well, she needs clothes and more menstrual rags.

Whatever you have in that category really right now would be the most helpful. I can have Steven or Corey get us something to eat and drink. It's been a long few days of traveling, and I'm sure she's as tired as I am."

The rest of the afternoon went as expected. Bethany brought me more than enough to take care of myself. I figured out the room had its own bathroom, and that was where the alcove lead to. Jake must have not been exaggerating when he told her he was tired. After he helped me shower and clean myself up enough to look presentable, like I wasn't a stray Gypsyin he just pulled from the wild, he crawled into bed with me to rest. I only remember spending a couple of weeks with him before Luca took me but, in all that time, I never remember him sleeping as soundly as he was this time. It was like he'd waited weeks to take a nap. I guess the more I thought about it, the more I realized that conclusion might not have been that far off.

I wasn't all that tired myself. I was just enjoying laying there next to Jake, watching him finally be able to sleep deeply, when I heard the door begin to open. Initially, I was concerned it would wake him up, and he obviously needed his rest so I was prepared to shush whoever it was behind it. Then that thought quickly changed when I realized I didn't know who was actually behind the door. The last thing I wanted was to meet one of his parents without a proper introduction. Before I had much time to worry about it, I saw a familiar head peek from behind the door, quickly releasing any of my fears.

"Kaleah…" Lane whispered, seeing Jake was asleep.

"What?" I mouthed, looking at him, trying not to make any noise and stay as still as possible. It still hurt to have any pressure laid against my stomach, so Jake wasn't sleeping right next to me as he had been before.

"I'm leaving now," Lane thumbed toward the door behind him then made other hand signals as he whispered, "Do you need anything else before I go?"

I couldn't really hear him, but surprisingly, I had a good concept of what the signals meant. Maybe Jake had taught me before I lost my memory. "No, but thank you," I mouthed back as I slightly shook my head, then ended it with a nice smile so he knew he was good to leave.

"Okay," he whispered again as he made the okay signal with his hand, then he slowly closed the door again.

"He really likes you, you know…" Jake whispered, startling me, before I could even relax back against my pillow. I looked over. His eyes were still closed, but he sounded like he was fully aware of what he was saying.

"Sorry if I woke you up. I was trying not to move." Seeing he wasn't as asleep as I thought, I took the opportunity to adjust my position and get more comfortable next to him.

"You're fine. I'll sleep when I'm dead." He said it with a small grin while still keeping his eyes shut.

I didn't respond right away. I just lay there staring at him, trying to memorize every little detail of his face. I never wanted to forget it again. I felt awful. That was exactly what happened the last time I gave myself the serum. He told me what happened and why I did it, so I understood. I wasn't mad at myself. I just wished it could have been different. I wished I hadn't lost all the memories of how I met him, how I fell in love with him, practically everything having to do with him.

"Have I ever almost lost you, like you almost lost me?" I asked finally, feeling curious.

"If there *was* a time, do you think it would be beneficial or detrimental if I told you?"

"Is that the way you decide whether you want to tell me something or not?" I suspected he wasn't always the most upfront about all of our history together.

"Hmm," he slightly chuckled, "You're too smart for your own good," he said with a big smile when he finally opened his eyes to look at me.

"There's a lot of things that you still haven't told me yet, aren't there?" I wasn't upset. I understood. Part of me felt like if we were going to be a team though, I needed to be involved in all of our decisions, the same as he was.

"Baby, the things I still keep from you are only because it'd be dangerous for you to know right now."

"You don't trust me to know? Did I give you reason before the serum to not trust me?"

He didn't say anything, he just looked into my eyes and then shifted his focus from one to the other and then back again. "No…" He said finally.

"Then why are you afraid for me to know now? It feels like you're treating me like a kid, not like your partner."

"You're right…" he sighed, then hesitated as he rolled onto his back to stare at the ceiling. "I can't help it, it's just… I know something about you that would cause you to be in serious danger here… I know I have issues being a little controlling… but if I'm the only one who knows the secret, I know no one else can accidentally find out. I feel like it's the only way I can protect you… even if it's from yourself sometimes."

"Is that secret the only thing you're keeping from me?" I took a hold of his hand that was lying on his chest and laced my fingers with his.

"That and anything that has to do with that… yeah." He squeezed my hand a little after he said it.

"I hate that I can't remember you. I think that's what bothers me the most. I understand that you have secrets you want to keep. I just feel distant from you… I want to feel what you said we had before I erased myself. Are there other things you haven't told me, like about your past… other women you've been with and stuff?"

He rolled back over to look at me again as he moved himself in closer and rested his free hand against my waist. "Baby, if I keep anything from you, it's never anything like that. It's only things that have to do with your past, things that I don't think are safe for anyone else to know."

"Okay… I just…" I didn't know what I was trying to say or ask. I just felt something was lacking, and I wanted to resolve it.

"Ask me anything. What's bothering you?" He reached his hand up to move the hair from my face, then left his hand resting with his thumb on my cheek.

"I don't know anything about your past relationships... Plus, I'm just your girlfriend... I mean... I was Luca's *wife*," I said with a small grin, but figured he would know what I meant by it. "If we loved each other enough to have a baby together..." I didn't know how to go on, I could tell my thoughts weren't concise so I could feel myself getting frustrated with not knowing how to tell him exactly what was wrong or how to continue.

"Okay... do you want to know about my past relationships or do you want to know more about ours?" He began to stoke my cheek with his thumb, then looked down at my lips.

"Both," I said, wanting him to continue before he decided to deviate and kiss me.

He smiled as he looked back up to my eyes, "Okay... Well, my entire life I've only had four girlfriends, if you don't make me count elementary school," he chuckled slightly then began to go on until I interrupted him.

"How many, if you count that?" I asked, intending to make him.

"Uh... that's not fair," his smile grew larger.

I didn't say anything I just stared at him.

"Fifteen..."

"What?" I let out a loud laugh.

"Well, does it count if they agree to it? 'Cause most of those were just girls that I told everyone we were together," He smiled again, knowing he was teasing me.

"Whatever, keep going."

"Okay... where was I... Oh yeah, back to the four of you..."

"So you're going to lump me in with the others?" I asked, teasing him back but genuinely wanting him to tell me how I differed from the rest.

"Okay then... back to the two cheerleaders, one fiancée, and you..." He said it playfully, continuing our banter, but this time the words he used caught me off guard.

"What?" I'm sure my face changed. I wasn't really liking the turn it took.

He must have caught on, his face quickly followed, "I'm sorry, baby, did me saying it like that bother you? I didn't mean it anyway—"

"It's fine," I wanted him to continue, but secretly it hurt a little. "I didn't know you had a fiancée."

"We don't have to talk about it if it's going to bother you," he said now continuing to sweep his fingers though my hair.

"Not talking about it is what bothers me. I can handle it. I want to know these things." I paused, trying to think of how to ask him to continue. "Have you ever had a relationship with Bethany?"

"No, I couldn't, she's a Gypsyin..." He grimaced as soon as the words fell out of his mouth. He knew he spoke too quickly, and I could take what he said wrong again. "I mean—"

"It's okay," I blinked slowly, trying not to look away.

"No... it's not okay, that's not what I meant. She's like a sister to me. When my parents first got her... ugh... There are laws, Gypsyins and Coldiers can't... Ah shit, none of this is coming out right."

"Is that why you told me I have to keep it a secret that I'm a Gypsyin?" I asked, seeing he was getting frustrated with himself.

"Well, that's one reason, there's a bunch more, but yeah," he said like he wanted to go on and keep trying to correct his mistake.

"It's okay... tell me about me then," I thought maybe he would feel better if we changed the subject a little. "How many men have I been with? Like, did I tell you about my previous boyfriends?" As soon as I asked, I could see the subject was almost, if not more, difficult for him than when he messed up telling me about Bethany.

"Um... to be honest, you didn't remember much about your life before the war, so you never told me if you had a lot of relationships or not." He seemed a bit relieved after he said it.

"Oh, okay, so you don't know if I was a virgin or not when we met, or like was I married before?"

His hand quickly froze and stopped stroking my hair as it had been. I figured he knew something, but wasn't sure if he was about to tell me or not. "Well... from what you told me, I wasn't your first, but I was the best guy you'd ever been with. You loved me the most. I was the most handsome and yeah… all that good stuff." He ended it with a smug grin. At that point, any part of me that wanted to really know the truth, I set aside. I felt like I was content with his version. Even if it was likely overly inflated, I wouldn't press him further.

3

MY EVERYTHING

"Okay, tell me more about us then!" Understandably, I figured if he wasn't in the mood to rehash my past with other men, maybe he would still be good with telling me more about our relationship.

"Well, that's a little open-ended. What do you want to know that I haven't already told you?" He let his hand return to stroking my hair.

"If I'm a Gypsyin and you knew it wasn't allowed..." I kind of shrugged, suggesting what I was asking but not finishing the question.

"You can't help who you fall in love with." His answer was simple, almost too much so.

"Have you ever been in love before?" I knew as soon as I asked it that it was the perfect question, and I'd hoped maybe his answer would help me resolve whatever was bothering me.

"I thought I was... with the woman that I was with before you. Enough that I asked her to marry me. I was planning a future with her." He stopped to lean in and kiss me, likely to release the tension he was beginning to feel with the difficulty of the subject. "But the moment I met you I knew there was something different between us I'd never felt with anyone else, this odd kind of chemistry... There was this pull and even though I tried to fight against it, I just couldn't help myself. It felt like you belonged with me... You know how you hear people talking about soul mates? Well, I always thought it was a bunch of crap that they just made up to make themselves feel better, so they'd believe they weren't making a mistake. Then I found you... it felt like the universe made me just for you, and you just for me... Like we were each specially made as a match to the other one's soul..." He stopped, but I wasn't sure why.

"So you weren't in love with your fiancée?" I asked, giving him fuel to continue.

"Yes, and no... I think I was in love with the *idea* of what I wanted us to be. I wanted a family. I wanted a person to call mine. It was really just me filling in the blanks of what life was supposed to look like, but it was nothing like the love I have with you."

"But... in the future... if you wanted... you can't marry me, can you?" I asked as I reached up and took a hold of his hand to stop him from stroking my hair so he would concentrate and really think about the question before answering.

"Legally? No..." he said what I was afraid to be true, "that doesn't have to mean anything, though."

"You just said that's what you wanted. You're in love with the idea of filling in life's blanks. You can't marry me, and now we might not ever be able to have kids together, so—"

"Why are you doing this?" He stopped me. "Legally, we can't, but that doesn't mean we can't otherwise, like spiritually or whatever... That's enough for me."

I didn't respond. I didn't want to say anything that would hurt his feelings, but I was upset. It wasn't enough for me. I wanted to be more than that. I didn't want to just be a spiritually promoted girlfriend. I wanted his last name. I wanted to be Mrs. Miles, someone he could show off. Not just the Gypsyin he had to hide to keep safe.

"Is that what's bothering you, baby?"

I didn't know how to answer him, but it was. Knowing our relationship could never be more than it was bothered me along with so many other things. It felt like I'd only really known him for less than a month, so it also bothered me that I would even want to marry a man that I hadn't known long.

It bothered me that he remembered his past and that helped him know why he loved me and I didn't have that for myself. I was bothered that even though he acted like he didn't think of Bethany in that way, I could tell she thought of him that way. How would she feel if she ever found out I was the same as her and that was the very reason he couldn't be with her, yet he's now with me? I had so many mental complexities that were all happening at the same time. I didn't know how to answer him.

"I want my memory back." I don't know why I said it. That wasn't the answer I had just thought of, but apparently it was bothering me enough that I used it in the correct answer's place.

He began to stroke my hair again; he didn't say anything he just nodded like he wanted me to know he was listening.

"I hate not remembering you, not remembering my past… I want to remember who I used to be with, so then when I think of you I can see why I love you so much, just like you can with me. I hate feeling powerless, like I have to rely on you for everything. Like I need you to tell me how to feel since I can't remember enough to know if my feelings are accurate or even appropriate… Ugh, I hate it!" I didn't want to cry. I could feel it coming, but I didn't want it to, so I did everything I could to hold it at bay, waiting for his response.

"Would you believe it if I told you one time you said you hated that you remembered everything, and you just wished you could forget it all?" His voice was sincere and sweet like he knew it was hard for me, and he was trying to be tender.

Hearing him say that, at first, I didn't believe it. It didn't make any sense to me. "Why would I not want to remember you?" I asked, hoping he would clarify.

"It wasn't me… you hated the things from your past, the things I won't tell you about. That's exactly why I won't tell you about them. You finally have a chance to be free from them and make a new future, just like you always wanted… So make a new future with me now, fall deeper in love with me again. We can create new memories together.

You said that to me yourself the first time you wanted to erase yourself and I wouldn't let you."

"What?" He hadn't ever told me about a time that I wanted to be erased and him stopping me.

Before he could answer, there was a knock at the door. "We can finish this conversation later, all right? Don't be upset with me, please…" He said as he stroked my cheek again with his thumb. I nodded, agreeing to his request. He smiled, then leaned in to kiss me again before he finally responded to whoever was knocking. "Who is it?"

"Um, it's Bethany. I'm sorry to bother you, Sir, but your mother is home, and she wants to see you and um… miss Kaleah."

"Tell her we will be down in a few, then. Thank you, Bethany," Jake politely hollered back.

"I don't know why, but I want to be honest with you… I'm scared of your mother," I said, refusing to let go of his hand as he started to pull it away to sit up in the bed.

"What? Why? You haven't even met her yet." He looked down at me with a mildly amused yet confused look on his face.

"I don't know. All I can think about is hearing Lane say she's wicked. Maybe I dreamed it… I'm not sure." Before I could go on trying to explain myself, Jake started to laugh like I had made a joke.

"Wow… you know you're a remarkable woman. Have I told you that yet today?" I was beginning to think he meant it sarcastically except his face looked like he was being genuine. "Kaleah, I really mean it," he continued. He must have noticed I was confused by what he was trying to say. "You talk in your sleep, and now you have proven my suspicions are correct. You can hear conversation in your sleep as well… That's truly a gift," he said with a warm smile as he turned to sit on the edge of the bed.

"Okay… I don't know what that kind of thing would be good for, though." I stopped to think about it. "You know, maybe I should have been an agent like you," I slightly chuckled, thinking about it and how silly it sounded as I waited for Jake's response, expecting something similar from him. He didn't say anything, though. He just leaned down to put his boots back on. "How are you going to introduce me to her?" I asked, trying to break the awkwardness I felt at that moment.

"Carefully..." he said, finishing with his boots and standing up. "If calling you my girlfriend bothers you, what would you like for me to call you?"

"I guess that's all I am, so..." I shrugged, but realized he probably wasn't looking at me so he wouldn't see it. I got up and walked over to the bathroom to look in the mirror and make sure I looked presentable enough.

"You're more than that. There just isn't a good label for it right now. You're my Kaleah..." It felt like he was saying it just as much for himself as he was for me. He walked over beside me, checking himself in the mirror now as well.

"If you had a chance to introduce me to Luca again would you tell him I was just your girlfriend?"

His face froze with a slight lift of his brows suddenly like my question was thought-provoking. He stopped combing his fingers through his hair, looked over at me, and took a deep breath. "Hmm... You're right, if it's not good enough for him, it shouldn't be good enough for my family either... I get it." He looked away again, probably trying to resolve this new conflict of thought within himself.

He grabbed a hold of my hand as we slowly walked down the stairs together. I think it was more for emotional support than physical, though. Bethany was at the bottom of the steps looking up, watching us descend. She had a sweet smile on her face, but there was a part of it that looked forced. Something in me felt bad for her, though I wasn't sure why. I think it was the lack of understanding what role Gypsyins actually played within the city. I wondered if they had their own homes, car, relationships, or just what. I felt like I was a piece of both worlds that didn't fit into either, like I was a pretender who shouldn't have been able to be with Jake, like I didn't belong.

"Miss Kaleah... Mr. Miles... The table has been set and dinner will be served shortly," she spoke like a servant, not what I'd think hired help would, but what did I know.

"Please, Bethany, you know you don't have to call me that," Jake spoke to her in a lighter tone, releasing her from her polite society role.

"I'm afraid I do, Sir," she said as her eyes darted far toward the right. "Your mother is waiting for you in the dining room." My fear of his mom was now heightened further than it had been. She must have been one scary woman if Bethany was even scared of disobeying her.

Jake just nodded as we passed her and walked toward what I'd thought was a large sunroom, but it wasn't. It was apparently the dining room. It was massive, with a wall of windows on three sides. Lined up in front of those were identically sized, delicately carved porcelain statues of scantily dressed Greek figures. Then right in the middle of the room, there she was, sitting at one end of a large, long wooden table. She looked like she was drowning in a sea of space. The table could probably sit upwards of twenty people, yet it was just her sitting there all alone.

"Jacob!" she said, as our entrance caught her eye. Her voice was surprisingly pleasant and not really anything like I'd expected. "Oh, this must be your girlfriend. It's nice of you to let me finally meet her. Bethany has been telling me so much about her already." Jake slightly squeezed my hand as she said it. I wasn't sure if he was tense or if he was trying to help me remember to play along with what we previously discussed about how it should go.

"Well, I don't know what she would have already been telling you but here she is… Mom, this is Kaleah," Jake said as he turned toward me then put his arm around my waist. "My Kaleah… my everything."

She smiled, though it looked a bit smug, and I wasn't sure why. "Okay…" she said, then acted like she was waiting for him again.

"Kaleah," he said, addressing me as he stepped away to pull out a chair for me to sit, "this is my mother, Elizabeth, but you can call her Liz."

"Mrs. Miles," she stopped him as she gestured for him to take a seat. "She can call me what everyone else does. Mrs. Miles is fine."

He sat down next to me between the two of us. I could tell she was his mom. Some of his facial features matched hers. She had straight, thick, shoulder-length sandy blonde hair. What I couldn't pull my attention from though was her makeup. She wore it like the war had tried to make it illegal to do so and she was going to do everything in her power to rebel. It was so heavy, what skin I thought I saw might have not even been her skin at all but just a super thick layer of beige powder dusted all over her face.

"Where's Dad?" Jake didn't respond to her telling me I couldn't call her Liz like he said I could.

"He's still at work. Sound familiar?" She said, then looked from him to me with a sly smile like she was trying to hint at something and I should pay attention. "The longer you're with him, you'll see it, Kaleah. He's a hard worker, just like his father, but that doesn't always translate to the best home life if I'm being honest." She looked back at him as she finished saying it.

"Mom… please, this isn't the best way to—"

"I'm sorry, Jacob, you're right… I haven't seen you or heard from you in seven months, and with the line of work you chose for yourself, I didn't even know that you weren't dead… So, I apologize for feeling a little put off that you would suddenly show up out of the blue and act like everything is perfectly fine… Not to mention, you told Bethany not to tell me that I lost a grandchild…" She gave him a stern look, suddenly at the moment I realized where he must have gotten his.

I sat back a little in my chair, relieved that even though I was part of the subject matter, I didn't actually have to be a part of the argument itself since Jake said he would do all the talking if I didn't feel comfortable.

"Are you done?" Jake asked, probably not wanting to get interrupted again.

"I don't know… I'm pretty upset. What do you think?" She asked but then kept talking herself. "No actually there's more… We never resolved the argument we had the last time I saw you. Before you left to go on your *secret mission*, whatever the hell you said that was, I don't know why you couldn't tell me. Then there's the fact that you just left Katherine without a goodbye."

"Mom, when I left we'd been split up for over—"

"I'm not done, Jacob… I don't care. You just left her and didn't say goodbye. She wanted you back. She came here looking for you, trying to make amends… On top of all of that, you come home and I find out that you're doing things with *her*," she said as she pointed at me. "You aren't even married. I raised you better than that."

"Stop it, now!" Jake hissed, getting upset. "You knew me and Kat were intimate, and you never said anything, so don't start with me. This isn't about that, and you know it." He said through clinched teeth.

"But you were going to marry Katherine… I don't know anything about Kaleah."

"That's why I'm here, Mom," he started to raise his voice. "So you can meet her! She's my life now… I love her… I never felt this way about Katherine." He stopped and took a deep breath.

She didn't say anything at first. She just looked at him with surprise likely either from him speaking to her like that or because of what he was saying. "Fine," she said finally, relenting. "Well, who are her parents, then? You sure she's not just with you because of who you are and what our family is worth?"

"Don't talk about her like she's not even here," he said as he reached down under the table to hold my hand. I was happy he said it because it was exactly how I felt. "Her parents are Coldiers from Tennessee… and not that it's any of your business but no, she's not with me because of anything but the fact that she loves me… She didn't even know about how wealthy we were until two days ago. She doesn't care about that stuff."

"Well, what about my grandchild?" She asked coldly. I couldn't think of why, but it hurt the way she'd said it.

Jake stood up and pulled my hand for me to stand up with him so I did. "Mom, if you insist on arguing with me, we can have this conversation together later without Kaleah having to hear it. The world doesn't revolve around you! That's why I asked Bethany not to tell you… because *Kaleah* lost *her* child!" He paused for a moment. "Tell Corey he can bring our food to my room. If you don't want us staying past the night, I understand, we can go to Lane's. We don't need to be here." After he said it, he turned and brought his hand to my waist to guide me to walk out.

We only made it to the end of the table before she finally responded, "If you're staying in my house, you're going to abide by my rules, Jacob Adrian… You're not going to speak to me like that, do you hear me?"

Jake turned to look back at her like he was going to say something, then looked back at me, "Go back up to the room, baby, I'll be there in a minute." Then he leaned in to give me a kiss before turning away again to walk back toward her.

4

UNEASY ACCOMPLICE

"Are you asleep already, baby? You haven't eaten yet." I must have dozed off while waiting for Jake to return from finishing his argument with his mother.

It took me a second to think about what he was saying before I turned over to respond to him, "I'm not hungry… I only went to sleep 'cause there isn't anything else to do in here."

He walked over closer to the bed and set down a tray loaded with food. It looked like Corey brought an entire feast for just the two of us.

"How are you not hungry? You've barely eaten anything today. Come on… sit up and eat a little while we talk."

I really wasn't all that hungry for whatever reason, but I figured I would oblige him. I pulled myself to a sitting position and leaned against the giant wooden elaborately engraved headboard. "How did it go?" I asked, referring to how the argument got resolved.

He smiled, "I won… but I always do," he said with a mischievous grin as he sat down on the bed next to me.

"Oh, you do?" He piqued my interest. I was curious what hidden skill he'd been using against her I might not know about yet. "How so, because she seems like she's pretty controlling?"

"Where do you think I get it?" He asked, initially cracking a smile as he picked up one of the plates of food.

"You act like it's a good thing to have," I said, picking up a small plate for myself.

"It's only bad when you have selfish motives..." He didn't clarify it much, but I understood what he meant. "Either way, I get what I want... How do you think I got you?" He sounded like he was joking, but I wasn't quite sure.

"I don't know... How did you? Did you coerce me like you did her?" I smiled so he would know I was joking now, too.

"Baby... to tell you the truth, I don't think I have all that much power over you. It's the other way around. I'd do anything for you. Making you happy and keeping you safe... that's all I live for now," he paused, lost in thought. "So honestly, I don't know how I got you to love me, but I'm glad I did."

I wouldn't admit it to him, but hearing him say that filled something inside me that I needed to hear. I didn't feel like I was controlling at all, but the thought that I was in charge of him, who apparently was in charge of his mother to some degree, felt quite nice when I thought about it.

"Maybe it was your muscles." I said playfully, but deep down I kind of meant it. I didn't know exactly what it was that made me love him initially either, but I was sure his exquisite muscular physique likely had something to do with it. I would think so, at least.

He laughed, "Oh you like those, do you?" He took another bite of food after he said it.

"You have no idea..." I meant it. He really probably had no idea. I picked at my food a little, thinking about eating it, but didn't really want to. I figured he would stop asking me to if he at least thought I was eating. So I just used my fork to cut up a few pieces like I had given it a valiant effort even though I hadn't. "So... we don't have to go to Lane's now, then?" I made sure not to sound disappointed since I wasn't. I was starting to like the feeling of all the grandiose things that came along with his parent's house.

"No... I understand why Mom was upset with me. I just needed to talk to her about it to get everything straightened out, and we're cool now. I'm her baby boy… She wouldn't admit it, but she can't stay mad at me. That's how I get whatever I want." He had to stop from taking another bite because his smile was too large after saying it. "The last time I saw her was actually only a few days before I found you. We'd had an argument about me leaving New York and working for the agency in Nashville… she didn't like that. She wanted to know where I was going and what mission was so important that it couldn't wait. I didn't even know how important it would actually have turned out to be either, but look at you… It was obviously the most important mission of my life, and I'm glad she didn't make me miss it."

"Aww," I wasn't sure if my face was red from blushing, but I felt flattered. That was sweet. "So, is she happy to hear you're back in New York, then?"

"Yeah, knowing you're the only reason that I'm staying here helped her warm up pretty quickly to the idea of me being with you instead of Katherine," he said with a small chuckle then took another bite of food.

When he said that, something hit me and I realized we'd not really talked about our future. The only thing we really discussed was needing to come to the city for safety, not if this was where we were going to stay forever and if so, what we would end up doing here. "What are our plans for the future here, then?" I thought I might as well ask while I had the question in my mind.

"Well, first things first… you need to stop pretending to eat and actually eat!" He caught me. I nodded and took a bite, waiting for him to go on. "Next… we have to take baby steps before we can run… So, I have a doctor coming tomorrow to look at you and make sure you're going to recover well. I had Steven make an appointment with our family physician, don't worry you'll like him. He's an older man… really sweet guy."

I suddenly felt a bit sick and if I hadn't wanted to eat before I definitely didn't want to anymore. For whatever reason, the idea of a doctor seeing me felt pretty traumatic mentally. "I don't want to see a doctor," I said quietly, putting my plate back down on to my lap.

Jake didn't say anything at first. He just turned and looked at me like he was thinking of why I would respond like that and what he should do about it. "Okay… I understand why it would probably be hard on you to want to see one," he said softly like he really did understand, and he was being sympathetic. "But I'm not going to let the trauma of what Luca did to you stop me from making sure you're going to be safe, healthy and heal well." He finished with a stern tone like he wasn't about to allow me to argue with him about it.

That didn't stop me from trying though, "But I just—"

"I can be in the room with you if you're uncomfortable. I won't leave you if you don't want," he said, cutting me off before I could attempt to give him anymore excuses.

"Fine…" I knew it wouldn't do me any good to try to argue again, so I just agreed to it.

The morning came early and with it, the dreaded physician's appointment. I was hoping when he did finally arrive, seeing he was an older man and nothing like Luca might help, but nothing was helping with all the nervous tension I was feeling while we waited. I even woke up before Jake did, which was uncommon. I just lay there in the bed, staring at the windows. It was still dark, but I could see the glow of streetlights which I hadn't seen before in the grotto lands.

I tried not to move much, knowing I would probably wake Jake up since he was such a light sleeper. He seemed to be sleeping deeper than usual, though, just like he did during his nap the day before. I figured he must have finally felt comfortable and safe, probably for the first time since he'd met me. I loved it when I was able to snuggle up next to him; it felt like the safest place I'd ever been when I was in his arms.

"Mr. Miles! How are you, Sir?" I could hear the doctor speaking to Jake downstairs once he finally arrived. I had returned to our room after breakfast using the excuse that I needed to rest, but in reality I think I was trying to hide. When they finally entered the room, I was surprised. I was expecting to hear them coming up the stairs first but didn't, probably because the stairs were carpeted.

"Kaleah, baby, the doctor is here to see you," Jake said from behind me. I would have stayed there and pretended to be asleep if I'd have gotten away with it, but I figured they'd already seen me startle a little at their entrance and would've quickly caught on.

I turned over to look at them and began to sit up when the older gentlemen finally spoke, "Oh no, my dear, you're fine to stay laying there. I can examine you as you are."

I could tell from that brief response, Jake was most likely right. He sounded like a sweet man. Unfortunately, that didn't make me feel any less tense, though. I didn't say anything, I just lay there watching as they both walked around the bed over to my side.

"He's just going to look at you and ask some questions about how you feel, all right? You'll be fine. I'll stay here with you both," Jake said probably hoping it would help me relax.

"Mr. Miles has already explained to me what things have transpired to put you in this predicament," the doctor said as he set his bag down at the end of the bed near my feet. I looked over at Jake, not sure what he had already told the doctor, but now wondered if it was the truth or if I was supposed to go along with some half-lie he'd already concocted. He didn't say anything to help give me a clue to which; he just nodded his head, reassuring me again that I would be okay.

Neither of them said much more as the examination commenced. The doctor would just give me a brief description, telling me what he was about to do and why. Thankfully, he really didn't ask many questions, so I didn't have to say much. If he had, I was afraid I would talk too much and give secrets away. After he was done, he took everything he'd pulled out of his bag and began to put it all back.

I was expecting him to tell me what the diagnosis was or if I was fine, but he didn't say anything for a moment. He just zipped his bag back up and stood there for a second, looking at me like he forgot to check something. He took a couple steps forward toward the head of the bed and then took a hold of my arm like he might have been wanting to check my pulse but instead, before I realized what he was doing, he pushed my sleeve down to my elbow.

"Jacob!" He scolded as he stood there staring at my tag-less arm, sounding like an upset parent. I pulled my arm away as quickly as I could and pulled my sleeve back down, then looked over at Jake, hoping he didn't think it was my fault. I didn't know if I did or said anything to make him suspicious, but I was instantly frightened that I might be in danger now that someone knew what I really was.

"Doc, that's not what I brought you here for," Jake said as he moved around toward me, making the doctor take a couple of steps back.

"You didn't tell me she was a Gypsyin. I can lose my license if I provide her medical care without seeing her papers."

Jake's shoulders suddenly became tense. The muscles in his back looked like they were instantly more defined through his shirt than they were three-seconds before that. "Look Doc, you've known me my whole life… You know what kind of man I am." Jake prefaced whatever he was about to say with reminding the doctor which role they each played, "She isn't just some Gypsyin I found somewhere. She doesn't have any papers, and she's not going to… She's a human. She's not my property, and that's how she's going to stay." Jake paused, waiting for the doctor's response.

The doctor clenched his jaw like he was thinking about what to say.

"If it's going to be a problem, I'm sure my family wouldn't have any issue finding another physician to take care—"

"No! I'm sorry, Mr. Miles, you're correct." The doctor quickly thought of a response. "She *isn't* property. I won't say anything to anyone if you won't."

"That's better," Jake said, sounding a lot less intolerant.

"Um… of course. Well… uh… from what I can tell, she's lost a lot of blood and that's likely what's making her feel weak and want to sleep so much. She's anemic and will need iron. I'm sure this has all affected her appetite or lack thereof, as well. Uh… she shouldn't bleed for more than a few more days. If it continues after that, let me know. If she has any symptoms of a fever, then—" he paused as he looked at me like he was scared to continue, "Um… Well, if that happens, then she might not have expelled everything from the pregnancy and would require a procedure to have it removed… Jacob, if that happens, this whole thing could get out of hand quickly. Not only does she not have papers, but they'll know she's not been sterilized and—"

"Doctor!" Jake quickly cut him off, seeing he was saying more than Jake probably wanted me to hear or even know about. "Why don't we finish this discussion in another room, shall we?"

The doctor nodded, like the idea of getting away from me was just as pleasant for him as it was for me. He picked up his bag, turned and walked toward the door with Jake behind him.

"I'll be back, baby, just stay here." Jake said briefly, turning back toward me, then they both walked out the door and shut it behind them.

As I sat there, feelings of shock began to consume me. Sure Jake just wanted me to stay there. He was probably pretty upset that I just found out what I did, or maybe even scared of how I would react. Honestly, I was afraid of how I would react too once all the new information had a chance to really sink in. I tried to thoroughly review the conversation in my head so I could come up with my own conclusions before Jake came back in to tell me what he wanted me to think it all meant. *Papers…* Gypsyins were supposed to have papers? Jake said he didn't want me to have any because I wasn't property to be owned. At that moment I got it, like a light bulb lit then exploded in my head. *They not hired help; they're slaves!* They—*we* were slaves, my kind… my people!

"Oh my gosh…" I sat there staring at nothing, trying to think about what it all meant and how it affected me. Was that why he didn't want to be with Bethany, because she was sterilized and couldn't have any children anymore? The thought crossed my mind before I realized it was deeper than that. They weren't supposed to be with us at all. Coldiers weren't supposed to be with Gypsyins. The danger of my situation sunk in farther than I ever imagined it could have. No wonder it was imperative that no one found out what I was. *Is Jake in danger for hiding me away like this? If he gets caught, could he go to jail?* I didn't even know what kind of jail they had anymore. My lack of memory at that moment was more than frustrating.

Would it all be okay if I just had papers? Why didn't he want me to have papers? They seemed innocent enough. Was it just because he didn't want me to feel like he owned me? I could understand that, though part of me didn't mind the idea if it meant we could both live without fear of being caught.

What else wasn't I aware of? I wondered. Were there other laws pertaining to Gypsyins that made it dangerous for me to be there? Was that why he didn't want to take me to the city? I had so many questions.

Before long, I heard a knock at the door. Initially thinking it was Jake, I was about to holler and tell him to come in when I realized it couldn't be him. He wouldn't knock on his own door. I got up from the bed and quickly made my way over to it. I looked down to check and make sure I was presentable first, then opened it. At first, before the gap was able to get very wide, I saw another large tray of food. I assumed it must be Corey bringing lunch.

"Miss Miles," a large man greeted me, likely not realizing that wasn't my name, but probably not sure what else to call me since we'd not yet been introduced.

"Yes… My name is Kaleah… Thank you," I said as I finished opening the door all the way. "You can set it over there on the bed." I turned to point, then stepped aside, inviting him in.

"Yes, ma'am, neither you nor Mr. Miles have been down to have your lunch yet, so I thought I would bring it to you like I did dinner last night. I hope I'm not intruding."

"No, of course not! Its Corey, right?" I asked, but figured I was correct.

"Yes, Ma'am," he said. He reminded me of a large teddy bear. He looked soft and squishy, like he had plenty to eat, since he was most likely their cook. He had extremely freckled skin and the brightest red curly hair that I had probably ever seen in my life. He didn't say much else, he just set the tray where I asked him to and turned to walk out.

"Thank you!" I said again as he started to leave. I knew he was the last of the Gypsyins in the house that I hadn't met yet. I wanted to stand there and nicely interrogate him, asking him everything I could think of about what it was like being a Gypsyin in New York. I knew I couldn't, though. I didn't have to be exceptionally intelligent to know that was a very dumb thing to do and would likely only bring undue attention to myself. It could potentially put both Jake and me in more danger than we were already in to start with as well.

"Kaleah!" Jake called as he exited with the doctor from another room along the hall.

"Corey brought us lunch," I said still standing in the doorway watching Corey slowly walk down the stairs into the grand foyer at the bottom.

"Good! Go back into the room. I'm going to see the doctor out, and then I'll be up as soon as I can to eat with you."

"Okay," I said, watching as they both came near me, walking toward the stairs. I looked over at the doctor as he began to walk past, intending to smile at him as a small gesture of gratitude, but he wouldn't look at me to receive it. He kept his head down with his face turned away.

"Go eat!" Jake said again before descending the stairs, seeing I was hesitating to listen to him the first time.

I nodded, then shut the door.

5

PAPER CHAINS

J ake returned. He didn't look all that thrilled with the conclusion of what he spoke with the doctor about.

"When were you going to tell me?" I asked right away, figuring we might as well get the conversation started so we could get it over with as quickly as possible.

"Never…" He said like he was half serious but left room to say he was joking, probably depending on how I decided to take it. Then he sat on the edge of the bed in front of me with the tray of food between us.

"How do I get papers?" I knew I probably didn't understand all the implications but in my life-lesson-less mind it sounded like it was a safer option than what we were doing.

He narrowed his eyes, looking puzzled. "What?"

"I'm a Gypsyin, wouldn't it just make it safer if I had papers? Like the doctor sa—"

"No!" he quickly cut me off. "I don't care what you think you heard the doctor say. You don't understand it, so you don't get to decide."

I could see he was frustrated, but I didn't like the way he was acting. "Then help me understand it."

"You're not getting papers because I refuse to own you or anyone, for that matter. It's that simple!" He said it with his stern face like that statement needed to be the end of the discussion, because it's what he'd already decided.

"You're just looking at it wrong, it's only papers… Really wouldn't it be like marriage and a marriage contract? A married couple kind of own each other, don't they?"

"That's different, and you know it, Eva! I can't even believe you're trying to tell me this. I thought I was going to come back in here and have to console you over the fear that I might want to actually do it someday."

"Well, sorry to surprise you!" I didn't really mean it. I wasn't sorry at all.

"What's new? You've been nothing but one surprise after another since I met you." He didn't say it like it was an endearing quality that he loved about me, but more like it was an irritating characteristic he wished I didn't have.

I didn't say anything. That hurt my feelings, so I didn't know how to respond to it. I just looked down and began to play with my food, rather than eat any more of it.

"I'm sorry, I didn't mean it like that…" it must not have taken him long to see I took it badly, whether he meant it that way or not.

"What do you plan on doing with me, then? If you won't get papers for me, do you just expect me to stay in this house and hide forever, like I did at the cave? Was that why I erased myself, because you kept me trapped?"

"Just because I accidentally said something that hurt you, doesn't mean you need to respond with something trying to hurt me," he spoke calmly.

"I'm sorry, you're right." I looked back up at him. "I just wish you wouldn't keep me in the dark about everything. You say you're just trying to keep me safe, but it feels like saying a pet is safe the longer you keep them in a cage."

He sighed like he knew I was right. "Fine… What do you want to know?"

I instantly felt relieved. I wanted him to trust me with the information, so I was happy he decided he could.

"Okay," I said, thinking about what I wanted to ask first. "Well, don't take this wrong, but it's something I wondered about so I want to ask."

"What?" He didn't sound the most enthusiastic, but he was willing and that's all I needed.

"If Bethany is a Gypsyin, she's been sterilized, right? I assume that means they can't have kids... Is that the reason you weren't interested in being with her?"

His face contorted in confusion. Maybe he wasn't expecting that to be the first thing I wanted to know. "What is your deal with Bethany?" He said as he started to eat, probably feeling like he could finally now that the worst of the conversation was hopefully past us. "Yes, she's been sterilized. That's the standard procedure when they bring new Gypsyins into the city. After that, they wipe their memory, then assign them. Or well... more like sell them to the highest bidder."

He paused to take another bite of food as he looked at me. I knew he hadn't finished answering the question though, so I didn't interrupt his silence with another one. I just sat there and waited. He swallowed, then went on. "As far as me being interested in her, no. That has absolutely nothing to do with it, not to mention I wasn't ever interested in her to start with, so you can just get that out of your head. She was fifteen when my parents got her four years ago. She's like a sister to me, a way younger sister, and that's all."

"Oh, okay..." I wasn't expecting that answer from him, but it was satisfactory to what I wanted to know. I liked that he wasn't interested in her. I wasn't sure what exactly made me concerned that he was. Maybe it was the way she acted around him the first time I saw her. Either way, I was happy with his answer and stopped to think for a second about the next thing I wanted to ask. "Can you get in a lot of trouble for doing... uh, like you know... with a Gypsyin? Like, could they take you to jail if they found out?"

He quietly laughed a little to himself then looked back up at me, "I'm sorry, I know that's a serious question... you're just so cute the way you asked it." He sighed as he lowered his fork like he didn't want the chewing of his food to hamper coming up with the perfect answer.

"Okay…" he said finally, waiting to take another bite. "Yes, it is technically illegal for us to be intimate… well, without papers. It is with papers too, but you know people do it. That's probably the whole reason for the sterilization. So the real problem is you can have my child… They made the laws because they didn't want a conflict with bringing Gypsyins in and then if they had kids, whose side would the kids be on. You get it. The whole thing is really f'd up to be honest. That's why the doctor was upset when he found out you were a Gypsyin that just miscarried." He stopped like he thought he finished the question.

"So… can you get in trouble, then?" I reminded him there was still more to answer.

"Oh… right," he said, then put his empty plate down and moved the tray over so there was nothing between us. "I'm not the one we have to worry about if we got caught." He paused again to scoot himself forward, so he was sitting straight in front of me. "I rank high enough in the agency that I can get away with that kind of stuff if I wanted… It's just… they would take you away from me though, that's what I would be worried about the most. If they did that, then they would send you through a Gypsyin processing unit." He stopped and took a deep breath as he looked away.

"Go on…" I said, knowing he had more, but was probably just scared to tell me.

"You'd be sterilized, then erased again and have your name changed… There'd be no way for me to ever find you…" I could see his hand start to shake as he said it. "And if I ever did find you, it wouldn't matter. You'd be owned by someone, with no memory of me…"

I reached down to take a hold of his hand, hoping it would make him feel better. Neither of us said anything for a minute. We just sat there in silence, letting the gravity of the situation really sink in.

"Is that why you didn't bring me to New York before now?" I asked, breaking the silence.

"That was one reason, but there were a lot of others too… The problem is this is the safest place for you now." His face started to turn red as he began to clench his jaw slightly the more tense he became. It was easy to see he was getting upset.

"Well, how can we make it safer here for me?" I didn't want to mention the papers again, but in a roundabout way was alluding to them. Maybe if he saw they were the only way, he'd finally agree to them.

"Eva, dammit, I know what you're trying to do, and you're not getting papers. I said no!" He apparently saw right through the question to my real motives.

"Why do you call me Eva when you're mad at me?"

He looked back up at me while letting his face relax a little. "I'm sorry, baby, I'm not mad at you," he said as he leaned in to wrap his arms around me and pull me toward him. "I'm just scared… okay?"

I pushed him backwards a little so he would lie back onto the bed, then I lowered my head to rest against his chest, while I curled the rest of my body up next to him. "Okay…" I said. I didn't need to ask him anything else, just laying there with him was enough. He brought his hand around and started stroking my hair.

"I know you're still learning to love me again, but do you at least trust me, Kaleah?" His voice was faint and sweet.

"Yes…" I wasn't sure why he was asking, but I did. Every ounce of me did.

"Then believe me when I say you are the only woman for me. You're the light in my world, baby. I won't leave you, no matter how hard things get. I'll protect you with my life…"

"Okay…" I said softly. I did believe him, even when the things he said didn't make sense. I decided I would just keep believing him, trusting he had the best for me no matter how it looked.

The next morning, I woke up with a knock at the door. I was alone, covered completely and tucked in nicely; I'm sure just the way Jake left me. "Who is it?" I asked, raising my voice, though it cracked halfway in the middle.

"Bethany, Ma'am… May I come in? Are you decent?"

"Yes… Come in!"

She opened the door slightly and peeked her head around the door, then finished entering the room once she saw I was up and awake. "Ja… Mr. Miles has asked that I come check and make sure you are ready for a surprise he has for you." She said, still standing just inside the door.

"Uh… okay?" I still felt a bit groggy. "Where is he?" I asked.

"He's downstairs eating breakfast." She wasn't giving me much information to go off of, but it was easy to conclude his surprise probably didn't have anything to do with food if he wasn't waiting for me to eat.

I got up and sat on the edge of the bed, then she went over to the dresser and helped me pick out a set of clothes. Clothes that were originally hers since she'd been the one to bring them to me when we first arrived. I went to the bathroom and got dressed, making sure she wasn't able to see my arm. She was still in the room when I came back out. I wasn't sure why at first, but then it became obvious once I saw her hair kit sitting on the dresser. It didn't take long for her to change from orderly to giddy as soon as she realized she was the one who got to do my hair for me, since I had no idea what I was doing.

Initially, she didn't say much other than some small talk but that quickly developed into a deeper conversation once we began to talk about Jacob and all of his amazing attributes. It was hard for me to gauge her at first. I knew how Jake felt about her, but I thought it would be a great opportunity to really get a good idea of how she felt for him.

The more we talked, the more I noticed something similar about her that I saw in myself. There was a childlike innocence she displayed especially with the way she spoke. The more I thought about it, the more I realized that was probably a side effect of us both having been erased. She wasn't dumb but the more I talked to her, the more I saw she had the same perception of life that I did—one that was lacking a complete knowledge of our past. Without it, we didn't have a good idea of how dangerous the world really was. It hadn't been as obvious to me until I saw the same thing in her.

She did love Jake, but not the same way I did. When she talked about him, it was like you would an older brother. I tried my best not to mention anything having to do with Gypsyins, even though I could see another opportunity, just as I did when Corey was around. I wanted to know what she thought, how she felt about the things that had happened to her, if she was sad that this was her new life. Oddly enough, though, from what I could tell, she seemed happy, almost oblivious to what she was.

Jake never mentioned it, but seeing her act that way made me wonder if there was another part of the Gypsyin processing that he might not have wanted to allude to. A part where they brainwashed the newly erased to believe that they were lesser, almost non-human. Maybe that was the way they could make them more docile and less likely to fight back against their oppressors.

The longer I sat there watching her do my hair, the longer I had to think. I started to see why Jake might have been so hostile toward the idea of me having papers. *If there is anything in me that felt like he owned me, giving me no choice but to be his, then how will he know if I am being genuine when I tell him I love him?* Whether there were more reasons or not, I could understand that one. He needed my love to have a choice. If there was none, it all meant nothing.

"You're really beautiful," Bethany said, looking into the mirror at me with amazement, possibly at her work, or maybe me, I wasn't sure.

I dismissed her statement with a bashful shrug. Then she began pulling makeup from her kit until I politely stopped her. For whatever reason, I didn't like the idea of makeup. She seemed to take it well and put it all back along with the hair stuff she was now done with.

"Jacob must really love you…" she said with a large smile as I stood up. The statement was innocuous enough but the way she said it was like there was more meaning behind it, so I gave her a look, curious about what exactly she meant.

"How so?" I asked.

"He never did the same things with Katherine that he does with you."

I was more puzzled by that statement. What had we actually been doing but sleeping all day? I'm sure my look changed because she started to sputter to correct and clarify what she was telling me.

"I mean… like Katherine never spent the night here with him. I barely ever saw her with him honestly… He didn't really talk about her all that much either, not until they started planning the wedding, and then it wasn't long after that when he decided he wanted to move to Nashville. I didn't think he wanted kids before either, not until you came—" she stopped like she wasn't sure if she was about to say something that would hurt my feelings.

"It's okay, you can go on," I said.

"He was always working… like even after he sold his house and moved back in here, we still barely saw him. But he acts different now that you're around, like he doesn't care about work like he did, he just wants to be here with you. More than all of that, though, it's the way he looks at you… I don't know how, but I can just tell… it's different. It's like… oh, I don't know," she giggled.

"Thank you," I said with a smile. It was good to hear from someone other than Jake how much they thought he loved me. I couldn't tell her that I had had my memory erased and that I couldn't remember much of him. Everything in me wanted to feel the same love for him I was sure I must have felt before, so hearing her tell me how much he loved me helped. If he felt it so strongly, I at one point, had to have as well, and hopefully would again soon.

I walked down the stairs, not sure what I was about to be surprised with, but excited nonetheless at the idea of even getting a surprise. Jake must not have realized I was behind him as I entered the living room. He turned and froze when he saw me. His eyes lit up in a way I hadn't remembered seeing before.

"Kaleah?" He said, standing there stunned with his mouth slightly ajar. "Wow, baby, you look… amazing."

"Thanks," I said, smiling the same as I did when Bethany complimented me, then moved to sit on the couch.

"Oh no, we have things to do," Jake said quickly, before I was able to sit all the way down.

"All right?" Knowing it was a surprise I didn't want to ask directly what he was talking about but figured he would tell me what I needed to know, when I needed to know it.

"First, I have a tailor waiting for you. When he gets your measurements, we can get clothes made just for you."

I bit my lip, trying not to smile too large. If that was the only surprise, it was enough. Having my own clothes sounded amazing. "Are we going into the city, then?" I asked, thinking the tailor was probably waiting for me at his shop. Then I second guessed myself as I wondered if stores even still existed and, if they did, why wouldn't we just go buy clothes my size instead of using a tailor? Or maybe that was the way rich people got their clothes. I didn't know.

"Oh, no, baby, he's out in the garden. I asked Corey to take your breakfast out there for you. I figured you would enjoy the sun while you ate."

"Oh, okay…" I was thankful for the clarification, but felt a bit frustrated with myself. I wasn't sure if my ignorance was from having my memory erased or—what I thought was more likely—from previously being poor and not having a single clue about the way wealthy people lived their daily lives. I couldn't get past the idea of why he would be in the garden with my food.

"Then after that and breakfast, I'm going to take you to the city."

"Really?" I said loudly, refraining from clapping my hands like a little kid although I felt ecstatic. I thought when he said someday he meant like—never. Similar to when a child asks for candy and the parent says, 'maybe later'. They're really just making them stop asking all the while hoping if they wait long enough, the kid might just forget about what they actually wanted.

"Yes, but you have to promise to listen to exactly what I say? That's the only way I can keep you safe. Don't go off on your own again, okay?"

I nodded, keeping a large grin on my face. I knew he was referencing what happen at the grotto lands but tried not to let that make me feel bad, even though I realized it was my fault. "I promise," I said finally after the initial excitement cleared and I had calmed back down.

"That's my girl," he leaned in and kissed me on the forehead, then reached down and took a hold of my hand to lead me to the garden.

6

APPLE JUICE

"The garden didn't look like I thought it would," I said, walking behind Jake out to the car.

He chuckled, "Okay?... What exactly did you think it would look like?"

"I don't know," I did, but I didn't want to say since I felt stupid. "Okay... I thought it was like rows of carrots and tomato vines and stuff like that, not a patio with gorgeous shrubs."

He laughed louder as he reached behind him to take a hold of my hand and help guide me around the array of cars that we just encountered inside their garage. "That makes sense. You might have never seen a garden like ours before."

"Which one is yours?" I was distracted from the previous subject by seeing so many nice vehicles all in one place.

"None of them. I took my car to Nashville. It's probably still parked at my house."

"You have a house in Nashville?" I asked, feeling quite surprised. I wasn't sure if it was something I had previously known or not, but hearing about it now was a bit shocking.

"Yeah... Well, I do if Miller hasn't gone and confiscated it already," he said as he moved closer to a small sleek, shiny blue car sitting near the end.

"Miller?..." The name sounded familiar, but I didn't have a good idea of who he was to Jake. "Oh my gosh, it feels like I don't know you at all." I couldn't help but feel slightly agitated again that I couldn't remember things like I wanted to.

"I know, baby, it's a process," he said as he went around to the passenger side door to open it for me. "It'll take time, but you'll re-learn everything, promise."

"Don't make promises if you can't keep them," I said as I climbed in and sat against the smooth black leather seat.

"I don't," he reached in over me to secure my seat belt for me.

"Wait..." I said, looking around. I started to remember something. It was the car... I remembered being with him before in a car.

"What, baby? What's wrong?"

"It's the car, I remember you... then there was another man. He was scary, though." I couldn't help but start to feel a bit frantic by the flashback. "Why was I running from you? You attacked me..." I said finally looking back up at him.

"Oh my gosh, baby, that's great!" He replied like he didn't hear the last thing I said.

"What's great? The 'you attacking me' part... or the 'scary man' part?" I asked, now more confused by the whole ordeal.

"Ok, well first, I've never attacked you, so let's just get that straight," he said as he stood back up and shut my door before walking around and getting in to drive. "Second," he said like he didn't just take a long break to walk around the car. "It's great because that means you can remember things. The man was a bad guy, but don't worry about him. He died of unnatural causes so he'll never bother us again." He pushed a little button, and I heard the garage door start to open.

"Do you say things trying to confuse me?" I asked playfully, although I meant it.

"Sorry... I didn't attack you. You were afraid of him because you saw he was a Coldier. At the time you were scared of anyone who wasn't me so you ran from him, but you were still my prisoner so I had to kind of tackle you to stop you from getting away." He said it nonchalantly as he began to pull the car out of the drive.

"Oh, ok," that seemed like a fair enough reason for what I thought I remembered. "I'm not sure about you tackling me though, I bet that hurt... You're a big guy."

He chuckled a little. "Nah, you're resilient."

"Whatever..." I couldn't help but roll my eyes. "Is it normal for me to have flashbacks? Will everything come back?"

He didn't respond for a second, he just looked like he was thinking as he started to drive, "Well..." he said finally, "No, it's not normal, actually. But I suspected something was different about the way you were erased this time since you told me you had other memory flashbacks when you were with Luca... Not to mention you can still fight and a few other inconsistencies."

"Okay, what does that mean, then?"

"I don't know... I'm not a Sicari. It was their serum that you took this time, not the Coldiers'. It would be easy to assume they work the same way but now that I think about it, it makes sense that they wouldn't be identical. They were likely made by different doctors, chemists, whatever... I understand the way ours works because I talked to the doctor who helped develop it. Yours... uh, I mean the one that you took last, the Sicari's... I don't know how it works. I guess we'll just have to wait and see."

"Well, if it wears off won't that mean they could track me again?"

"Ugh," he sighed like he didn't like the idea and hadn't thought of it himself yet. "Maybe... It shouldn't be that big of a problem now that we're already in the city, though. The Sicari aren't likely to send agents through the city to look for you when all they have to go on is a wide range of where you'd be. I doubt they would risk it. The problem would be if they had your exact address," he paused to look over at me, then take a hold of my hand before looking back at the road, "Don't worry about it though, baby, that won't happen. You're safe when you're with me." He said, then brought my hand up to kiss the back of it.

"Is that why you're taking me into the city, so I'll be with you?"

A small grin started to creep up on his face like he hadn't told me something. "Well… it's something like that."

"Where are we going?" I wanted to know. I didn't care if it ruined the surprise. Though, looking at his face, I was now suspicious it wasn't the same kind of surprise I originally thought it was.

"We're going to the city like I said we were… That's where Lane lives so I'm taking you to his house for a while to hang out while I go to the agency downtown. I have to report that I'm back in the city."

"What?" I said disapprovingly, seeing my suspicions were correct. "I thought I got to really go into the city with you, not just go to a babysitter's."

He started to laugh, "I'm gonna tell Lane you called him a babysitter, that's funny."

"No, it's not funny. You tricked me." I turned to look out my window and let go of his hand.

"What, are you mad at me now?" He asked. He probably did care, but I'm sure my answer would have no effect on making him change his mind about where I was going.

I didn't respond. I just kept looking out the window.

"Look, you can't go into the agency with me. That would be the last place I would take you, and I don't want to leave you at my parents' alone. I thought you'd enjoy going to Lane's. He has books you can read… uh and probably other fun things you—"

"You know," I interrupted him, "I'm sure that's exactly what you tell a kid when you drop them off at the babysitter's for the first time. You're going to be a wonderful father…" I actually meant it, but I said it sarcastically because I was mad.

"Fine, be mad at me… Say whatever you want if it makes you feel better. But I know what's going to keep you safe, and I don't care if you're upset. You're going to do it and get over it."

I didn't respond. I didn't feel like talking to him anymore. That was the last thing he said to me the rest of the way to Lane's house, too. We both just sat there, letting the silent tension build between us as he continued to drive. Before too long, we arrived. The building wasn't what I expected. It didn't look like a house where someone would live. It looked like a place where people would have their business or their office. He pulled into a spot straight in front and got out of the car and started to walk around.

He stopped and talked to a suited man who was standing outside the entrance. Then, after a moment, he handed him the keys before walking over to my door to open it. He reached his hand down toward me to help me out, but I didn't take it. I pulled myself up, which was actually pretty difficult and still a bit painful—I regretted it and wished I had just let him help me like he offered to.

He didn't say anything, he just put his hand around my waist to help guide me to where I needed to go. I suspected it could also have been to make sure I didn't do anything ignorant again, like walking away from him, since he knew I was upset.

We walked into the building still without saying anything to one another then got into the elevator. He pushed the number 22 button and stepped back to stand next to me. After a minute of riding, the elevator stopped, and I heard a low buzzing sound. Jake stepped forward and pushed another button then spoke into the speaker.

"Lane, we're here."

After a moment, the doors opened. I was expecting to see a hall or lobby, but there wasn't one. It was his apartment we walked straight into.

"Hey guys!" Lane quickly came around the corner to greet us, then stopped to observe both of our faces, probably trying to decide what was going on. "Uh… is there a problem?" He asked, looking at Jake.

"Nope, no problem," Jake said as he brought his hand up to the small of my back to push me forward gently.

"Then why do you two look as happy as hogs at a bar-b-que?" Lane asked, looking over at me, like he expected me to answer. I didn't feel like talking yet though, so I didn't respond, making Lane divert his eyes back to Jake for an answer.

"She's just upset 'cause she thinks you're gonna be a shitty babysitter. Prove her wrong, will ya?" Jake said finally like he was trying really hard not to laugh.

"What?" Lane chuckled, eyeing me with furrowed brows.

"I never said that, Jacob!" I turned and started to walk off into what I figured was the living room.

"She gets her afternoon nap at two, all right, Lane. Make sure she doesn't miss it, or she'll get really grumpy," Jake continued as I walked off. This time, he didn't stop himself from laughing.

"Screw you, Jake!" I yelled out from the room I had walked into, which was actually the dining room.

"Wow, you gonna let her talk to you like that?" Lane asked jokingly.

"Ah, it's fine. That's nothing compared to Eva's mouth." He chuckled again. "I love you too, honey! You sure you don't want to come give me a kiss goodbye?" He hollered back at me.

I didn't respond. I was still trying to maneuver the maze that was Lane's apartment, still looking for the living room.

"Ok… joking aside, don't let her go anywhere, hear me?"

"Yeah, man, you got it."

"I'm serious, Lane! Don't let her try to manipulate you either like what happened with Luca. She's not gonna hur… Um, well, she shouldn't hurt you. She can get feisty sometimes, but you should be fine. Whatever you do, she doesn't leave this apartment!"

"What if I need to pee? You sure he's not allowed to put me on a leash to go for a walk?" I yelled back, figuring I might as well insert a bit more sarcasm into the conversation.

"Pee on his rug, I don't care. He needs a new one, anyway. That thing's hideous," Jake bantered back.

"Hey now!" Lane chimed in. Apparently, he was cool with the insults until one was thrown his way.

I didn't hear anything else for a minute. I figured Jake was probably talking to him quietly; I wasn't sure. Then, before long, I heard the buzzer on the elevator door.

"You promised me, Kaleah, remember? Stay with Lane. You'll be safe. I love you, baby." Jake hollered one more time, reminding me what I agreed to, then the buzzing quit, and I figured he was gone.

By then, I had managed to find my way to what I assumed was the living room. It had a row of bookshelves filled with books and a couple of lounge chairs with a couch offset by a wall of windows.

"Kaleah?" Lane called for me, probably curious where I had gone. I thought about not answering him and hiding to freak him out, but realized it wasn't his fault I was upset. Plus, even though it sounded fun, I knew it was childish, and I was trying to steer away from that kind of behavior, even if it was all I really knew thus far. I really didn't want to be immature, but it was so hard for me when I couldn't remember how to act mature.

"I'm in here!" I yelled so he could hear me wherever he was.

"Oh, hey," he said as he finally walked into the room a few moments later. "You like to read? Is that why you're in here instead of the living room?"

As soon as he said it, I realized his house must have been like Jake's parents' and had way more rooms than any one person needed. "No, I don't like to read... and I thought this *was* the living room," I said, looking around at all the shelves of books.

"No?" He sounded shocked. "You don't like to read?"

It was obvious by how many he had; it was probably his main pastime, but I couldn't actually say that I did or didn't like it since I didn't remember one way or the other. "I don't know," I finally admitted, after thinking about it for a few seconds. "I can't remember if I even know how."

"What?" His level of shock seemed to increase with each of my statements. "Surely you do, you're not that much of a Gyp... uh..." He stopped himself, realizing what he was about to say was offensive.

I didn't respond, instead I acted like it didn't bother me, even though it did. After thinking about it for a second, I realized something. Lane might have not been openly prejudiced toward me, but there was probably still something in him that thought Gypsyins were lesser-than, just like what I saw when I spoke with Bethany. I started to wonder where he would have gotten that idea from, maybe it was the agency. Jake didn't act that way at all though, so I wasn't really sure.

"I'm sorry, I didn't mean to upset you," he said after I'd been silent for a minute. Maybe I wasn't as good at hiding my feeling as I thought I was.

"It's fine," I was hoping we could just move on. "Why don't you show me your favorite book, and I'll see how well I can read some of it?" I smiled.

His face lit up, "Awesome, okay… well let me look. I don't really have a favorite. I love poetry though, do yo… uh right, you don't know. Here I know what to pull. Give me a second and I'll find it. The whole book is poetry. I'll see if you can read my favorite poem from it." He stood there staring at the wall, running his hand along the spines of the books slowly.

"Yep… right where I left it, everything is in alphabetical order," he sounded proud of himself. He opened the book like he knew the exact location he was looking for and, with the flip of a couple of pages, went right to it. "Here," he said finally, handing the book to me. It was thick and heavy, not what I would have expected from a book of poems.

I looked down at the page and began to read. It wasn't difficult at all. I knew exactly what it said.

Honorable Men

The raising of the second sun

Had cast no shadows upon what begun

The men were frail, with elegant ghosts

Close to the ground they lay all the most

Clutched in their hands machines to kill

But no one himself with a dying will

Noises of nothing rang in their ears

Along with shattered cries and isolated tears

The sky grew dark with an ancient appeal

As puddles of rain leveled the hill

Each minute went by, none like the rest

As the thunder screeched the morning's crest

The hollowed out limbs fell from the trees

As the gunfire shot into the shattering breeze

The smell of death ran through the air

As men sat crouched with denying fear

The worried had waited, longing for home

But knowing much sooner they would be all alone

Time was near, with their minds to be set

Would they be honorable, or would they choose to regret

Days and hours they took to believe they were men

For one more second's worth, it would soon all end

They rose to their feet with no hope left

As they said their last prayer and soon went to rest

"What does it mean?" I asked. It was obvious I could read, but now I wondered if I had an issue with comprehension.

"Yeah, it's a bit cryptic, but that's what I love about it. When I first read it I had to make myself slow down and reread it a few times, then I understood what it meant." He said it looking down at me like he was reading it over my shoulder while I had silently to myself.

He didn't actually answer my question about what it meant, but I figured maybe it was a man thing, since it was about men. I closed the book and handed it back to him. I wasn't in the mood to read man stuff.

"Is that why you don't have a girlfriend?" I asked before letting the words go through my mental should-I-say-this filter. I felt bad as soon as I said it, though. "I'm sorry that sounded mean…" I made a yikes-look on my face so he knew it was an accident that I let my thoughts slip out of my mouth.

"It's okay, I guess now we're even." He said kind of laughing as he took the book and put it back up. "I need to reevaluate the way I think about Gypsyins. I'm sorry I said what I did, I'm sure it sounded extremely haughty, which I can assure you, I'm not. As far as the girlfriend thing, you shouldn't believe everything Miles says about me."

I appreciated the apology. I didn't remember what Jake said about him actually, but I knew he was single so I thought I might as well ask him about that. Since the subject came up, I was now intrigued. "Well... you're good-looking. *Why* aren't you with anyone?"

His face quickly turned a faint shade of pink. "Uh... would you... uh... like something to drink?" He said quickly like he felt uncomfortable. There was a glass pitcher with what looked like apple juice in it and a couple of glasses already sitting on one of the shelves between the books.

"Sure," I said, happy to have a glass. Apple juice sounded great.

He turned and picked it up, then poured what I thought was a chintzy amount. I figured beggars can't be choosers though and accepted it from him without saying anything but a polite thank you.

It didn't taste like apple juice at all, but despite that, I loved it. Maybe it was the way wealthy people liked their juice, tart and dry. Maybe it was really expensive, I didn't know. He didn't seem to pay much attention each time I continued to ask for more of it either, so I was happy to get away with drinking way more than I figured he would have wanted.

The conversation continued quite oddly. When he said I shouldn't listen to everything Jake said about him, that made me think about all the reasons he wouldn't be with someone, so I asked if he was gay. I made sure to prelude it with the fact that I would understand, but he didn't take that well either. He was pretty emphatic that even though he was single, he still liked women and only women. He said he'd had many girlfriends in the past, but he hadn't more recently because he just hadn't found the right woman yet that he wanted to spend the rest of his life with. I was beginning to lose track of the conversation at that point, though, so I wasn't sure what else he said about the subject.

It didn't take long until I, for whatever reason, began to feel a bit spacey, and noticed it was harder to concentrate. It wasn't a sensation I was used to at all, so I wasn't sure at first what would have been causing it. Before long, I finally gave up looking for the source and gave in to the feeling since I didn't really mind it.

"I'm a woman... Jake said you're scared, uh, of us... and that's your problem. Are you scared of me?" I asked, trying to get to the bottom of his problem so I might be able to help him.

"No… well, kind of, but it's different," he said as he relaxed back into his chair. "I'm really more scared of Miles than I am of you. It's like he trusts me to watch his most prized possession, and I'm secretly terrified I'll lose you or break you somehow… So yeah, he'd kill me if anything happened and that's kind of scary." He followed it with an anxious laugh.

"Oh, fair," I could see where he was coming from. "So you kissed… uh, you've kissed a girl then, right… like before?"

His face turned pink again. "Well yeah." The way he said it sounded believable, but I wasn't all that sure I believed him since he blushed when I asked.

"I'm not believe you…" I hiccuped. "Here, let me show you how it's supposed to be done," I said as I stood up to walk over to him. A couple of steps in, I stumbled a little. I assumed the floor in that room must have been uneven.

"What?" He gripped the arms of his chair, leaning back, now with a scowl, looking shocked that I would want to help him with his girl troubles, but I knew it would have only been the polite thing to do. "Oh my gosh… Kaleah? How much have you drank?" He asked frantically as he looked down at the jar of apple juice.

I knew he was just probably too bashful to openly accept my help and was trying to get out of it by changing the subject. "Come here, Jake," I wasn't sure why I called him that, but at that moment he did look an awful lot like Jake. I figured that would make it easier on me when I showed Lane how it was supposed to be done.

"Holy shit, he's gonna kill me… Ugh, this is exactly what I was talking about." He said as he began to jockey himself behind his chair, trying to keep me away from him.

"Nooooo…" I was trying to encourage him to see the bright side with me. "He won't mind, he knows you need me… my… uh, women help."

"It's okay… it's okay, Lane," he must have been talking to himself 'cause I was pretty sure my name wasn't Lane. "Miles only said she couldn't leave. He never said she couldn't drink…"

I didn't respond to whoever he was talking to. I just kept trying to get close to him, though he must have been more athletic than I was. He hopped and skipped around the furniture way better than I could. It didn't take long before I couldn't stop myself from laughing hysterically. The idea of his house not being fun quickly changed in my mind the longer we unintentionally played tag with one another.

"Kaleah!…" He must have been getting winded. Each phrase he yelled at me had a long pause between them. "Stop!"… "Oh my god!"… "I'm so dead!"

I continued to chase him around, but now not as much to still kiss him as it was just fun to see if I could catch him.

"Please stop…" he sounded like I was starting to scare him, "you could fall and get hurt."

I was beginning to wear out myself, so I slowed down then sat on a couch that was in what I assumed was probably his actual living room. He must have figured I was tired enough to be done as well because he sat down on a couch across from me like he felt safe.

"I don't know how long it's going to take for that to wear off, but… uh shit… Can you take a nap now or something? I don't want Miles to come back and see you like this." He leaned back, breathing heavy with his face beet red from running and jumping around.

I started to laugh again, thinking about the nap and what Jake said earlier, "Only if I can watch cartoons and eat cereal," I said jokingly.

He perked up like he was hoping I was serious, and he might just do it if he thought that would fix me. Suddenly, I heard the buzzer from the elevator, and Jake's voice through a tiny speaker, "Lane, I'm back."

I looked over at Lane as soon as I realized what I heard and what that meant. His face was frozen with fear, looking at the direction the voice came from like he was terrified to open the elevator doors. Then he quickly looked back at me. "Kaleah, act normal, please… for the love of all things holy, don't let Miles see that you're drunk," he said quietly, then turned and walked over toward what I thought I ran through earlier—the kitchen.

"Ohhh… what?" I said aloud, thinking about what he just told me. "What was in that apple juice?"

The elevator doors opened and Jake was standing there all decked out in his handsome black uniform with one hand behind his back. I could barely see him from where I was sitting, but that was enough to know I liked what I saw. He was so hot; I wanted to touch him. Then I remembered what Lane said and tried to refrain myself from doing anything stupid to alert him to my altered state of mind.

"Uh… Hey, buddy. How'd your trip to the office go?" I could see Lane had greeted him in a way like he was trying to see how long he could keep him away from me.

"Fine. Where's Kaleah?" Jake asked right away.

"Uh… She's good, uh she's not taken her nap yet, she could really use it though—"

"Lane," Jake quickly cut him off, "I didn't ask about her nap. Where is she?"

"Um, yeah uh…"

"What's wrong with her?" Jake snapped, not sounding happy, like he knew Lane had broken his toy and he was scared to tell him.

"In here!" I yelled out. "I'm in the um, couch-y room."

"Lane!" Jake growled. He still sounded upset, but I wasn't sure why.

"What? She's fine."

"She doesn't sound fine!" Jake hissed as he got closer.

I thought I sounded fine. I started to second guess myself. I didn't want Lane in trouble, but I didn't know how to hide my mouth, either. Jake came into the room and just stood there looking at me, trying to analyze what he thought he heard and what he was now seeing.

"See she's still here, just like you asked. She never went anywhere." Lane said as he looked at me with wide eyes like he wanted me to play along even though I thought I was.

"Kaleah, baby, have you been drinking?" Jake said softly as he pulled his hand around finally from behind his back. He was holding a large bouquet of flowers. He took them and sat them down on a table just inside the doorway then walked over and sat down on the couch beside me.

"Uhhh…" I looked over at Lane, not sure what I was supposed to say. He had moved to stand behind the couch across from us, likely so he could run if Jake tried to chase him as I had earlier. "I had apple juice out of the… book room. Does that mean… was it, uh, can I not have apple juice?"

Jake didn't say anything, he just looked at Lane with a mean face.

"Hey, man, you never said she couldn't drink apple juice," Lane said with a grin, doing everything he could to not burst out laughing.

"Dude, I'm glad you think this is funny, 'cause now we're staying at your place tonight."

"Yay, sleep-overs… I love sleep-overs," I couldn't help but express my excitement at the new development.

Jake looked back at me. "Apple juice, huh?"

I smiled and shrugged.

"All right, well, at least you don't still seem mad about earlier, so I guess I can handle it." He said, looking at me then turned to address Lane, "For future reference though, Lane, how about you hide all your apple juice. Next time you baby-sit, maybe just stick with chocolate milk."

"Uh, yeah man, no problem. This wasn't my idea… seriously she's kind of scary. She was chasing me all over the place." I could see right after Lane said it he looked like he regretted it.

Jake leaned forward and brought his hand up to rub his face as he let out a disapproving groan.

"Did you get me flowers?" I couldn't help but feel distracted looking over at them.

"You can stay in my spare bedroom," Lane interjected, talking to Jake again.

"Why thank you, Lane," Jake said still looking down toward the floor, leaning his forehead into his hands. "That's the least you can do now that you made it where I can't take her back to Mom's."

"They're really pretty, I like them a lot," I said still referencing the flowers that I was sure were probably mine.

"You know what?" Jake said, sitting up finally and looking at Lane, "You can make us dinner tonight too, 'cause this shit's your fault."

The rest of the night went well. To no one's surprise I maintained my great mood until we finally went to sleep later in Lane's guest room. I think that's what made Jake not so mad at Lane; he was in a better mood once he saw I wasn't still mad at him anymore.

7

MAN ENOUGH

"They're good, just eat 'em already," Lane apparently didn't like that I was picking at the plate of eggs he had cooked me for breakfast.

Jake laughed, "You tell her, man!" He said, probably happy he wasn't the only one willing to get on me about my eating habits.

"Look, just 'cause you both eat meat like it's going out of style like freakin' cavemen, doesn't mean I have to." I countered back, irritated that they would gang up on me.

"Ah, protein's good for you though… You know before the war Lane was going to be a chef," Jake said smiling really big before he stuffed more food into his mouth. "He loves to cook." I could barely make out what he said. He wasn't the best at talking with his mouth full.

"He cooks, he reads, he's got his own place, he's really hot… maybe I should be with him instead," I said, looking up at Jake with a grin so he knew I was joking.

Lane about spit the food out of his mouth as he started to laugh, then covered his mouth and swallowed, trying not to choke.

Jake apparently didn't think it was as funny as Lane did. "Well, it'd be your loss, 'cause I'm sure he's not as good at *other* things, if you know what I mean," he winked with a smirk as he took another bite of food.

"Well, aren't you Mr. over-confident…" I jested back at him.

Lane didn't say anything but began to laugh again, this time successfully. Apparently, he was enjoying seeing me tease Jake.

"Stop laughing, Lane! She doesn't know what she's talking about. We haven't really done much since she was erased." Jake grinned, acting a bit defensive while still keeping the playful mood. "The Eva before that couldn't get enough of me." He winked at me again like he felt his rebuttal was satisfactory.

Not long after breakfast, Jake must have figured I was back to myself enough we could finally leave and return to his parents' house. We didn't make it far before the conversation in the car became a bit tense between us again.

"But I love weddings!"

"You don't know that, and I told you already, you're not going!" He was acting all hard-nosed again.

"But you said the man insisted that I be there. How'd he even know about me?"

"Mom must have told him I came back and was willing to stay in New York for you. I don't know why she even told him anything. I knew they were friends, but… Ugh, it pisses me off."

"Why? Because I was invited too, and you don't want me to go?"

"No… because he ranks higher than me, he's almost at the top… and the only reason he invited me was because he wants me to work again when I told him I was done with it," Jake's voice was thick with frustration and his knuckles were almost white from how tight he was gripping the steering wheel.

"Who's even getting married?" I asked softly, changing the subject back to the wedding.

"His daughter," Jake said shortly. "It's an Elite's wedding—the daughter of a high rank. That means it's going to be elaborate, massive…

swarming with agents, probably no less than five hundred of them. If I thought taking you to the agency was bad, taking you to an Elite's wedding would be… ugh… no. My answer is no, you're not going. I'm sorry."

"Fine…" I said softly willing to drop the subject. I wondered if Jake's real problem was he didn't like getting ordered around, and he felt like he didn't have a choice but to follow orders this time. I knew it probably wasn't something I should bring up at a time like that, though. It would likely only irritate him more to think I had him all figured out.

I t wasn't long before we were back at his parents' house, pulling into the drive.

"Dad's home…" he said, surprised. I didn't see what he was looking at that gave him that idea, though.

"Is that not normal?" I asked, sensing the odd way he said it.

"Uh, no actually, it's not." He pulled the car around in front of the entrance like Lane had the first day. "He pretty well lives at his office, so to see him here in the middle of the day is, uh… strange."

That made sense, considering I hadn't met him yet, and we'd been there for a few days already. I wondered if I should have expected him to be as unruly as Jake's mother was, but the thought quickly passed as Jake opened my door to help me out.

"I guess this is as good a time as any for you to meet him," he said as he reached down for my hand, then looked over at Steven as he approached from the side. "Steven, would you mind getting the flowers out of the back and putting them in a vase with water in our room? Thank you!"

As we went inside, I didn't know what to expect, what his dad would look like, act like, or why he was even there to begin with. As we walked into the living room, Jake looked around like he was trying to find someone, when he finally caught Bethany coming into the room from another entrance. "Hey Beth, do you know where my dad is? I want to introduce him to Kaleah," he said in a sweet tone.

"I thought I heard you were back," she smiled. "He's in his study. He's waiting on you, actually."

"Really?" Jake tilted his head. "All right, thanks," he said as he took a hold of my hand and lead me through a couple of rooms before we reached a large closed black wooden door at the end of a hall. Jake knocked a couple of times, then turned the knob to enter without waiting for a response.

"Hey, Dad," he said as he walked in before me, then moved over and pulled me up next to him.

His dad was sitting there behind his desk. He looked like an older version of Jake. "Hey, Buddy," he said with a smile that was identical to Jake's. His voice was higher, with a raspy hoarseness, but he sounded friendly. I had a feeling I was going to really like him. "Who you got with ya? It's Kaleah, right?" He looked over at me with his eyes gleaming like a proud father, approving of his son's catch.

"Kaleah," Jake said, pulling out a chair for me across from his dad, "this is my father, Duke. Dad, this is Kaleah, my... girlfriend." Jake gestured for me to take a seat.

"Nice to meet you, sweetie. I've heard so much about you already." Duke smiled then motioned for Jake to take a seat in the chair next to me.

"Only good things, I hope," I said, smiling back while trying to sit up straight like a lady and be as polite as what I thought high society called for.

"Yes, yes... well," he brought his hands up and rested them on his desk like he was waiting for Jake to get comfortable before he had a talk with us. "Elizabeth has her opinions, I have to disregard most of those though," he gave a wry smile then went on, "it's other people's opinions I take more seriously."

I assumed when he said that he was referring to the other Gypsyins in the house, since they were the only other people that had really met me yet, but I didn't know.

"Jacob, my boy!" He said now looking at Jake, "You're decisive, as you should be. I know you've already made up your mind about what you want your future to look like. Tell me… What are your plans with Kaleah?"

I looked over at Jake, trying to see how he would respond. I knew from the conversation with his mother the dynamic between them, but he hardly ever spoke about his dad so I was curious now to see what their relationship looked like in comparison. I was also quite curious how he was going to answer that question as well.

Jake was sitting up straight just as I had been. He wasn't putting off the same energy as he had when we were at the table with his mom, either. This time he acted as if he was sitting across from a military commander, someone he knew was in charge of him. Someone with real power, not just a lust for control.

"Well… I love her so I want to spend the rest of my life with her, whatever that looks like."

I looked back at his dad. He pooched his lips like he was thinking, then made a face like he wasn't quite content with the extent of Jake's plans. "Jacob…" he said finally after staring at him for a moment, "There's an order to life… If you keep that order, things go well for you. We have values… standards to maintain."

"Yes, Sir, I understand." Whatever he said Jake must have gotten the idea, even though I still felt a bit clueless.

"Good, so you're going to marry her and repurchase your own house before trying to have another child then, correct?"

"Yes, Sir," Jake said then swallowed like it was a promise he didn't know how to keep even though he just made it.

"That's my boy," Duke said, then looked back over at me with a pleasant smile, as if none of that just happened. Then, as he stood up from his chair, Jake immediately stood to mirror him. They both then looked down at me like I was expected to do the same.

"Oh, sorry," I said, expressing I didn't know any better, then stood up.

Duke walked around the desk and over to me as he opened his arms wide to offer a hug so I turned and moved toward him to accept one. "If my son is willing to have a child with you, don't worry my dear, he's man enough to commit to take care of you as well," he said, releasing the hug. As he stepped back, he slid his hands down the outside of my arms toward my hands to hold them. I immediately felt a little tense, hoping he hadn't felt that I didn't have a tag. I smiled like I appreciated what he was saying, though.

"Actually, Jacob, would you mind if I had a little chat with Kaleah alone?" He said finally letting go of my hands and moving back around the desk to his chair.

I turned around to look at Jake; he acted like he knew he didn't have a choice. "Um… okay, sure," he said, then looked at me with a look of warning in his eyes, silently telling me not to say anything that I wasn't allowed to say. I nodded like I saw and was agreeing to do my best. He walked out and shut the door while I sat back down in the same chair across from Duke.

"Kaleah… that's a pretty name. Unusual though, I don't think I've ever heard it before. Is that your real name, a nickname or just what?" He asked as he leaned back in his chair and crossed his fingers against his stomach.

"Oh…" I was taken aback a bit by the question even though it seemed simple enough. I was scared he was going to ask about something more intense about my past, or something I couldn't remember. "Um… no, it's not actually. My real name is Eva," I paused, realizing that wasn't quite accurate either, and I didn't want to give him false information. "Well, that's my last name. My full name is Jordan Ellice Eva."

"All right well, miss Eva, where did you grow up? Around here?"

"No," I was trying to concentrate on his questions so I could only give the answers I knew Jake would want me to give. "My parents are Coldiers from Tennessee."

"Good… good. Would you like a drink?" He said as he stood up and walked over to the end of the room where he had a glass jar very similar to Lanes.

"Oh… uh," I knew what it was now and didn't want to hear Jake lecture me anymore on the subject and why he didn't want me to drink it so I figured I would try to refuse. "I can't, Jake said I shouldn't."

"Oh well, that's admirable. There's no harm if you only drink just a little though, please I insist." He said as he poured the liquid into two different glasses then walked back over and handed one to me. I took it and just sipped a little, thinking surely Jake would understand if I told him my refusal hadn't worked.

"Do you love my son, Kaleah?" He asked after he sat back down before he took a sip himself.

"Yes," I said then smiled. I meant it even if I didn't feel like I knew him all that well again yet. I did love him and was excited about the idea of falling into an even deeper love with him over time.

"Good!" He smiled back, happy with my response.

After talking a while longer, I left his office feeling satisfied with my answers. I didn't feel like I said anything Jake would be upset with. The alcohol, on the other hand, I wasn't sure if I wanted to mention to Jake. Considering he had just made it clear to me the night before that he didn't want me to drink because it made me irresponsible or some crap like that. I wasn't paying all that much attention to his lecture though, since I was still a bit inebriated.

"How'd it go?" Jake perked up as I entered our room. I looked at him strangely. He was sitting on a velvety gray couch that hadn't been in there before. "Oh, I was tired of having to sit on the bed all the time, thought we could use some more furniture..." He said nonchalantly like it wasn't a big deal.

"It went well." I walked over to the couch and sat down on the far end away from him. I didn't want to get too close, thinking he might be able to smell the alcohol. I wasn't sure, but figured I would play it safe.

"What are you doing?" It didn't take him long to notice.

"Nothing..."

"Then come here," he said as he patted the cushion next to his thigh.

I rolled my eyes up a little like I was thinking about if I wanted to do it or not. "I... uh,"

"What's wrong?" He asked as he moved himself over next to me instead.

"He made me…" I said, assuming he could now smell it on me.

"Made you what?" He looked at me oddly, probably not sure if he should be concerned or not.

"I'm sorry. He insisted that I drink. I told him you forbid it and it—"

He started laughing before I could finish. "Oh, baby, you're fine." He wrapped his arms around me and pulled me toward him to rest against his chest. "I didn't forbid it, silly. I just don't want you over-doing it, especially when I'm not around, that's all."

"Oh, ok," I said, lowering myself to rest my head in his lap and look up at him while we talked.

"You didn't say anything that would make him think you're a Gypsyin, right?" He asked finally. I knew it had to be the main thing he was concerned about.

"Nope, the subject never came up, so I wouldn't think so," I said, feeling pretty confident that I passed the test.

"Good, that's all that matters really," he smiled and looked at me like he wanted to kiss me, but knew he couldn't reach me without changing our position.

"So… what do you think about what he said to you?" I asked, as I reached up to fluff his hair. It looked so soft and inviting to my hand.

"Well…" He took my hand to hold it instead as he sat back and looked away. "I've been thinking about what the doctor said as well, and it would probably be a good idea to get you some birth control." He didn't sound all that comfortable talking about it, and was trying to avoid the real subject matter of my question.

"So that way you don't have to marry me. Just make sure I can't have your kids, right?" I didn't mean for it to sound as snarky as it did, but I didn't apologize.

"What? No, baby… that's not what I was saying!" He leaned forward to look back down at me.

"That's what it sounded like," I said it softly so he knew I wasn't mad.

"Well, that's not what I meant, so don't take it like that."

"Well, you shouldn't have lied to him then." I knew it might have sounded a bit harsh, but I had to say it, since deep down I meant it.

"What are you talking about? I didn't lie to him." He said, defensive.

"You agreed that you were decisive and already thought about our future. Well, from everything I can see that was a lie. You don't act decisive at all, and you definitely don't act like you want to marry me."

"I can't, Eva," he raised his voice. "I told you, we can't."

I sat up and looked at him, "You're right… Why buy the cow when you can have the milk for free?" I don't know where the saying came from but when it popped into my head, it was the perfect analogy for how I felt so I used it.

"Are you freakin' serious?" He looked genuinely puzzled by my response. "Baby, I love you! I'd marry you tomorrow if I could."

"If you can't, then how will you keep the promise you just made to your dad?"

He didn't say anything at first, he just looked away again like he didn't know how to answer. "I don't know," he said finally, then leaned forward to rest his head in his hands.

"Well, I guess you could buy us our own house. That's a start."

"Dad's old school. He won't allow it without a wedding," he said dejectedly, still resting his head in his hands. "That's probably the only reason he's still with mom. He doesn't agree with divorce either."

"Isn't it your money? Why do you need his permission to get a house?" I reached over to rub his back. I could tell the subject was harder for him than I previously thought.

"It's not that simple, baby. Yeah, I have my own money, but… it's just not how things work. When he dies, the entire company goes to me. I don't really want to upset him. Not to mention he's my dad and I genuinely want to make him proud of me." He sat up a little like talking was helping him feel better. "And it's not that I don't agree with him, either. He's right. I wouldn't be a real man if I didn't make you an honest woman," he said now turning to look at me again.

"What if you just tell him I'm a Gypsyin then? Maybe he'd understand—"

"Eva…" the way Jake said it made me prepare myself that he had gotten upset again at the suggestion. "That's not an option, baby. I know you don't understand, but it's just not," he said it softly like he wasn't upset at all.

"Okay…" I continued to rub his back.

"I don't want you to worry about it, though. I'm going to figure it out, okay?"

I nodded, then leaned over to rest against his shoulder. "Okay."

8

SHITTY PRISONER

"**K**aleah, is there nothing productive you could be doing right now?" Liz asked after her third time walking through the living room for no apparent reason. I was sitting on the couch waiting for Jake to return since he had to leave to run errands.

"I… uh… I was just—"

"Please, spare me your excuses. I refuse to harbor a lazy person in this house, let alone one my son claims to love." She stopped beside the couch with a cocktail in her hand as she stared down at me, assessing my apparent laziness. "I don't mean for this to sound crass but I am having a difficult time seeing what Jacob is so head over hills about when it comes to you."

I was stunned into silence. I couldn't believe she was so transparent with her disapproval of me.

"Go on… tell me. What is it you possess that has his head in the clouds these days?"

"Liz, you barely even know me. I'm not lazy, I just don't have—"

"It's Mrs. Miles, please address me as such. I will not tell you again… Also if you're about to claim that you are bored then I would be more than happy to give you a portion of the Gypsyin's chore load. Surely you possess some useful skills. Cooking perhaps?"

"Um…"

"Oh my gosh, Kaleah…" She sighed dramatically. "You are no better than a Gypsyin. I swear, I don't know what is wrong with that boy. Katherine was such a darling, she was able to cook. Such fabulous cooking abilities, that one." She said, looking off past me, daydreaming.

"Mrs. Miles, I don't think it's fair to compare—"

"Oh, please…" she huffed, bringing her eyes back to mine, now with an even bigger scowl on her face. "Fair? You want to talk about what is fair? Do you think it's fair for my potential future daughter-in-law to bring practically nothing of value to the relationship?" She paused for emphases. "Absolutely not! If we're going to discuss what is fair, I'd dare say you sinking your claws into my son is unfair to him. If you weren't around, he could have a woman that loves him who is mature, able to cook, clean… Hell, she even has her own house. What do you have, Kaleah? A pretty face? That will only get you so far—"

"Mrs. Miles?" Bethany hesitantly broke into the conversation as she walked closer to the couch. Her eyes flicked to mine briefly, then back to Liz's. "There is a delivery you need to sign for at the front door, Ma'am."

Liz gave her a curt nod, then looked back at me again with an evil look on her face. "Good thing Katherine was invited to the wedding. Shame you won't be able to go." She smirked, then turned and walked away.

"Miss Kaleah?" Bethany asked with concerned in her eyes, likely seeing I was on the brink of tears. "Can I…" she trailed off, probably uncertain how to help.

"I'm fine." I said, getting up to go back to our room. "I'd just like to be alone right now, if you don't mind."

"Kaleah?" Jake called. It sounded like he had opened the door and was now inside the room.

"Go away, please. I don't want to talk right now. I already told Bethany that. I just want to be left alone." I pulled my legs in tighter than they already were while trying to keep the blanket over me, but the curve of the couch made it want to keep slipping off.

"Bethany told me mom wasn't being very nice. She didn't tell me what she said, though. I'm sorry I wasn't there, baby," he said. His voice was getting louder the more he talked. I assumed he wasn't listening to my request and kept walking closer instead. "Will you turn over and talk to me? I'm here now." I felt him touch my back like he had sat down on the floor beside the couch.

"It's too late." I didn't want to talk.

"Too late? What do you mean? I wasn't gone long. You know I just had some errands I had to run in town. Are you mad that I didn't take you with me?"

"No, I'm mad that you left me here with her. We haven't even been here three weeks, and this is the fourth time she's been mean to me."

"Is she being mean, or is she just saying things that you don't like?"

"She said that I wasn't good enough for you."

"Those exact words?" I didn't know where he was going with the questions, but they weren't helping, so he might as well not have been trying to talk to me since it wasn't doing any good.

"Just go away!"

"Kaleah, please… I'm not trying to defend her. I'm just asking so I know."

"No, she didn't use those exact words." I was getting more upset trying to think about what she did say to repeat back to him. "She said that I wasn't very mature, and you needed a woman that was mature. Then she talked about how Katherine could cook and clean. Katherine already has her own house, and she was practically perfect, not to mention she's going to be at the wedding that you won't let me go to."

He didn't respond, and I had my head buried in the crack of the couch so I couldn't see how he took what I said.

"So… no, she doesn't have to say those words, but I still get it, I'm not high society… I'm nothing, I'm just a stupid Gypsyin."

"Kaleah… that's not true."

"He's lying to try to make you feel better. You know it's true. You aren't good for him."

"Yes, it is. Now leave me alone. I don't want to talk to you anymore." I knew the voice was right. I'd been hearing it more frequently over the past few weeks. It had to be right.

"Baby, please turn over… I hate it when you're upset like this."

I didn't want to, but he asked it so sweetly I figured I might as well. Something inside me wanted to see his face even though he wasn't listening to me every time I asked him to leave. I uncurled myself and rolled over to look at him.

"What do you need to hear to make you feel better? Do I need to go have a talk with my mom?"

"No!" I knew that didn't work. The last two times he went and talked to her, she just twisted it back around and made it sound like I was overreacting. "I hate it here. This place is awful." The house itself was nice but having to be around his mom all the time made it feel like living in hell.

"Okay…" He said it so easily I was a bit surprised. I figured I would have to argue with him to get him to finally see my side. "I can talk to Lane and see if we can stay at his house for a while until I figure out what to do next. Would that make you happy?" He smiled and brought his hand to my face to tuck my hair behind my ear.

"Uh-huh," I murmured under my breath.

"She shouldn't talk to you like that. I'm sorry I wasn't here to stop her."

"Okay…" I said, accepting his apology.

"Good… Here, now give me a hug." He wrapped his arm around my back and dragged me off the couch onto the floor with him.

"That's not a hug!" I gasped, trying to push the blanket out of my face.

"See… you didn't really want me to go away." He teased, pulling the blanket back and quickly moving his face down to kiss me.

"Yes, I did." I said, playfully pushing my hand against his chest.

He leaned back and looked into my eyes, studying me.

"What?" I asked, curious.

"Nothing," he said softly, as he looked down at my lips, "you're just the most beautiful woman I've ever seen… and I can't believe you're all mine."

I smiled and started to say something, but I wasn't able to get any words out before he leaned in to kiss me again. We had done nothing but kiss since he rescued me from Luca, and I could tell we both were probably thinking we were overdue for something more.

The way he was kissing me this time differed from the other kisses he normally gave me during the day or at night before bed. This one was passionate with intent behind it. It was slow and methodical. He moved in hard, pushing his lips against mine before sweeping them up as he pulled away. Then he gently moved back as he took my lower lip and sucked it into his mouth only to release it again before extending his tongue down into my mouth. He slowly moved his free hand down to my waist, rubbing it gently before slyly slipping it in under my shirt. His touch and the rhythm of his kisses were almost hypnotizing, drawing me in while the rest of the world faded.

"Do you feel like you're ready?" He asked as he lifted his lips from mine briefly. I knew what he meant. I figured he wanted to make sure I had recovered and it wouldn't cause me any pain.

"Yes," I said softly under my breath as I leaned forward, trying to entice him to return his lips to mine as I pushed my hands through his hair.

"Good!" His voice was gruff, close to my ear. "You mean so much to me, Kaleah. I love you so much." He continued as his lips trailed down my neck.

"Jake?" I asked, almost breathless.

"Yes, baby…"

"Is this forever? I mean… you know… us?"

He stopped and brought his face back up to study mine again. "I won't make promises that I can't keep. But…" he paused to search my eyes, "yes, as far as I'm concerned, this is forever. You're my life. What we have isn't usual. It's timeless."

I smiled and nodded, holding myself back from bursting with emotion as I felt a tear slowly trickle down my cheek.

His mouth quickly crashed back down onto mine. He could speak of his love for all time, but showing me was now his aim. It was like I was air to a drowning man who had just burst through the waves and opened his lungs to take me in.

At this moment there was nothing else in all the world, just him and me and what we had together. If this feeling was the byproduct of his love for me, then I decided I wanted it, all of it, and I would give him all of me in return. I would choose him, I would let go and let myself be most certainly, absolutely, utterly, entirely, madly in love with him. Because I already was… and now I knew it.

B reakfast the next morning was delicious as usual, what I ate of it, anyway. The more I talked to Corey the more comfortable I felt being there, even though I still didn't like Jake's mother and did whatever I could to keep my distance from her. I found myself frequently in the garden; it was peaceful there. I enjoyed what small aspect of nature they were able to achieve within such a large building-dense city.

I was excited about the idea of temporarily moving to Lane's house. The last few times we'd gone there the past few weeks had been more enjoyable than the first day. He didn't have any Gypsyins standing around at his beck and call, which I thought was nice. It felt more normal that way.

"Hey, baby, what're you doing out here? I've been looking for you… I asked Corey, but he said he didn't know where you went." Jake said as he walked closer to me while I sat on the ground next to a large white statue.

"Just thinking…" I continued to pick at a small weed that was trying to creep up through a crack in the patio's floor.

"About what?" He sat down next to me and leaned against the short wall that was behind us.

"Life… I guess, I don't know. This place is boring," I said, looking up at him, attempting to smile.

"Wanna go to town with me?" He smiled, knowing the suggestion alone would liven me up.

"Yes!" I didn't have to try now; my face smiled with ease. If it was his goal, it'd worked. Before I let myself get too excited though, I figured I would check to see if he was trying to trick me again. "Just to Lane's though, right?" I assumed that was likely the extent of what he was willing to do.

"No, I was planning on taking you somewhere else I think you'll like." He said, studying my face, probably anticipating my excitement.

"Yay! Okay… Do I need to go get ready, then? Should I ask Bethany to do my hair?" I perked up probably just as he had hoped I would.

"Sure, baby, do whatever you need to make yourself feel comfortable." He released me, then quickly put a hand on my arm to stop me again. "Just make sure you cover your arm really well though, okay? Like wear one of the new shirts I had made for you that makes it difficult for your sleeve to be pulled up."

"Okay," I said, trying to give him my full attention, willing to do whatever he asked of me.

He didn't let go of my arm, instead he just sat there and stared for a moment. Then he leaned in to kiss me as he brought his hand up to the back of my head. The kiss started passionately again the same way it had the day before. He brought his other hand up to my waist to gently pull me toward him.

"Kaleah," he whispered softly in his husky voice. "Do you even realize what you do to me?"

I didn't respond. I didn't want to pull my lips away from his long enough to say anything back.

He moved his hand from my waist just under my shirt to rest it against the skin of my back as he continued to kiss my lips before moving to my cheek.

"Jake?" I said softly, with my lips now free.

"What, baby?"

"Are you happy?"

"Only when I'm with you," he whispered softly into my ear.

"You really mean that? You're not just saying it? Surely there are other things that make you happy…"

He pulled away to study my face as he paused in thought, "I mean it." He said sincerely. "Life before you was pointless…"

I was still stuck in my head about what his mother had said and it bothered me. He was never shy to reassure me of his feelings for me, yet it felt like he was in a delusion. Like whatever I had to offer him was enough for him but me and the rest of the world saw it differently.

"What are you thinking about, baby?" He asked, reaching up to caress my cheek with the back of his hand.

"My past…" It wasn't exactly the truth, but it wasn't a lie. I had also wondered more about my past and the thought that maybe it held more insight into what I had to offer him.

"Oh, yeah?"

"Um-hmm," I nodded. "When you first found me in the woods, how did I act? Was I shy, nervous… uh… or—"

"Rabid," he said suddenly with a large grin.

"No, I wasn't." I pushed against his shoulder, knowing he was teasing me.

He caught my hand before I could pull away and held onto it. "You were scared, yet at the same time entirely brave… I've absolutely never seen the combination in anyone else like I saw in you that day. Even though I could tell the world you'd been living in had broken you, shattered you really, there was still this undying will to survive. Even though you were willing to go with me, and knew it was your plan all along, you still chose to put up a fight—to be feisty—just because…"

I could feel the love and reverence for me as he spoke. At the same time, I sensed he was also speaking about a part of me that was now gone and he longed for.

"Do you miss her?" I asked, curious.

He looked away and softly sighed. "Who? The Kaleah I first met?" He asked like he knew exactly who I was talking about.

"Yes."

"You know, it's weird. Every time you are erased, when you come back I get a new version of you. You're still the same just… altered. Your personality is similar, but…" He paused, pulling his hand away to lean his arms against his legs as he fidgeted with his fingers. "…it's also not." He stopped again and blew out a large breath. "Kaleah… it's so hard to explain. It's like you keep dying and every time you're resurrected I'm left with the same emotions—grief, regret, anger… then relief."

"Regret?"

He looked at me suddenly, taking my hand again. "Not like that. I've never regretted what we have or have had. Never regret for my decisions to be with you, to love you… It's always regret for how we got in the situation for you to be erased again, that's all."

I nodded in understanding but couldn't stop my mind from taking his admissions and twisting them. Thinking about all the pain that I have put this poor man through. His mother's words kept coming back to me, making me wonder if she was right. Was I being selfish by holding on to him?

"Where are you planning on taking me?" I asked, changing the subject.

"That's a surprise. You'll just have to wait and see." He eyed me as he ran his thumb over his lower lip, pensively.

"I'm surprised. I thought you'd never take me anywhere since you think I'll get caught and forever be a prisoner." I smiled teasingly. "You're just jealous. I'm such a good prisoner that you don't want me to be anyone else's."

He shook his head. "You were a shitty prisoner," he said, looking over at me, grinning as he played along. "Super rebellious… always running away. Out of all of my prisoners, you were the worst. Definitely shitty."

I started to laugh, then leaned over to cozy up to his side. "I guess I'm not all that keen on taking orders."

He smiled then reached over to push the hair out of my eyes, "It's the Eva in you… She's somethin' fierce."

I smiled, not sure exactly what he was referring to, but figured it was something good so I didn't inquire further.

"Now… you're gonna go get yourself cleaned up and ready to go to town," he said before kissing me on the head and lending me his hand to help me up.

"Yes, sir," I said with a smirk, then winked.

9

FINDERS KEEPERS

J ake said the city was never really the same after the war. Not only did it now have more strict rules, but it also had more demand on goods with less supply. Though, from what I could tell as we drove through it, it didn't appear to be dying—quite the opposite, actually. There were people everywhere. Gypsyins, Coldiers, I couldn't tell exactly who was who. They all blended in with each other.

I wasn't sure why but I felt safer with large crowds of people around. Maybe I felt like it would be easier for me to blend in, less likely to be noticed. It must have been the opposite feeling for Jake, however. The more people we saw and drove past, the more and more tense he appeared, gripping the wheel harder and readjusting in his seat over and over.

He never told me where we were going. He just said it would be a surprise, a real one this time. No bait and switch. I watched the people walking down the sidewalks as we passed; they looked normal just like me. There weren't a huge number of them in uniform like what Jake wore, but they didn't all have their arms visible either.

"If a Gypsyin gets papers, how do they know the papers go to that Gypsyin?" I thought I would ask while I had an epiphany fresh in my

85

mind. Why can't I share papers with Bethany? It seemed like a brilliant idea.

Jake didn't answer right away. He seemed super focused on the road and not on the question. "Hang on, baby, ask me again when we get there."

I didn't remember whether I had ever driven before or if I even knew how, but I could understand why he wouldn't want to talk while he felt anxious. "Okay," I said quietly, feeling determined to remember the question, since it was such a good one.

We drove for another few minutes until we finally arrived at wherever it was he was taking me. He stopped the car and parked in front of a large building. It looked like it was made of nothing but reflective windows.

"No… you know what, I don't want to do that," he said, talking to himself as he bent forward a little to look up through the windshield at where we were.

I didn't say anything. I didn't want to distract him. I figured he knew what he was doing and didn't need me asking questions. He put the car back in drive and went forward again, but just a few car lengths until we came across a large hole in the side of the building. I assumed it was a garage and as he turned to pull into it; I saw that I was correct. Initially, I was divided between the thought of how I even knew that and the feeling of wanting to congratulate myself for knowing more than I realized I did. It was short-lived once we finally parked and started talking again, though.

"Going through the garage will be safer than using the valet at the front doors," Jake spoke finally, free from the anxiety.

"Oh, okay, yeah I guess that makes sense."

"What were you asking me about now?" He looked over at me as he relaxed against his seat.

"Oh, right… Why can't you use papers from one Gypsyin with another?" I asked not really wanting to bring Bethany into it yet unless he didn't have an answer to the question and it was actually a feasible solution to our problem.

"Fingerprints…" he said like he'd already thought about it, "you have to give them your prints when you fill out the paperwork."

"Ok… but like theoretically, if someone asked to see my papers, and you showed them another Gypsyin's, they aren't going to sit there and look at my hand and analyze if the prints match… right?" I thought the question made enough sense.

"No, you're right, they can't verify them on the spot, but if they're suspicious, then they'll take you into the agency to have them verified… So yeah, you could do it and maybe get away with it… once, twice, but it's not worth it. The problem is when—not if—you do get caught. If someone is suspicious that you're doing it, they could report you… If we got caught, it's not the same consequences as just having a Gypsyin without papers. It's much worse."

"How?"

"Both Gypsyins are put to death, the one the papers belonged to and the one without the papers… They'd hang you, Kaleah." His voice lowered to an uneasy hum. He couldn't look at me when he said it. "They take counterfeit papers seriously, very seriously."

"Oh," it was easy to see now why he hadn't brought it up before as an option. "Well, what happens to the Gypsyin's owners?"

"They're heavily fined and they lose both Gypsyins, and for most, that punishment is enough to deter people from trying it."

"Okay… never mind then."

"That was a stupid question…"

"You ready?" He looked back up at me finally and smiled.

I nodded. "Where are we going?"

"You'll see… it's still a surprise." He winked, then opened his door and walked around the car to my side where he opened my door and offered me his hand to help me out. I took a hold of it to pull myself up but he didn't let go once I was done. "We have to walk across the street and down a block. It's crowded… stay close to me, all right? Whatever you do, don't let go!"

"All right," I said, feeling a bit skittish, but followed tight against him as he began to walk in front of me, parting the crowd of people as we went.

He was right; it was crowded. There were so many people, something in me started to panic. I gripped his hand tighter, noticing my palm was getting sweaty.

"Jake," I shouted up to him as he continued to lead me but he didn't turn to respond. He must not have heard me.

I couldn't help but feel overwhelmed. Everyone's voices were getting louder. Then, without realizing it I could distinguish more sounds, more than I usually could. The clicking of heals, the thud of boots, the swishing of pants all like a crescendo as it mixed with the loud chatter of everyone's voices—everything was beginning to overwhelm me.

"He's going to lose you!"

"Stop it," I finally yelled at the voice, knowing it wouldn't matter over all the other noises, anyway.

I looked down after I yelled it. I was stopped. Jake was no longer pulling me anymore. I slowly lifted my hand to stare at its new vacancy, blinking blankly, trying to think about what happened. Shit… Did he let go? Did I let go?… Where is he?

Panic ensued. My breathing became fast and shallow while a light sweat broke out all over my body. Bile began to rise in my throat at the thought of losing him.

I didn't move, I just frantically looked around. There were people so close, only inches from my left and my right, quickly passing by, some bumping into me where I stood.

"Jake!" I screamed, hoping it might help him locate me among the horde of people that I felt were now suffocating me.

"You should run!"

"I can't do that." I didn't know why I kept hearing that voice but I didn't think it was right this time. That didn't sound like a good idea. I looked around again, trying to see anything that looked like what he was wearing or anyone who looked like him. People continued to bump into me almost on all sides. It was all I could do not to be knocked over and trampled.

"Kaleah?" I heard Jake's voice. He must have been shouting for me as well.

I called back to him, hoping he could hear me enough to make his way back. Then I felt someone from behind grip my shoulder tightly. Instantly I felt relieved as I turned to make sure it was actually him who finally found me like I assumed it was.

"Ma'am, are you lost?" It was an agent. He was dressed just like Jake, wearing nothing but layers of different tones of black, but it definitely wasn't Jake.

A wave of terror mixed with nausea begin to overtake me starting at my knees but working its way up quick enough to my throat that I couldn't speak as clearly as usual, "Uh... yea... I'm... no, I mean... no, I know..."

"You sound lost," he said as he released his grip from my shoulder and brought his hand down to grip my upper arm even tighter.

"No... Stop! I know where I'm going!" Finally something in me kicked in enough to sound confident in my lie. I thought about calling out to Jake again, but didn't know if it would help or make the agent want to take me away faster.

"Fine," he said, loosening his grip a little. "Let me see your tag, then you're free to go."

"Uh..." I looked down at my arm, hoping I could stall just long enough for Jake to make his way to me. I halfheartedly tugged on my sleeve, pretending like I was trying. "My sleeve is too tight. I can't pull it up."

He gave me a look like he didn't believe me and even if it was true; he wasn't going to let it slide on principle. "Woman... I don't care if you show me here or at the agency, but I'm gonna see it one way or another." There was a harshness in his tone and a coldness in his expression that felt familiar to something I've seen on Jake, though I couldn't remember when.

I didn't respond. I didn't know what to say to get myself out of the trouble I could see I was now in. I just looked around again, hoping I would see Jake so I could call for him.

"Fine then, if that's how you want it, that's what I'll do." The agent said, looking at me with little to no compassion in his eyes as he moved to my side. He gripped me tightly at the waist with one hand and my upper arm with the other, then began to push me forward.

"No… Okay, okay, I'll show you, I'm sorry. I'll show you," I said, trying to stall again. Somehow I knew if I didn't stay where Jake lost me, he might never find me again.

"She's with me," a strong voice spoke from behind us, but it wasn't Jake's. I began to turn around to see who it was that was claiming me but was beaten to it by the agent.

"What's your rank? I found her, and she won't show me her tag… It's protocol," he said after he spun around to address the voice.

"Henry Lane, Recon Scout Agent, Pillar 14, 11th rank. She's with my brother, TC Agent Miles, so I suggest you take your hands off her before he sees how you're manhandling his girlfriend." Lane said, standing tall, staring the man down without breaking eye contact even a little.

The man immediately loosened his grip and slightly pushed me away as he did, "Oh, Sir, of course… I'm sorry. I didn't know." He stuttered a bit. From the fear I now saw in his eyes, he clearly recognized Jake's name.

Lane smiled finally as he let himself briefly look away from the man over to me then back, "You're just doing your job, I understand." He said as he moved forward, narrowing the space between me and him then took a hold of my arm as the man had, though his firm grip was comforting rather than scary. He nodded at the man, then the man nodded back, seeing he'd been released, and turned to walk away.

"How did you find me?" I asked, seeing the other agent had left and I could talk to Lane freely.

"Why aren't you with Miles?" He asked without answering my question first. His voice wasn't as lively and cheerful as usual but it wasn't as stern as Jake's sounded when I was in trouble either.

"I was with him. My hand slipped away from his and I couldn't find him again with all the people." I didn't know why I had to defend myself but I did nonetheless.

"Let's go," he said now stern like Jake would. He gripped my arm tighter and began to walk while pushing me in front of him.

"Are you mad at me? Am I in trouble? Jake's probably looking for me... Where are we going?" I turned to talk so he could hear me as I kept walking. I felt extremely confused the further we walked and not hearing him answer any of my questions. Before long, we finally stopped outside what I assumed was a bakery from the strong yet pleasantly overpowering smell of bread in the air.

"I'm not mad at you," he said finally, without looking at me. He just kept looking around like maybe he was watching for Jake. I wasn't sure. "But seeing this and what Miles has told me, you do seem to have a knack for getting yourself lost."

I didn't feel like that was a fair statement but I didn't argue with him. "What are we doing here?" I was hoping he was about to tell me of a preconceived plan he and Jake devised for such an occasion.

"This is where he was taking you," Lane said like maybe I was right about them having a plan. "He's probably still out there looking for you. But he won't know I have you until he finds us."

I guess I was only partially right. "Ok, well, how do you know he will come here? If you hadn't found me, I wouldn't be here... He never told me where we were going. It was a surprise."

"I know that," he said as he relaxed against the brick wall of the building next to the restaurant. "I guess I just figured he might have faith in my superior tracking skills."

I didn't respond because I didn't understand what he meant by it. I'm sure my confusion was showing on my face, though.

He finally looked away from the sidewalk down at me. "It's an inside joke," he said now smiling. "I like to tease him and tell him I'd make a better track and capture agent than him." He looked back toward the sidewalk, still watching for Jake. "Until you came along, I never got a chance to prove it to him... But now that I found you before he did, I plan on rubbing it in his face," he chuckled like he was excited about the opportunity. "After he's not upset about losing you first, of course..."

"How'd you know he lost me?"

"I'm a Recon Scout. It's my job to watch people..." He said, then smiled even bigger. "It's because I'm an awesome babysitter, even if you don't think so," he looked over at me again.

"Thank you!" I realized I hadn't said it yet, but really did appreciate him saving me from whatever crap could have happened if the other agent had taken me with him.

"My pleasure... I'll take any chance I get to hold something over Miles." He smiled again probably thinking about the fun he could have teasing Jake after this. "This probably won't be good for you, though."

I didn't know what he meant by it but felt a little anxious after he brought it up, "What do you mean, will he—"

He must have noticed the trepidation in my voice. He interrupted before I could finish, "He won't be mad at you, if that's what you think I meant. I was just trying to say this is exactly why he didn't want to bring you to the city. It's easy for something so simple to happen and then you get lost... stolen, erased... All I meant was, he probably won't want to bring you back again for a while, that's all."

"Kaleah!" Jake's voice yelled loudly from the direction we came but I still couldn't see him through all the people walking by.

"Jacob Miles," Lane cupped his mouth with his hands and quickly called back in a loud commanding voice, one I knew I wouldn't have been able to match even if I tried.

After a few moments, I saw him finally, clad in his all-black attire, a good head higher than most. He was walking but then once he made eye contact with me; he picked up his pace to get to me as quickly as he could. His face started to brighten up like it was reflecting a beam of light until he looked over at Lane who now was displaying a huge smirk on his. From that, Jake's face dulled a bit back to an 'oh shit—what could have just happened' face. He looked back at me, relieved to see me but probably not expecting the backlash from Lane on having lost me to begin with.

"Oh my gosh, baby, you scared me," he said when he finally got to me, completely ignoring Lane and leaning in to embrace me. He held me tight against his chest, running his hands up and down my back briskly as he nuzzled his face into my hair and breathed in deeply.

"I'm sorry." I hoped he didn't feel like Lane and think I just had a talent for causing problems.

"I know, baby, you're okay." He hugged me harder, not ready to let go just yet.

"You are welcome," Lane interjected, prompting Jake to finally release me and pull away, only slightly, to look at him.

"What, you want a cookie?" Jake asked sarcastically as he leaned over and brought his arm around my back to grip me tightly at the waist. I'm sure in a way that was more difficult to lose me again.

"Yeah, man, for sure! I mean, I guess that's probably not the best pay for the high quality babysitting I've been doing lately but hey… I'll take what I can get," Lane laughed loudly, thinking he was funny.

"Well, too bad," Jake said like it was hard for him not to laugh as well but he was doing an excellent job holding it back. "Where did you find her? After her hand slipped, I looked all over but all the people around were pushing me so bad, I couldn't see where she went."

"I didn't go anywhere," I said finally, speaking up. I knew he wasn't blaming me but I wanted to get my side of the story in before the whole thing was about to be told just from Lane's perspective.

"Yeah, she's right. She didn't move. Once I saw you two had lost each other, it took me a minute, but I was able to get to her before anything bad happened," Lane said matter-of-factly.

"Wait? You were watching us?" I asked, now confused and taken aback a little at what all that entailed. It made sense with how fast he'd gotten to me, but it was still surprising now that I'd thought about it.

Both Jake and Lane looked at each other like they weren't sure who was the one that should fess up.

"It's no big deal, baby, I just asked Lane to watch from a distance… You know, so if anything happened to you, I would have backup." Jake said, looking down at me, trying to get me to relax about the idea of being spied on.

"Yep… and you saw if I wasn't there what could have happened?"

Lane said, looking at me, then winked. "I mean like since Jake couldn't find you, you could have gotten really lost if it weren't for me." He smirked again after he said it, probably figuring it was now a good time to rub it in.

I realized with the wink he was probably indicating he didn't intend to tell Jake how close of a call it really had been with the other agent. If that was the case, maybe Jake wouldn't be as likely to not want to bring me back again. I appreciated the gesture and felt it was a good tradeoff for them teasing me about having to be babysat so I didn't say anything to the contrary.

"Since you're already here, Lane, why don't you come in and eat with us? It was supposed to be romantic but just your presence alone has already screwed that up… So you might as well come in and get your cookie," Jake said gesturing to the door.

"Dude, that sounds great." Lane didn't seem bashful at the invitation as he turned to open the door and walk in, holding it open for us. "You know, if you guys are gonna be living with me, I'm gonna have to have some better house rules in place."

Jake gently pushed me ahead of him and then stood next to me while we waited for someone to take our order. "What are you talking about, Lane?" He asked still looking ahead.

"Well… you guys can't be making a bunch of noise… Uh, you know, my walls aren't crazy thick," Lane said with a huge grin.

"Don't be jealous, Lane," Jake turned to smirk back at him. "It's not my fault I got myself a hot woman and you don't."

"Well, that's until you lose her again," Lane retorted back without missing a beat. "Next time you lose her, when I find her first we might just play finders keepers," Lane said it like he was joking then looked at me again trying to hold himself back from laughing but wasn't as good at it as Jake.

Jake turned to grin at him. "You couldn't handle her," he said as he reached down to hold my hand. "She's almost too much woman for me… but… because I'm more man than you, we're good." He chuckled, then turned back to the display case.

IO

ANOTHER GIRL

"Miss Kaleah? Are you out here?" Bethany called for me. I wasn't technically trying to hide, but I knew I was probably hard to find and I liked it that way. Until Jake returned, I would do whatever I needed to do to stay as far from his mother as I could.

I hesitated to answer her. I wasn't sure I wanted to reveal where I was, but soon gave it up when the curiosity of what she wanted from me had become too much. "I'm over here!" I yelled finally. I was sitting next to the fountain, in the same place in the gardens I had been the day Jake came out and found me.

I faintly heard her little feet delicately moving closer to me. "Oh, there you are… Are you all right?"

I knew that wasn't the reason she'd originally come looking for me but it was polite of her to ask, so I thought I might as well reply to the question before finding out why she was really there. "Yes, I'm fine. I like the sunlight out here; it makes me feel better."

"Oh, ok… There is a gentleman here to see Jac—Mr. Miles… Do you know where he is? I haven't been able to find him. I've looked everywhere." Her speech was courteous and dainty.

"Um, yeah…" I started to respond, but was mentally interrupted by the thought of who would come to visit him. "He went to town. He said he had to pick up something he'd ordered."

"Is he with Lane then?" She asked.

"I… don't know." Jake was pretty vague that morning about where exactly he was going so I didn't know what to tell her.

"Oh…" She sounded like she wasn't sure how to proceed. "Well, do you at least know when he might be back?"

"He said later this morning, but other than that I'm not sure. He lives on Jake time so that really could be whenever," I said, trying not to smirk since my clever description of his time management skills amused me. "I can talk to whoever is here, though."

"Okay!" she said, relieved. "He's sitting in the receiving room. Follow me."

I pushed myself up, using the statue sitting next to me to lean on, then realized that was a bad idea when I felt it move a little. I made a mental note not to sit there again as I finished standing, then followed her back into the house.

"Andry!" I said, when I recognized the over-sized man sitting on their little sofa. "Do you remember me?" I walked around to sit on the couch across from him then dismissed Bethany with a nod and a smile.

I don't know how long he'd been waiting in there but it looked like I had disturbed his nap time. He opened his eyes and looked a little puzzled, maybe wondering why he was talking to me and not Jake. "Kaleah… yes," he smiled finally like he'd recognized who he was really looking at. "Is Miles not here?"

"No, not yet, sorry… Was there something important that you needed him for?" I asked as I adjusted myself to lean back on a large pillow that was sitting there likely only for decoration.

"Um, yeah I have a message for him." His voice was deep and gravely like what I'd think a bear's would be if they could talk. The longer I sat there looking at him, I noticed other things that I hadn't previously. He had dark brown skin and a thick black beard with a shiny bald head. Though large in stature, he didn't look overweight, but was definitely thick and muscular. He looked quite cuddly actually, though, also quite intimidating. I wouldn't want him as an enemy, that's for sure.

I thought about what he said for a second, curious if he would give me the message or if he felt like he needed to wait for Jake to return. I also wondered about Luca and once they got him to Nashville, what happened to him from there? I knew it wasn't a question he would answer and probably not a good one to ask either so I didn't. "If you're in a hurry, you can give me the message. I'll tell him once he gets back." I offered, knowing it was probably a long shot.

"Oh... I'm sorry, it's not something I can uh... I'm afraid it's personal." He grumbled, likely not knowing how to respond to me. He was probably trying to walk a fine line of being polite, at the same time, telling me it was none of my business.

I thought Jake hadn't been keeping any more secrets from me but realized that was unrealistic, knowing him. "I understand," I said as I let my eyes drift slowly away from his so he might sense my disappointment.

It didn't take long for me to see he really was a tough nut to crack. We sat there in an awkward silence for a few minutes. I was close to getting up and excusing myself, seeing that the conversation had ended and I wasn't getting anywhere, when I finally heard Jake's voice billowing through the house. I couldn't quite understand what he was saying, but he sounded like he was in a lively mood, one that wasn't all that common for me to witness.

"Jake," I yelled for him so he knew where we were.

However, before I was able to get too loud, Andry suddenly stood up and in his deep husky voice intervened, "No, I got it..." he said as he turned to walk toward Jake's voice. He acted like he'd been in the house before and knew exactly where he was going as well as felt comfortable going wherever, without permission.

Seeing he was leading the way, I immediately got up to follow him. He clearly towered over me more than most men, so all I could see walking forward was his back.

"Take this up to my room, will you? I don't want Kaleah to see it, so if she's not in there already distract her until I'm done." Jake was speaking to someone, probably not realizing yet that I could hear him. After following Andry past one more room and into the next, I heard Jake again, "Andry, my man, I was expecting you. Got any news for me about the girl?"

As soon as I heard him ask, I wanted to duck and hide, realizing I probably wasn't supposed to hear whatever Andry's news was but I wasn't far behind the giant so I figured I would be caught.

"Uh... Boss," Andry said as he raised his arm, thumbing toward me behind him. Then he swiftly moved over to the side, revealing to Jake that I was standing right there.

"Hi," I said softly with a small smile like I knew I was caught even though I wasn't actually trying to be sneaky or hide in the first place.

Jake cringed like he was thinking about what he just said and if it was too much for me to have caught on. "Hey, baby," he said clearing his throat, trying to pretend that whatever he said didn't matter. "Um... I have some business to talk to Andry about, uh..." he trailed off, probably trying to think of a nice way to tell me to go away.

"I'll leave," I said before he could finish. I knew he wanted to talk to him in private. I didn't like the idea that they were most likely talking about more secrets he'd been keeping from me, though.

Jake didn't say anything, he just narrowed his eyes, but then relaxed and nodded like he didn't know if he should stop me or just let me go. "All right..." He said, though sounded a bit stunned that I would be so willing.

I realized he might not have known he'd have to deal with the consequences later but if he was still keeping secrets that's exactly what was going to happen when we were alone again. I turned to walk out and started in the direction that lead back to our room then realized I couldn't go there either so I moved back through the living room to go back out to the gardens. I sat down next to the same not-so-stable statue that I had decided to stay away from and leaned back against the fountain's wall.

"You're alone… He doesn't really love you, or he wouldn't still keep secrets."

I didn't want to listen to it, but the voice was right to some extent. Not only was I literally alone at the moment but I felt alone as well. It didn't matter how many people were around or how many were currently in the house; I was lonely. I knew it didn't make much sense. Jake was with me so much of the time but I just couldn't help the feeling of being forsaken, not even as much by him as just by the world. I didn't belong here. I was nothing, just a Gypsyin, a nobody.

"Leave him. You can find someone who treats you better than he does. Someone that really loves you, and doesn't just pretend to…"

I didn't like that idea either. Whether I felt like the voice was right or wrong didn't really matter, though. It still spoke to me, mostly when I was alone. Sometimes my mind would be clear enough to see the voice was nothing more than an enemy to my good nature. It always sounded like it had my best in mind but when I really thought about what it was telling me, it was clear it wasn't anything that was for my benefit.

The problem was when I already felt distant and upset, that's when the voice would come and I couldn't distinguish it from my own thoughts. I couldn't tell it to go away. I couldn't decide it wasn't good for me. Those were the times I felt inclined to believe it. It's like I had an enemy inside my mind that at the most opportune times did a fantastic job of convincing me it was an ally, and I knew no different.

I didn't have anything to do but sit there thinking about what I overheard him say before he knew I was there. I wondered what item he had taken to our room that he didn't want me to see. That could have been anything, so I didn't let my thoughts linger on it for too long until I considered what I heard him say to Andry. It was something about a girl… Why would he need to talk to Andry about another girl in Nashville, or was it Nashville? Maybe there was another one in New York… The longer I sat there thinking the more depressed I felt. I leaned against the statue and closed my eyes. Whenever I felt that way, generally a nap always made it better, at least for a little while.

"Eva, get up… you're a better fighter than that. Lewis hasn't even been here for a month… I know he's bigger than you but you've got more in you than that, I know it. So get off your ass and show me!" There was a large muscular man yelling at me from across the room. His words, although forceful, I knew were good-natured.

"Is this the Eva you were telling me about, Johns?" I looked over to where I heard another voice in the opposite corner of the room. The man who said it, slowly started to walk over toward me as he began to roll up his sleeves. His left arm had something on it. There were three small circles all lined up in a row. They were a deep red color that slightly glistened from the bright lights overhead. He motioned, telling the beefy man who had just pinned me to leave. "Get up!" He said as he stood there now looking down at me.

I stood up and looked at him square in the eyes, not liking the way he spoke to me.

"Well, she can follow orders at least," he said as he turned his head back to speak to Johns. Then, without fully turning back toward me, he spun around quickly, as if to surprise me with a punch in the stomach. Even though he was fast, I saw his intent before he did it and pivoted back on my right heel while leaning to the side so his extension only grazed me, nothing more. He looked up at me surprised, then tilted his head as he furrowed his brow. "You're fast," he said still staring, studying me.

I nodded, knowing not to smile. I didn't want him to think I was being disrespectful.

"I don't suggest you try to grapple with her." Johns spoke up again, talking to the man. "Unless you're sure she's the one you want, then I guess it's your choice if you want to test her out. From what I can tell, though, she's ready for the field. I haven't had a man who isn't twice her size like Lewis here, be able to pin her—she's too quick."

The man who tried to hit me just stood there, now smirking like he knew what he wanted. Then he looked down, eyeing my body, judging it. Maybe he was thinking about how small I was and if that would hinder my fighting, I didn't know. "Nah, she's great. I'll take her."

"I'm not a cow. If you want me as your partner, you need to put in a request just like anyone else." The words came out of my mouth without me thinking. I wasn't all that fond of how he was looking at me.

The man's smirk quickly disappeared and was replaced by a scowl. "Well, isn't that unfortunate…" His eyes flicked back up to mine as he made a tsk motion with his finger.

"What?" I asked, knowing I was talking to a superior but didn't care.

"You'd be perfect if you could just keep your mouth shut," he said, then turned around apparently done with the exchange, having changed his mind.

"Eva, dammit!" Johns must have seen the man's loss of interest and felt the need to scold me. "Reagan, wait…" he held up his hand, trying to get him to reconsider.

"Marcus can have her!" The man said as he turned back to speak to Johns while looking at me briefly over his shoulder. "After he's done training her mouth to stay shut, since you're apparently incapable, I'll reconsider her again when it's time for a re-assignment." He concluded, then turned to walk out.

Johns clinched his jaw, dragging his angry eyes back to me. "You couldn't just behave for once, could you?"

"Nah, that's not my style," I said not caring that I just lost him a decent commission.

"Eva, I swear," he looked at me like even though he was irritated, he still couldn't help but feel a bit of endearment for the real me, rebellious and all. "Fine, but when Marcus gets here, you better not pull the same shit with him! I'm not going to have my best not go to the best. Do you understand me?"

"I doubt Reagan would like to hear that," I said flatly.

"Second best then…" he shrugged. "You know what I mean. You're going to keep your mouth shut, hear me?" He stood there and pointed a finger at me, trying to be stern. He was clearly holding back a smile though, because the corners of his mouth twitched before he quickly looked away.

"I'm sorry I lost you your commission, Johns," I said sincerely. "But I'm not a cow," I smirked, so he knew even though I was sorry, I would do it all over again.

"Get outta here, go back to your dorm," he rolled his eyes. "Sorry, my ass…" he said, then turned to call Lewis and the other boys back into the room.

"Kaleah?" Jake's voice startled me from my dream. I couldn't help but feel perplexed as I lay there thinking about what I had just heard, seen, experienced… "You can't be comfortable like that, baby. You could have taken a nap on the couch."

I looked up at him, still feeling a bit groggy, then down to myself to see what he was talking about. Apparently, in my sleep I had shifted from leaning against the statue to curled up beside it, laying straight on the concrete.

"What's wrong?" Jake looked at me like he could sense something I couldn't yet.

"What? What do you mean? I'm fine," I groaned, dismissing his concern, trying to sit up.

"The face you're making… it just looks… I don't know, upset." He reached down and took a hold of both of my hands, preparing to hoist me up.

I immediately realized what he was sensing, as I remembered the flashback, dream, whatever it was, I had just had. I didn't want to tell him about it, though. I wanted to think about it and analyze what exactly it meant before he could tell me what he thought it meant. There was also a part of me that liked the idea of having my own secrets from him, since he was still choosing to keep some from me. "I'm fine," I said coldly as I reached my hands up, letting him pull me to my feet.

"Kaleah, don't lie to me." He said without stepping back so now we were just standing there staring at each other.

"Lie?" I scoffed. "I'm not the one keeping secrets, Jake. You're smart. You tell me why you think I'm upset." I said, trying not to look too cross, but I didn't know how successful I had been.

He just stood there looking at me like what I said took him off guard. "I don't know what you're talking about."

"Whatever, Jake, I don't have time for this," I said as I pushed past him and began to walk back toward the house. I didn't know where my sense of confidence suddenly had come from but I was suspicious the dream might have had something to do with the new attitude.

"What?" I didn't get far before he reached out and grabbed my wrist to stop me. "Eva? I don't understand why you're acting like this."

"You said you wouldn't keep secrets from me anymore, yet Andry apparently has a few to share with you that I'm not allowed to hear. Then you have Bethany take something to our room that I'm not allowed to see. You're talking about another girl with him. Then, on top of that, I just had a dream that told me I was more than you've been letting on." I didn't intend to say the last part but got carried away and it slipped out with the rest.

His face looked like he wanted to make it the usual stern wall he liked to hide behind but he must have known I was right and it wouldn't work this time. "Okay... you're right, we need to talk." He said with a sigh as he ran his hand through his hair.

"Too bad. I don't feel like talking to you right now," I said, now feeling more upset than confused. I pulled my wrist away and started to walk back toward the house again.

"Where are you going?"

"To our room. I hope whatever you asked Bethany to hide, she hid well." I said, without turning around.

"Eva, wait," his voice grew closer like he was now following me, "before you go in there, let me explain."

"No!" I kept walking but then, after hearing him behind me, picked up the pace a little. That made me want to get to the room even quicker.

"Seriously?" He sounded more annoyed than upset as the sound of his footsteps picked up their pace behind me.

It didn't take long before it turned into a bit of a chase. The activity helped my mood lighten a little and I could tell it was getting harder trying to stop myself from giggling at how we were both acting. As I reached the middle of the stairs, the thud of his boots grew even closer.

"Eva! I'm warning you. Don't you open that door!" He must have thought threatening me would work, but it only made me want to disobey him more.

When I reached the room, I turned the knob and opened the door as quickly as I could, only looking back at him to smirk like I'd won and I wasn't going to let him boss me around. I took a few steps in, then turned to slam the door behind me, showing him I was in defiance—if he hadn't already seen it yet.

As I turned back from the door, I instantly saw what he was hiding, pulling a silent gasp from my chest. I covered my gaping mouth with my hand, my body now frozen in place.

Only a few seconds later, he opened the door behind me and walked in slowly. Coming alongside me, he reached to hold my hand as he turned to study my reaction.

"I don't understand," I said, still frozen.

"I had it made for you. I thought you could wear it to the wedding." He stepped closer to me and reached up to push the hair out of my face then let his hand rest against my temple.

"It's beautiful," I whispered, unable to tear my eyes away.

"Just like you." He said softly.

"But you said I couldn't go." I let my eyes look away from the dress to stare up into his.

"I changed my mind," he smiled, letting his face relax, his eyes now fully focused on mine.

I quickly forgot entirely why I was mad at him and why I was running. "I love it," I said as I started to turn my head back to look at it again but he stopped me, leaning in with a kiss.

II

WILD MUSTANG

I slowly ran my hands from my stomach down across my hips. I didn't know what the fabric was, but it was so billowy and soft, I didn't want to stop touching it. It was black but had delicate little lines of silver thread running through it, crisscrossing randomly here and there, making it shimmer almost like the stars in a night sky. The top was tight with a deep v neckline, filled with a delicate black lace, allowing the ivory skin of my chest to peek from behind it. It cinched at the waist and continued to be snug down past my hips, where it finally fanned out and showed more of the beautiful black lace overlay near the bottom. The longer I stood there staring into the mirror at it the more I thought it had to be way too fancy for what a wedding would surely call for.

"It's beautiful on you." Jake was sitting on the bed behind me, staring. The intense focus of his eyes made me wonder if its beauty wasn't what he was actually thinking about, though.

"It's not too fancy?" I asked, ignoring the fact that he was probably more eager for me to take it off than to keep sitting there staring at it.

He smiled and moved his eyes hesitantly back up to mine, "You probably haven't ever been to a black-tie event before... No baby, it's not too fancy. Quite the opposite actually, I had to persuade the tailor to rein himself in." Jake chuckled as he let his eyes slip back down to my body again, "He was excited about making it for you, he suggested I get it in red but I said no, black would do… I don't want to draw too much attention to you… but from the look of it I might still be in trouble…"

"Huh?" I was listening, but I didn't know what he meant by being in trouble.

He smiled again as he stood up slowly then began to walk over to me. "I could make you wear a paper sack and still not be able to hide your beauty… I think I'll bring Lane with us, because seeing you now in this makes me regret my decision to let you go." He said standing behind me, then brought his hands to my hips.

"Was he invited?" I didn't know if that mattered, but was curious how it worked.

"I doubt it but if Voss wants me there. When I RSVP with three instead of two, I'm sure it won't be a problem." He moved himself around to talk to me from the front but the way he was eyeing the straps of the dress made me think he wasn't intending to talk much longer.

"Thank you for this… I'm sorry I ruined your surprise." I knew it probably wasn't something he was concerned with at that moment, but it was one of the things I wanted to get out of the way before we went on.

His focus quickly shifted from my neck to my eyes as he nodded, then returned them to my neck again. "You're welcome, baby," he said softly as he leaned in, bringing his lips to kiss my collar bone. "You didn't ruin anything."

It was easy to see what was now preoccupying his mind, but I hadn't been distracted by the same thing. All I could think of at that point were the other things he said we should talk about. "Jake?" I leaned away a little so he could see I wasn't in the same mindset as he was.

He moved with me as he continued to kiss my neck, then I could feel his hands move their way slowly up my back like he was looking for the clasp that held the dress on. "You're right... we shouldn't... until this is off..." He said between kisses.

"That's not my problem." I didn't move away again, but I didn't touch him back either.

He stopped fiddling with my clasp and brought his hands to rest against my upper arms as he leaned back to look me in the eye. "What's wrong, baby?" He asked. The look in his eyes said he was genuinely unsure of what I would be concerned with at that moment.

"Who's the girl?" I just came out and asked. We both knew I heard him mention her to Andry so there was no point in pretending, especially if he was expecting to make love to me again. I needed to know there wasn't someone else.

His face froze as his eyes trailed off and down, probably thinking about how to respond. "Who are you afraid she is?" He asked finally bringing his eyes back to mine while keeping his body close, not putting any space between us.

It was an odd way for him to answer my question but I didn't get the feeling like he wanted to be deceptive so I went with it. "I don't know... but generally if you keep secrets about other girls, it's not a good thing." I tried to keep my face as calm as I could so he wouldn't be afraid to tell me the truth even if he thought it would hurt.

"You think I'm cheating on you?" His brows furrowed, clearly shocked I could even come to that conclusion.

"No... but..." I didn't, but I didn't know exactly what to tell him I'd been thinking, "You have a house in Nashville that I didn't know about either... I mean it wouldn't surprise me if you had another—"

"Kaleah, baby..." He stopped me from going on. "There's no one else. I don't have another woman in Nashville. I don't have another woman here, or anywhere. There's only you. It's only ever been you, baby."

"Okay," I said quietly as I looked away. I believed him. After all, if there were someone else he had his perfect chance to leave me when Luca took me, but he came back instead. The more I thought about it, I felt relieved like I hadn't realized it, but that was really the only problem I had with him and Andry's secret. I didn't know what else it meant, but I didn't feel like I needed to probe him any more about it. If he wanted me to know, I figured he'd tell me in time.

It didn't take him long to take my 'okay' as an 'all clear' and begin to move back into his previous position trying to remove my dress. I could feel as the clasp released and his hands shifted over to gently tug on the straps, pulling them off my shoulders and down my arms.

"Why would someone get a commission for training me how to fight?" I asked, seeing it wouldn't be long until he was too involved to want to answer anything else.

His eyes quickly jumped up to mine as he continued to gently shimmy the dress down past my hips. "What?" The way he said it sounded like he knew the answer but was trying to stall.

I didn't repeat myself. I just stared at him like I knew he heard me and I was waiting for the answer.

"I can't answer you, Eva…" He took his eyes back to the dress as it grazed the floor. He wrapped his arm around the back of it as I stepped out, then took it to hang back up where it had been when I came into the room.

"Okay, I'll ask Lane then," I said nonchalantly like it wasn't a big deal, though I suspected it was.

"You will not!" He said quite assertively as he turned back toward me. "Do you hear me?"

"You're not my boss!" I didn't know where that came from but I said it.

"What?" Not only did he sound like he didn't like that I said it, he acted just as shocked as I was that I said it. "Yes, I am your boss and you'll do what I tell you 'cause it's for your own good!"

"What makes you my boss? You're not my daddy. You don't own me. I don't have papers, and I definitely don't see a ring on this finger saying otherwise either!" I matched his tone with mine.

"The fact that I love you and I want what's best for you." He said, lowering his voice like he realized I made a valid point. "What was in your dream? Is that why you've been acting like this?"

"Like what?" I asked, as I thought about it.

"Rebellious!" He said then sat back down on the bed. He must have realized this wasn't about to lead into what he'd been hoping for earlier.

"I'm not rebellious," I said, trying to give him the same stern face he always gave me.

"Bullshit, ya aren't!" For whatever reason, he started to remove his shirt after he said it. I wasn't about to let his muscles distract me though, even if that's what he was trying to do. "If I tell you to stop that makes you want to go. I tell you to be quiet, you get louder, on and on... That's what you do to me, Eva. It's like you have to fight me with every freaking thing."

I didn't say anything. I just stood there watching him. Now he was taking off his boots. "No, I don't," I said finally.

"Look, you're doing it right now!" He continued to banter with me as he removed his socks.

"What are you doing?" I couldn't take it any longer. He was distracting me just like I hoped he wouldn't.

"Wanna know why I'm the best capture agent?" He asked now sitting there shirtless and barefoot, staring at me.

"Uh... does it have anything to do with you getting undressing for them? Because that's just weird..." I was legitimately confused where he was going with it.

"No, it's because I take charge. I make people listen to me. I lead, it's just who I am."

"Okay?" I was still lost at what that had to do with me being rebellious.

"To be honest, I've never met a woman as rebellious as you..." He said as he stood up and started to walk toward me again, now making me feel a little uncomfortable. "It's f'd up but I think that's why I love you so much... you challenge me, like no one else ever has. You make me better. You're like a wild Mustang I finally caught," he said as he moved closer to stand in front of me. "Wanna know what I plan on doin' with my wild Gypsyin Mustang?"

I began to breathe heavier. Just his presence alone was overwhelming me, but hearing him speak to me like that was also pushing me over my 'don't get distracted' threshold. "What?" I asked softly, trying not to let him hear the tremble in my voice.

"I'm gonna tame you... make you mine..." He reached up and placed his hand on the back of my neck, then pulled me toward him. "Look at me, Kaleah," he said as he brought his other hand under my chin, moving my face to look at his.

"I can't." I closed my eyes. It felt too vulnerable to let my eyes look into his. I didn't know why but at that moment I felt powerless over him, like he saw right through me and I hadn't decided yet if I wanted to allow it or fight it.

"Just let go, Eva. You've had to be independent and strong for yourself long enough... If you let me lead you, I'll protect you... cherish you, provide for you, build you up... Let that be my job, baby."

His words hit me harder than I ever thought they could. Somewhere deep down they resonated, somewhere there was pain and emptiness, a place consciously I knew existed but only subconsciously understood. I opened my eyes to look at him finally. His expression was sweet and caring. I loved him. I wanted him to protect me and I wanted to be his. Whether I remembered it or not, I knew he was right. I felt like I'd been on my own, taking care of myself, alone and scared for too long. "Take me then," I said softly as I stared into his eyes. "I'm yours."

Without saying anything else, he leaned down and kissed me like he was sealing a deal I'd just made with him. After that, things happened so quickly. His moves were direct and precise like he had already planned out what he was going to do with me before we ever started.

He picked me up. I wrapped my legs around him expecting him to carry me over to the bed but he didn't; he carried me into the bathroom instead before he leaned down to let me rest back on my feet.

"What are we doing?" I asked, thinking it was odd where he brought me.

"Recreating the moment I fell in love with you... kinda..." he said with a mischievous smile as he turned the faucet of the shower on then guided me to stand under the water still in my bra and underwear.

"Uhhh, it's cold!" I didn't know what he thought he was doing, but I wasn't sure I still wanted in on it.

His smile got bigger as he stood there staring at me for a moment. "It's only for a minute. You'll be fine. Maybe it'll give you flashbacks." He wasn't getting all that wet himself, but seemed to be overly enjoying the fact that I was getting thoroughly drenched.

I liked it when he was in a playful mood so I followed along, pushing the hair away from my face.

"Anything yet?" He smirked.

I glared at him now, regretting my decision the colder I got. "What... the..." I was getting cold enough it was hard for me to cuss even though at that point I was trying to, "How did this... make... you love... me?"

"You'll see. You cold enough yet?" He asked, still just standing there outside the stream watching me.

"Seriou... Jaco... ugh," I couldn't finish anything I was trying to say. Plus, I could tell I was close to shivering.

"Okay, baby, that's probably good..." he said with a brilliant smile, obviously happy he'd thought of this. He reached in and shut the shower off and finally got close enough to me again to wrap his arms around me. "Now, I can warm you up." He kissed the top of my head as he moved his hands quickly up and down my sides and back, while he pulled me tightly against his chest.

I might have kissed him back or used my hands to rub on him or do something, anything, except I was too cold. All I could do was stand there and try not to shiver too badly, waiting for him to warm me up. I closed my eyes and let my head rest against his chest, letting him take care of me just as he said he would.

"That's my girl, just relax." He cooed.

We stood there for a moment like that. Even though I was cold, there was something about it that I was actually enjoying. I felt a sense of connection with him that I wasn't sure I had at that point even though we'd already been intimate numerous times.

"I can take you to the bed to cover up if you're still too cold," he said now sweeping my hair to one side with one hand and beginning to wring the water out with his other.

"No, I… I'm good… here." I wanted whatever he was doing to continue, just like he was doing it. I wanted to keep feeling whatever it was that I'd been feeling that was new to me. It was serene, almost magical. I wanted to get lost in him. Then, as I continued to relax into him, a thought hit me. *This is love.* Never before had it felt as tangible as it did in that moment.

"Okay, just tell me if you need me to turn the hot water on and I will. Okay?"

"Umm-hmm" I mumbled still trying not to let my teeth chatter any.

He went back to rubbing his hands up and down my back while he held me tight to his torso. It was soothing in a way and primal in another. There was a part of me that wanted to relax and let him take over and another part that wanted to embrace him back.

Before long, I could tell my body was absorbing the heat from his and I wasn't nearly as cold as I had been. "Will you get me a towel?"

He smiled as he continued to push the hair away from my face and look into my eyes. "Sure." He sighed softly, closing his eyes as he gave me one last tight hug, then turned to reach into the shelves while I stripped off my wet undergarments.

"Feeling warmer?" He asked as he brought the towel back and wrapped it around me.

I nodded with a smile as I looked up into his eyes, hoping he could see the love I had for him radiating from mine.

He reached down and picked me up again, but this time carried me like a bride. He walked back into the bedroom and gently laid me on the bed, then brought the down covers up to cover me. "Let me get a towel for your hair really quick." He said as he bent down to kiss my forehead.

When he came back, he gently lifted my head to place the towel over my pillow, then he went around and crawled under the cover to snuggle up against me.

I pressed my face to his chest and closed my eyes, feeling more content and relaxed than I could ever remember. It was such an odd sensation, considering how it all started.

"Kaleah," he said softly, as he lightly drew circles on my bare shoulder.

"Yeah, baby?" I didn't know what he wanted but felt like after that I would give him the world if he asked for it.

"Do you really love me?" He asked, sounding genuinely uncertain.

I pulled back to face him, then reached up to run my hand through his silky hair. "I do... If I didn't, I wouldn't still be here. I wouldn't give myself to you... I wouldn't sleep with you, want to marry you, have your babies... But I do, all those things... I do!"

12

EXTRAVAGANT BOREDOM

I hadn't been to a wedding before, not that I knew of, and definitely none that were as elaborate as the Coldier Agent's we'd been invited to. We hadn't been there more than half an hour and I was already beside myself with all that I'd witnessed without even seeing the bride yet.

I wasn't sure why Jake was so uptight about me going. There were so many people there I actually felt like I fit in quite nicely without standing out. Even though most of the men there looked like they were agents like Jake and Lane, no one acted suspicious of me or like they wanted to see my arm.

Jake did a thorough job explaining to Lane before we went in how I wasn't to be left without one of them at any point and Lane acted like he fully understood. Everywhere we went Jake walked on one side of me with Lane on the other. Anytime we spoke to anyone Jake would refer to him as his brother, which I thought was interesting. It made me think of the day when Lane stopped the agent in the city from taking me; he called Jake his brother. The label seemed fair enough; they acted more like brothers than anything else.

Jake also made it clear before we went in that I wasn't supposed to speak unless spoken to. I didn't know if it was just because he was afraid I could say something that might get me in trouble or if all women were to stay quiet. Seeing the amount of risk he was taking with me, I wasn't about to disobey him this time.

I didn't know if the design of my dress was more Jake's idea or the tailors but whose ever it was I thought must have been brilliant. The night I tried it on, the dress itself looked simple enough, with just small straps across my shoulders and a clasp holding it up. It didn't extend down to cover my arms, but I never thought to ask him about it. Then later that week he finally showed me the jacket that he'd had made to go with it. It just took the tailor extra time to finish.

It wasn't simple like the dress. It was intricate, detailed and tight— very tight, especially on my lower arms. It felt like the same fabric the dress had been made from, but without the silver thread. It was made to slip over my head and not be easy at all to take off. It was black with rows of elaborately woven straps each bordered by a row of black lace. I thought it was just as beautiful as the dress, maybe more-so. It was obvious Jake had had it designed to be extremely difficult for me to reveal my arm in the instance anyone insisted on seeing my tag.

It was evening when we arrived. I thought that was odd, and that weddings were normally earlier in the day but I figured it was another one of those things where I didn't know any better. For a while, most of the people just mingled and talked before slowly the room emptied as they were ushered in a few at a time to finally take their seats in another larger space within the building. I thought the first room was extravagant until we were taken into the room where the actual ceremony would be. I'd never seen a space look anything like it. The ceiling was high, almost two stories above us, and looked to be nothing but glass. The walls were covered by rows of grand columns all painstakingly decorated with strands of little white flowers.

I didn't have a problem keeping my mouth shut when the men were talking. I just stood there, ignoring whatever small talk they were discussing among themselves. I had too many other things on my mind to bother listening to them. Not only was I intrigued by everything I was seeing but I was also curious when and if I would see Katherine. I didn't expect Jake would actually introduce me to her if he saw her there, but I didn't know.

When we did make it into the ceremony room, it felt like we were sitting there in silence forever before we finally began to see the bridal party make their way down the aisle. I was bored, but I did the best I could to keep myself distracted by looking at all the decorations as well as what the other women's dresses looked like. Jake said he tried to make mine where I wouldn't stand out but from what I could tell it was still prettier than most of the others. I realized I was biased since he'd had it hand made for me and likely designed it himself, but I didn't care. The way Bethany had done my hair and makeup seemed on par with everything I was seeing as well, so for once I didn't feel self-conscious or like a fraud.

I was close to falling asleep when I finally heard music that, for whatever reason sounded familiar, and I got the idea that something big was about to happen. It was loud but somewhat hypnotic-sounding at the same time. It wasn't long before I was mesmerized by what I was seeing as the bride began to walk down the aisle. All I could think of was how amazing she looked, like a princess from a fairy tale.

"You'll never have that. He can't marry you!"

I believed it; I knew it was right. The longer I stood there staring as the bride effortlessly floated toward her knight in black-cloth armor, the more upset I could feel myself becoming. The stronger the feeling got, the closer I felt to tears. I knew no one would be looking at me now that the bride was there and the ceremony had started, so once we sat back down I closed my eyes. I couldn't let myself cry. Not only would it draw undue attention to myself—attention I was warned wouldn't go well—but I didn't want to mess up my makeup, either. Bethany spent so much time working on it, it would have been a shame if I couldn't have made it last until the end of the night.

Just like everything else had been to that point, the ceremony was long and boring. So much so, I'd started to wonder why I begged Jake to bring me to begin with. As soon as it was over, it was the same routine as we'd had with the first room now going into the next. The crowd slowly shifted from the ceremonial room to the banquet room, hall, auditorium—the big room that was full of more decorations, tables, and food—whatever they called it, I wasn't sure. We slowly made our way over to a table that was reserved specifically for us and then sat while we waited to have our food served.

Jake seemed to be in about the same mood as I was, lethargic and bored. Lane, on the other hand, acted like he usually did, upbeat and happy. Still determined to keep my mouth shut and not get myself in any trouble, I couldn't help but feel a bit impish the longer we sat there.

"If Miles hasn't already told you, you look prettier than the bride tonight," Lane leaned over and whispered to me while we waited for everyone else to finish settling into their seats.

"Haven't you seen what Jake does to other guys that hit on me?" I whispered back while keeping my face dead serious. I knew he was just trying to be sweet, but I thought I would play with him a little.

Fear quickly blanched his face as he started to stammer, trying to adjust what he said and how I took it. I didn't let it last too long until I finally winked at him and grinned so he knew I was joking.

His face relaxed as he briefly looked down and away. "You're mean," he groaned, looking back at me.

I couldn't help but laugh. "Thank you, Lane, what you said was sweet... I really don't know how you're still single." He blushed a little after I said it then looked away again. He was so kind and sincere, I was happy that he was Jake's right-hand man. I especially liked to play to his gullible side. Since Jake didn't seem to have one, I couldn't play with him the same way.

The servers came to take our order. Apparently, even as elaborate as the wedding was, they still didn't give us a vast array of options but I didn't mind. When I heard fish was one, that's what I chose. I was watching Jake as he looked around, waiting for him to make eye contact with someone. If it was a woman, I figured I would ask him if it was Katherine. Even if he didn't intend to introduce me to her, I knew he wouldn't lie if I were to catch him and straight up ask.

I didn't know who any of the men were or how he knew them. Sporadically, one or two would walk by and greet him like they knew him but he never introduced me or said anything about me to them. I wasn't upset about it, though. He never said he would introduce me to anyone, and I understood why he wouldn't, even if it did feel a little uncomfortable at times.

It wasn't long after our food came out that I noticed an older man a few tables away was staring at me. I dismissed the idea initially, thinking he was probably looking at Jake or Lane or someone behind me but every time I looked up I would catch him again, still looking almost straight at me.

"Jake," I said quietly still looking down at my plate. I didn't want him to get upset with me for talking but I couldn't remember if the rule was no talking at all or just not to other people except him or Lane.

"What, baby?" He asked not sounding upset at all.

"I think that guy over there is staring at me." I still didn't look up. If the guy was looking when I said it, I didn't want him to look away when Jake discovered who I was talking about.

He chuckled quietly under his breath and reached up to hold the hand that I had rested on the table. "You're going to get a lot of guys staring at you tonight, baby."

I thought it was kind when he said it, but didn't feel like the way this man was staring was for the same reasons Jake was referring to.

"You talking about the older gentleman in black?" Lane asked softly as he put his hand holding his fork in front of his mouth like he was chewing but he wasn't.

"You're *all* dressed in black," I said sarcastically, looking up at him. I wasn't sure if he was trying to get back at me for messing with him earlier or if he really did see who I was talking about.

He smiled, then looked over at me with a curious look. "I know, I was joking. But seriously, are you talking about the man with the green emerald pendant on his chest pocket?" He asked like he knew exactly who I was talking about.

"Yes," I said, looking back at Lane when I felt Jake tighten his grip on my hand.

"Are you sure, baby?" Jake asked as I turned my head now to look at him. He was staring straight ahead at the man like he knew who he was.

"Umm-hmm," I mumbled, looking back down at my food, trying to avoid looking up at the man.

"How do you feel about that, Miles?" Lane asked. The way they were acting was starting to concern me. I wasn't sure if I was in trouble, if that was a problem, or just what.

"I bet Voss has already spoken with him. Maybe he mentioned me, that could be why he seems interested in looking at us." Jake said as he took another bite of his food like it wasn't an issue.

"That might be the case, but she's right. Every time I look up he's looking at her, not either of us." Lane's voice grew serious like his inner agent was coming out.

"Well, unless he comes and talks to us, there shouldn't be a problem." Jake said still acting dismissive. However, I could hear a different tone in his voice like he was concerned but just not wanting to let on.

"Maybe Voss will introduce you if he comes to talk to you again later," Lane was now looking down at his plate like me, unwilling to look up to see where the man's eyes were this time.

"I doubt he wants to talk to me again. Not only is he busy with the wedding, when we talked before the ceremony, I made it clear I wasn't coming back. He didn't like it, but I don't care," Jake said as he continued to eat, but also looked like he was being more vigilant than he had been.

"If you want to talk to him why can't you just go talk to him?" I asked not really understanding what all they were saying.

"He can't do that, even if he is fourth rank." Lane thought he would clear it up for me, but whatever he said didn't make any sense either.

"Fourth rank?" I asked softly under my breath.

"Kaleah, baby… There are rules we have to go by when we want to address an officer that ranks higher than us. I'm fourth rank and the guy you said was staring at you is first rank. There are only three Coldiers that rank first."

"So he's like really important and powerful and stuff, get it?" Lane decided to continue what Jake was saying, thinking he could explain it better.

"Oh, okay." Lane actually did make it easier to understand, "Well, what rank are you then?" I asked, looking at him.

He swallowed the food that was in his mouth and smiled. "Eleventh," he said with a smile, completely owning it.

"Uh," I'm sure the look on my face reflected my confusion.

"There are thirty-two total," Lane said, answering my next question before I even asked it. "So no, I'm not as high as Jake but I'm happy with eleventh, that's not bad, really."

"Oh… holy shit," I said under my breath once what they were saying finally hit me. I had no idea Jake ranked so high or what that even meant.

"That's enough, Lane…" Jake said finally seeing I was beginning to understand. I didn't know why he hadn't ever explained that to me but I thought it was pretty neat and figured I would ask him more about it once we were alone again.

"All right… Are you two coming back to my place after this or are you going to your mom's again?" Lane continued with another subject like he wasn't just ordered around.

Jake gave Lane an uneasy glance as soon as he heard him ask it, then he looked down at me, seeing how I took the question.

"It's okay," I said, letting him know it didn't bother me, even though it kind of did. It'd been three weeks since he initially told me we could move to Lane's house. Jake had so much going on up to that point though, we hadn't had a chance to move yet and it'd started to be a subject of contention between us.

"Whichever she wants to go to tonight then," Jake said finally, seeing I wasn't going to press the issue.

"Excuse me," a strong, commanding voice spoke from behind me. I figured it wasn't speaking to me though, so I didn't turn around to look. I assumed either Jake or Lane would address whatever the man wanted.

Jake turned as soon as the voice spoke, then without any hesitation quickly stood up from his seat. "Yes, Sir?" He said boldly like he was speaking to someone in authority. I immediately looked over toward the man they said was first rank, but he was no longer sitting where he had been. I knew with that and how Jake responded, it must have been him that was standing behind me.

"E.J. Prescott, I'd like to speak with you."

"Of course, Sir, I know who you are. TC Agent Jacob Miles, it's a pleasure to meet you. What can I do for you, Sir?" Jake greeted him. I knew better than to turn around at that point and draw any attention to myself, even though I figured the man had likely already memorized my face with how much he'd been staring at it.

"Would you mind introducing me? Is this your... wife?" He had to be asking about me now, since I was the only woman sitting at our table. Surely, it was obvious to him we weren't married though, since neither of us were wearing wedding rings.

Jake hesitated but only briefly, "Yes, of course, Ev... Kaleah, sweetie," he said nervously as he addressed me. That didn't help me feel any less nervous knowing I would have to turn around then and talk to him. I briefly looked over at Lane as I started to stand up. He acted like he wasn't paying any attention just still eating his food, though I suspected it was just an act.

I turned around and there he was, standing directly behind me, just as I was afraid he had been. "Mr. Prescott, this is my girlfriend, Kaleah Eva. Eva, this is E.J. Prescott, Senior Command Agent of the Eastern Division." Jake's eyes widened and slightly glared at me as he said it, silently warning me to be careful. Then he turned back toward the gentleman to wait and see what he said next.

"It's a pleasure meeting you both." The man said, looking at Jake, before turning toward me to speak again, "Are you an agent as well, Eva?"

I wanted to respond but was afraid to. I didn't know if something would come out of my mouth that I hadn't intended, so I just looked from the man over to Jake, trying to use my eyes to insist he help me. "No, Sir... She isn't a Coldier agent," Jake said, bringing the man's attention back to him as he smiled.

"Oh, I just noticed you called her by her last name, so I assumed that was the case." Mr. Prescott said, smiling, then turned back to me. There was something about the way he looked at me. It was almost how Jake did, something deep about the way our eyes connected, like he was trying to read my soul.

"Oh, no, Sir," Jake nervously chuckled, "it's a habit, I'm afraid."

"Of course..." E.J. said, nodding his head like he completely understood. "Would you mind if I spoke with her in private?"

As soon as I realized what he had asked, I felt my heart begin to beat quicker, like it'd sunken to the bottom of my chest and was banging on the door of my stomach. I looked over at Jake. His expression was a shaken, apparently unsure of what to do. I knew he couldn't say no, but probably everything in him was doing whatever it could to stop himself from saying yes.

"Of course, Sir!" I said finally, seeing Jake was hesitating too long and likely to get himself or both of us into the trouble that he tried so hard up to that point to keep me from.

Jake's eyes quickly shifted from Mr. Prescott's over to mine like he hadn't planned on it going down that way but knew it was too late and he couldn't stop it. I tried to act as confident as I could to show both him and the gentleman that nothing was going to happen and it was merely a chat... *That's all I hope it'll be, anyway.*

13

FIRST RANK

When I agreed to speak with him in private, I thought it would still be in view of Jake and Lane but just where they couldn't hear us. Instead, he walked with me over to a doorway and opened it like he had other plans. I smiled as he held the door open for me, then briefly looked back over at Jake to see how he was reacting. I couldn't tell if he was mad or not but both he and Lane were now standing like they intended to move quickly if that action became necessary.

"Please, Kaleah." The man said kindly as he gestured for me to go through the door before him. All I could think of was when Kyle took me into the hotel room and shut the door behind me. I started to feel frightened again with the idea until I remembered I ended up killing him when he tried to touch me. Once I had thought of that, any fear of walking through the door with Mr. Prescott quickly subsided and I realized I would be okay.

He gently let the door close behind us as we walked out into a large hall. Half the walls were stone like the banquet hall and the other half were glass like the ceiling. If it hadn't been dark outside I'm sure the sun would have lit up that space beautifully.

"Please don't be scared of me. I can see you might be. Is that the case?" He asked, now standing across from me. He wasn't super close like he had any bad intentions so for that moment I wasn't all that fearful of what he wanted with me.

"I'm not scared, but cautious, yes. I've had bad experiences with men so—" I stopped when I realized I wasn't filtering my mouth as well as I could and I needed to relax but not lose control with it. "No, I am not scared of you. Should I be?"

He smiled, "No, my dear, you're safe with me," he said then continued. "Are you a Coldier?"

Why would he ask me that? I hoped my face didn't reveal my anxiety as I hesitated to think about how I was going to answer the question. I didn't know what would be worse, getting caught lying to a first rank or being honest about being a Gypsyin without having any papers to show him if he asked. Internally, I was terrified when I realized if I said the wrong thing both me and Jake could be in serious trouble.

"I can see it's a difficult question for you," he said slightly lowering his brow, probably contemplating what was taking me so long to respond.

"I am," I said suddenly as I inadvertently swallowed. Lying felt like the least problematic choice at that moment. "Sorry, you make me nervous…"

He nodded with an understanding smile. "All right… It doesn't really matter, as long as you're not a Sicari." He didn't sound like he believed me, but didn't care, which I found odd but was relieved nonetheless. "Who are your parents?" He asked next.

I wasn't sure what called for the impromptu interrogation but I was doing the best I could to be honest. "They're Coldiers from Tennessee."

"Okay… Is that all you know about them?" He came across as kind, not aggressive at all when he asked.

"Yes," I said shyly, finally giving in. It was clear he was an intelligent man, and I knew any attempt at embellishing what little memories I did have would be obvious.

Something about his face changed as I said it but I couldn't distinguish what it was or what emotion he was now holding back. "That's unfortunate," he said now with a sad look in his eyes. "How long have you been with Agent Miles?"

"Um…" I tried not to hesitate too long again with the question, but was having trouble thinking about the answer. "About a year," I said finally. That time I was confident in my response time but didn't know the answer so I just said the first time that sounded realistic.

"Is he taking good care of you? Does he love you?" As he asked each question, he changed his position a little. With this one, he shifted his weight to his right hip and crossed his arms to rest them just below his chest.

"Yes… I've never been with anyone who's treated me better or loved me more," I said not really knowing if it was the truth or not, but figured he wouldn't know the difference either. I was ready to be done with the conversation, but knew better than to say or do anything that would come across as disrespectful.

"Do you love him? Are you planning on staying with him?" His eyes softened, but he didn't give me any indicator of why he was asking me so many personal questions.

I stopped to think about the question. "Yes, I love him very much. I want to marry him."

His expression turned cold after hearing that, but I wasn't sure why. "Kaleah…" he said like he knew he was starting to lose my attention, "Why are you in New York?"

What? I couldn't help but squint my eyes a little as he asked me. "Why are you asking me so many questions?" *Shit…* That slipped out without me thinking. "I mean, I'm sorry… I—"

"It doesn't matter," he interrupted my attempt at an apology. "I need you to answer me."

"Because Jake… uh, Miles, brought me here, to be safe."

"Safe from what?" His voice sounded a little more forceful that time.

"Gypsyins… Sicari… I don't know, okay? I don't know what you want from me. I don't know how to… uh," I stopped when I realized I was beginning to feel overwhelmed and lose my filter again.

"Kaleah, listen to me. What I'm about to tell you might not make any sense but you have to trust me, okay?" He said, waiting for my response though I was still uncertain why he thought I would trust him when we had just met.

"Okay," I said now curious what he was going to tell me, still not sure if I really trusted him or not.

"Stay with Miles… I believe he's a good man." He paused to make sure I was looking him in the eyes. "Don't ever go back to Nashville. Do you hear me?"

I was confused, but quickly got the idea he somehow knew things about me that I didn't even know. "Why? What's in Nashville?"

His face froze in shock. "How many times have you been erased?"

Oh shit, I thought instantly, wondering what I'd just done. I couldn't help but swallow again as I thought about how to answer him. "Uh… I don't know exactly."

For the first time, he looked down and away from me like he didn't know how to respond.

"How do you know me?" I asked.

He looked back up like he hadn't expected it. "You wouldn't be safe if I told you," he said, taking a step closer to me, lingering like he wanted to say something else but was stopping himself. "We're done now." He rested his hand on my shoulder, then began to guide me back into the banquet room.

When the door opened and I walked back through, I saw Jake now sitting back at the table without Lane. He immediately stood up when he saw me and began to walk over to us as we walked toward him.

"Agent Miles…" Mr. Prescott said as Jake got close enough to talk to him, "I hope I didn't cause you too much concern keeping her as long as I did. She's quite the gem."

By Jake's face he didn't know how to respond but he looked like he probably had been quite concerned. "Um, yes, it's… it's… yes, she is, Sir," he said, stammering his words slightly as he slid his hand around my waist as if to reclaim me from the man.

"Would you mind if I spoke with you in private, Agent Miles?" Mr. Prescott said, as he handed me off.

Jake looked at me, then back at the table, "Um, yes, Sir… Of course, just let me—"

"She'll be fine. It won't take long. We can just step over here if you don't want to leave her sight," Mr. Prescott said, seeing Jake's trepidation about leaving me alone at the table without him or Lane.

Jake nodded at him like he'd agree but I could tell he still wasn't all that happy with it. Then he turned and whispered against my ear, "Sit down and don't speak to anyone, okay, baby?"

"Okay," I said, looking around for where Lane had gone then turned to go back and take my seat again.

Mr. Prescott did as he said he would and only took Jake over to the side of the room to speak with him, not out in the hall like he had with me. I wasn't sitting there for long when I saw Lane walking back to the table. I could see that he had spotted Jake and Mr. Prescott talking, then he smiled as he made eye contact with me like he was letting me know he was coming back as quick as he could.

"I bet that was fun," he said lightheartedly as he pulled out his chair to sit down next to me.

"Not really," I said, observing the cold food still left on my plate.

"What did he say?"

"I'm not allowed to talk to you," I said, referring to Jake. Since he told me not to talk to anyone, I figured I'd use that to joke with Lane.

"What… why? He's never even met me." He sounded baffled, just as I intended.

I laughed, seeing his reaction. "I'm just kidding, but he did tell me a bunch of classified stuff and told me to keep it our little secret. If I told you then I'd have to kill you." I winked with a smirk.

"Yeah, okay, now you're just messing with me," he said, smiling as he bumped his elbow into mine.

"Fine… you're right. So anyway, Jake said he saw Katherine. How'd that go?" Not only did I want to change the subject, I also thought it might be a good chance to trick Lane into telling me things I knew Jake wouldn't.

"Oh, yeah… it went well… By the way she was acting, she clearly still loves him," he said it upbeat like it wasn't a problem.

"What?" I was shocked and, at that point, a bit concerned.

"Naw, I'm just messing with you," he said, giving me a playful smile. "She's not here. I guess she decided not to come when she knew Miles intended to." He let his face relax. "You shouldn't be as good at that as you are, you know?"

"What?"

"Lying…" he said as he began to casually look around.

"I'm sorry, I just—"

"No, I understand," he said, interrupting me. "I realize he doesn't tell you everything… It really is for your own good, though." He leaned back in his chair, about to relax, before something caught his eye. "Here, come… dance with me," he said as he stood up.

I looked over at what made him want to consider it then back at him, "But… Jake said… I—"

"It's fine. Come on…" he said, offering me his hand.

"Okay?" I looked over at Jake still standing with Mr. Prescott and wondered if he would have a problem with it when he saw I wasn't still at the table where he told me to stay. Then I took a hold of Lane's hand and let him lead me to the area where there were multiple couples already dancing.

"I don't know if I remember how," I said as we stopped. He brought one of his hands to rest at my waist while keeping a hold of my other.

"It doesn't matter, no one will be watching us," he smiled, leaning in a little. I wondered if the boredom from the rest of the evening was getting to him and he just couldn't take it anymore.

"Where did you go when I left the room?" I asked as we began to slowly sway back and forth to the music's meandering melody.

"To an area where I could keep an eye on you… Jake's orders," he said with a small laugh. "He would have done it himself but he wanted to stay at the table for when you came back."

"Oh… well, thank you," I returned his smile.

"Lane!" Jake growled. We both stopped and looked around for him.

He had been standing behind me but by the time I got a chance to turn and see him he'd already positioned himself to take Lane's place. He wrapped one arm around my upper back and pulled my chest tight to his as he held my hand with his other.

Lane smiled as he stepped back, "Just remember, I taught her everything she knows about dancing," he said, then looked at me and winked before he turned to walk away.

I smiled then looked up at Jake who didn't actually look like he was in the same mood as Lane had been. "What's wrong?" I asked, letting him continue to move with me around the floor as Lane had.

"I tell you to sit and when I'm done and ready to come back you're not there... How do you think that makes me feel, Eva?" He asked, sounding a bit sour.

I knew it wasn't my fault, but didn't really want to throw Lane under the bus either. "Okay, I'm sorry."

He narrowed his eyes on me, then pulled me in tighter as he looked away. "All right... I'll deal with Lane later," he mumbled as we went on.

I let my head rest against his chest, then let go of his hand and wrapped both of mine around his waist. "Can you talk to me about what Mr. Prescott said to you, or... do you need to wait to tell me in private like I do?" I asked quietly so no one else around would hear me.

"I have a feeling my conversation with him was completely different from yours," he said now sounding less agitated than when he first took Lane's spot.

"Okay?"

"He mainly just wanted to know what our plans were... how I felt about you, if we were in love," he paused for a moment. "He told me you were a very special woman and that I needed to take care of you."

"He wants me to stay in New York," I said, thinking I didn't have to be as quiet since that part didn't sound top secret. "The way he spoke to me was like he knew me... I asked him how he did but... he wouldn't say."

"Interesting..." Jake said, as he slowed down a little. I lifted my head to look back up at him. I could see his wheels turning, trying to fit all the pieces together. "Did he act like he was interested in you? Did he come on to you any?" His voice got quieter again.

"No, it wasn't like that at all, really. He treated me like your dad did when I was alone with him," I said, trying to be reassuring. "Why, do you feel threatened because of his rank? I mean, he is older but you know how I'm attracted to powerful men." I softly giggled, so he knew I was joking.

"You're cute," he said with a straight face so I didn't know if he was being serious or sarcastic. "We can talk about it more when we leave, don't worry about it for right now."

"All right," I said then leaned my head back in to rest it against his chest again as we continued to dance. It was peaceful and soothing and romantic, even if we were surrounded by a horde of agents.

W e didn't stay much longer. I think Jake was eager to leave, probably for multiple reasons, but likely a big one was so we could continue to compare notes about what Mr. Prescott spoke with each of us about. Lane seemed excited that we were going back to his house. He said he enjoyed having our company. When we got there, Jake said he had something he wanted to show me so we dropped Lane off at his floor and continued to take the elevator to the top of the building. Jake showed me how to slip past a few do-not-enter signs so we could get to the roof.

The view we saw as soon as the door opened was so beautiful it felt like it literally took my breath away. The sky was majestic all lit up with different beams of light. It looked like something in the distance had been set on fire, creating a large orange glow within and probably beyond the city. Somewhere in my mind I could faintly remember what an open night sky full of nothing but stars looked like and I was sure what I was now seeing could rival if not beat its beauty.

"Kaleah..." Jake said softly, I assumed, staring at the skyline as well.

"Yeah, baby?" I didn't look at him. I couldn't pull my eyes away from it all.

"Will you marry me?" As soon as I heard the question, I turned my head toward him. He was kneeling next to me, with one knee up and both his hands out, holding a small wooded box.

I didn't know what to say. I just stood there looking at him, completely overcome with shock. "But... you said—"

"I said I'd marry you tomorrow if I could," he stopped me before I could go on. "So say yes so when that day comes we'll be ready," he smiled, then opened the box to display what I thought was the most beautiful ring I'd ever seen.

I couldn't say yes. I couldn't get my mouth to work. All I could do was nod as tears began to stream down my face. He smiled the largest smile his face could probably make as he stood up. "Yes," I breathed, finally. I wanted to say it over and over then scream it for the whole city to hear.

"Kaleah, you don't even know what you do to me," he said softly, leaning down to kiss me. "You just made me the happiest I've ever been in my life."

We wrapped our arms around each other, and I buried my head into his chest. "I love you, baby. I love you so much..." I said, squeezing him tightly.

"Let me put it on your finger now," he said after a few moments of us silently holding each other, then he kissed me on top of the head.

"Okay..." I said shakily, pulling back and offering my hand to him. "What does this mean, though? Have you found a way around it... not being... uh...?" I was still so emotional I didn't know what words to say.

"It means I can start telling people you're gonna be my wife... You're now my fiancée." He said with the most sincere look in his eyes as he slid the ring onto my finger. "I'm tired of only being able to call you my girlfriend. You're so much more than that, baby."

I smiled and lifted my hand to stare at it.

"Mrs. Miles... Do you like that name or will you want to be called something else?" He asked as he began to stare deep into my eyes, like only he does.

I wrapped my hand around the back of his neck and stared back at him. "When all I am is yours, there's no other name for me... and no one else I'd rather be except Mrs. Miles."

"Good," he said as he leaned down to kiss me again, "Mrs. Miles it'll be then!"

14

COST OF LOVE

"Hey love birds… I gotta go to work."

"She was still asleep, Lane. Thanks…" Jake said as I began to stir when I heard Lane's voice.

"Oh, I'm sorry." Lane whispered as I opened my eyes to look over at him. "Aww, were you laying there staring at her, Miles? You're so sweet… She probably thinks it's creepy, though. I don't know if I would keep doing that."

"Lane, I'll let you give me relationship advice when you're in a relationship… Right now, shut the door and go to work."

"Well, here's another piece of advice, you should lock it next time. I don't know what I could have seen when I opened it." Lane said as he lightly tapped the knob.

"Then don't open it next time," Jake scolded, ready for Lane to leave.

Lane grinned like he knew he'd teased Jake enough and had probably pushed him as far as he was going to go, "Congratulations, Kaleah," he said now looking back over at me. "I'm not sure if I would have said yes to him if I were you, though… He can be a handful."

"Get out, Lane!" Jake shouted, trying not to smile.

"Yes, Sir!" Lane grinned again, then turned, about to leave, but stopped. "Oh, one more thing... next time you stay could you both keep it down a little more? You guys about kept me up all night last night... I can't do my job very well if I'm tired."

"Sorry, Lane," I said, realizing he was probably talking to me more than he was Jake.

Lane smiled and nodded like he appreciated the apology then walked out, shutting the door behind him.

"I didn't know he went to work," I said, looking back over at Jake.

He started to laugh, "Oh, baby, you really are cute," he said, then stood up from the bed.

"What are you doing?" I asked, "You don't have to work, so where do you think you're going?"

He smiled, reaching over to his bag to pull out a fresh pair of pants then bent down and continued to put them on. "Apparently, you can survive on nothing, but I'm starving."

I laughed, "Fine." I figured letting him go for a bit wouldn't kill me.

"Go back to sleep, baby. It's still really early. I'll be back in a few."

"Okay," I said, smiling and resting my head back against my pillow. I wasn't about to refuse the opportunity to sleep more.

"I know who you are... and now you don't." The man laughed. "Stupid woman, you should have just given me the intel like I asked. But no, you wanna be all tough... Well, guess who isn't tough now?"

I looked down. He'd bound both my arms and feet and had me sitting on the floor next to a large desk as he sat across from me in a puffy leather swivel chair.

"I don't understand why I'm here... What do you want with me?" I whimpered, feeling confused and scared.

"Ugh... it's the same question every time. It's getting so old," he said, leaning back and putting both feet up on his desk, crossed at his ankles. "You know... I can tell you this 'cause you won't remember it next week when I erase you again... I regret erasing you the first time… I really do. Upset is an understatement for how I felt. You'd have rather died than give me the intel." He began to seethe as he continued. "You little shit. I've never had anyone not talk when I interrogated them. Now the intel's gone forever, and it's your fault."

"Please—" I didn't know what else to say, but I wanted him to let me go.

"Shut your mouth, girl!" He yelled at me then sat back against the seat again to continue whatever he was ranting about. "Think you can take it to your grave, do ya? I made other plans for you, Princess. I'm gonna make you pay. How, you're probably wondering…" He stopped to pick at his teeth with his fingers before going on, "I'm gonna take something from you. Something that means as much to you as the intel meant to me."

"What?" I asked weakly, holding back from trembling.

"You stupid little shit, your body's broken. I've had you for seven damn months now and nothing… You know how irritating that is? It's not me either! I let the other guys take their turn with you too, but nope… I don't know what's wrong with you but you just won't take. Maybe it's the serum… stupid shit… probably shouldn't keep erasing you all the time but I can't help myself. Doesn't matter though, I gotta Plan B. If I can't actually take what I want from ya, I'll make it look like I did. Same effect, sweetheart… You won't know the difference once you're erased again!" He stood up after he said it and started to walk around the other side of his desk.

"I'm sorry, please just let me go," I begged, hoping he'd have mercy.

"Oh, you'd like that wouldn't you? Not happening, Princess! Right now I'm gonna go talk to your dad. You just stay put and be a good li'l Gypsyin…"

I looked at him now more confused than before.

"Yeah… you little princess… wouldn't you like to know more? It's his fault you're in this mess. He shouldn't ever have gotten that position. It belonged to me… If he thinks he can send his daughter over to do his dirty work and not get caught… Guess he's not that smart after all! You're both gonna pay…" He continued yelling at me.

"He knows I'm here?" I couldn't remember him, but hoped he was someone who could help me.

"No! You think I'm an idiot? I gotta plan for what I'm gonna do to you, and if you won't cooperate then, I'll just... He won't even know it but he's gonna help me, he'll give me what I need."

"Please, just let me go..."

"Kaleah, baby."
"Please..."
"Kaleah, wake up!"
"Let me go..."
"EVA!" I felt something suddenly jar me as I opened my eyes. Jake was standing above me, looking down with concern all over his face. I didn't say anything. I didn't know what to say. I knew it was just a dream, but it felt so awful and real. "Who was it?" Jake asked like he knew it was another flashback.

"I don't know," I said, trying not to cry.

He sat down on the edge of the bed. "Okay... What did he look like? Tell me."

I still couldn't really say anything. I wanted to cry so badly I wasn't sure I could stop myself.

"Come here, baby," Jake said, pulling me closer, then leaned down and scooped me up to sit in his lap. "It's okay," he whispered soothingly as he began to stroke my hair. "I'll never let anyone hurt you like that ever again." He tightened his arms around me.

"He had a mustache," I said finally, thinking about the man in the dream.

Jake tensed, then took a deep breath before he said anything else. "Just a mustache, no beard?"

"Uh-huh," I murmured as I leaned my face against him.

"Okay," his voice was tight. "Don't worry about him. He's nowhere around here so he can't bother you, all right?"

"All right..."

"Do you want to talk about it, what you saw?" He asked calmly as he began to rub my back with his hands.

"No," I didn't even want to keep *thinking* about it, so the idea of having to recount it to him sounded even worse.

"Okay, baby… I understand." He said softly, then rested his chin against the top of my head.

"What do you know about my dad?" I asked finally, after we sat there for a minute in silence.

"Not much," he said, then paused to think before he went on. "When you had your full memory back all you ever told me was he was a Coldier from Tennessee and that he was a lawyer, but right before the war he was voted in as a judge. You said you thought his name was Elijah. I think you still had trouble remembering a lot of your childhood even after the medicine though, so you didn't tell me a lot. Why? Was he in the dream as well?"

"No," I sighed, "I did something that made mustache man mad but he said it was my dad's fault too or something like that." I wasn't trying to be vague. I was just already starting to forget small details about the dream. I didn't mind it, though. I hoped over time I could forget it all together.

"I've looked for him… in the Coldier's archives. I didn't want to tell you unless I was able to find him 'cause I didn't want to get your hopes up, but while we're on the subject, I guess you might as well know. I couldn't find anything, though. There's no record of an Elijah Eva anywhere. I thought maybe you got your name mixed up, so I looked for an Elijah Jordan or an Elijah Ellice… but nothing." He stopped to brush my hair again with his hand. "I'm sorry, baby."

"It's okay," I said, feeling a bit better as the dream's negative effects started to wane. "I think I'm hungry now."

Jake perked right up when he heard me mention food. "Really? That's great. I could eat again as well, actually."

"Again? Where do you put it all?" I said, looking down at his shirtless chest and abs.

He didn't answer me, he just laughed as he leaned back against the bed and pulled me with him.

"What do you think you're doing, Mr. Miles?" I asked, wondering if he was trying to seduce me with his physique, since he'd normally already have his shirt on by that point.

"Lane won't be home until tonight… and even though we need to go back to Mom's today since I've got a few things I need to do there, right now we have all morning… alone… with nothing we have to do."

I knew exactly what he was trying to get at, since he wasn't really being subtle. "I'm not sure if I'm convinced," I said as I ran my hand up and down his smooth abs.

"Oh, no?" He said, tightening his stomach muscles as he sat up slightly to look at me. "What do you need to convince you?"

"Food…" I smiled, "'Cause I'm hungry, remember?"

He chuckled as he sat the rest of the way up, "Okay… you want food… wait right here and I'll go get you something," he said then stood up and walked quickly out of the room. I got the idea if what I wanted was stopping him from getting what he wanted, then he was more than happy to oblige me. I waited there for a few minutes as I lay back against my pillow, making sure to keep myself awake since I wasn't in the mood for any more dreams. Soon I heard him return, walking back into the room with a plate in one hand and a slender bottle in the other.

"I made myself blueberry pancakes earlier. I had some left over, so I heated them up again for you."

I gave him a big smile and I'm sure my eyes must have lit up when I saw him set the plate down on the bed. They looked amazing.

"I warmed the syrup up too," he said, pulling the blankets all over to one side of the bed.

"Will Lane get upset if we make a mess by eating in here?" I asked as I reached over to grab a pancake. They looked too good to wait on the syrup.

"I don't know, let's find out," he said as he took the bottle of syrup and intentionally drizzled it up and down my right leg.

"Jacob!" I scolded, shocked that he would do something like that.

"Don't worry, you keep eating. I'll clean it up," he said with a shameless grin.

It was obvious at that point what he was doing so I shrugged, figuring if anyone was going to get in trouble for the mess I could easily blame it on him without feeling guilty. I took the pancake that I was holding and rubbed it on my thigh, letting it soak up as much of the syrup as it could.

Jake leaned down against the bed, bracing himself on his elbows, and kissed my ankle then pretended to nibble on my leg. "Mmm, you taste amazing. I could eat you up. You're so sweet." He teased.

"You're trouble," I said as I sat there eating my pancake, watching him.

"Only when you're around," he mumbled, holding my knee and ankle and pretending to bite down on my calf like he was eating a giant turkey leg.

"You're gonna make me all sticky," I said, smiling like I didn't really mind, but wanted to complain anyway.

"We can take an ice-cold shower when we're done, then." He looked up at me, winked then grinned.

"You're funny," I said sarcastically.

"Just eat your food, don't mind me." He said, picking up the syrup bottle like he was ready to make more of a mess then bent down to kiss me on the lips.

"I guess eating in peace is out of—"

"I can make you a fresh batch later." He said as he moved his mouth down to my neck. "Lets get my shirt off you now. I don't want it to get all sticky."

I giggled as I thought about how we were acting. It was obvious he was happy. I made him happy and in exchange, that made me happy. That's all I wanted really, just for him to be happy.

Later that day, we finally made it back to his mother's house. I wasn't thrilled to go back there but after the events from the morning both Jake and I were in a terrific mood and I hoped she wouldn't spoil it, for either of us.

"Hey, Beth, is Mom around?" Jake asked after he took our stuff to our room and came back down to the living room where he left me to wait for him. He wanted to tell his mother that we were engaged and knew it wouldn't go as well if he didn't do it before other people found out first.

"She's in her studio. Would you like me to go get her?" Bethany asked politely. I couldn't get over how sweet and selfless she always seemed, especially with what the Coldier society had done to her.

"Yes, please," he said kindly, then walked around the couch to sit next to me and hold my hand. "It'll be all right, baby. You don't need to be anxious."

I wasn't sure how she would react, but to say I was anxious was an understatement. I squeezed his hand without saying anything, assuming he knew what I meant by it.

We had only sat there for a minute or two before she sauntered in from down the hall. She didn't have the most pleasant look on her face either, like she was suspicious we had some kind of news that she wasn't sure about.

"Mom, have a seat, please. We want to talk to you." Jake said as he saw her come into the room.

"Jacob, sweetie... You're making me nervous," she said, sounding friendly enough, but I was waiting for her inner monster to come out.

"It's fine, just sit, please."

"Bethany," she said as she sat down across from us and looked back over her shoulder to where Bethany was standing. "Bring us all a drink. I want a gin and tonic. Miles will have his favorite, a Whisky Sour and Kal... just get water for Kaleah."

"I'm not pregnant," I said without realizing I was speaking.

She looked over at me with a smug grin. "Well, how am I supposed to know that, Kaleah? When you sit down like you have news for me, it's an easy assumption, since you both insist on doing things out of wedlock."

Only because wedlock *this day and age isn't the same*, I thought.

"Mom, please..." Jake cleared his throat, diverting her attention back to him.

"Fine, Jacob. What do you have to tell me then?" She smiled after she said it but I could tell it looked forced.

"I asked Kaleah to marry me and she said yes," Jake said as he leaned forward, resting his elbows on his knees.

She started to laugh, but it wasn't loud, like she was amused but trying to hold it in. "Great!" She said suddenly, taking me off guard. "When's the wedding date, then?" She asked him, then looked over at me. There was something I could see in her eyes that looked devious.

"We haven't set it yet. I'm glad you're taking this so well." Jake said, then leaned back to relax against the couch like he hadn't expected her to react that way either, but wasn't suspicious when she did. I couldn't shake the feeling that the smile on her face only served to hide her true feelings.

"Of course, dear, I just want you to be happy." She said, looking down and away like she was thinking about what it all actually meant. "Jacob... would you mind if I spoke with Kaleah alone?" She said as she relaxed back against her couch and crossed her legs.

"Um, okay..." Jake said, looking over at me, "I'll give you a second." He squeezed my hand like I had done to him earlier and stood up. "I'll go help Bethany with the drinks," he gave me a reassuring look then walked out of the room toward the kitchen.

"Kaleah," Liz said softly with a forced smile, "I'm going to do my best to be nice because I do believe that my son loves you... but... well, let me ask you this... How much do you love him?"

"A lot." I was having trouble getting my words out. Just her presence was unsettling and making me feel nervous. "I mean, with everything I am, I love him."

She quickly gave me a face that looked like she thought I was just making stuff up or saying what she wanted to hear. "Well, good, that means that you'll leave him then."

"What?" I paused, confused and not understanding what she meant. I even considered maybe I had just heard her wrong.

"I'm glad that you love him that much. Let me be clear, you are not the right person for Jacob. He needs a woman, not a girl. He needs someone who is strong and independent and capable… I'm afraid you are none of those things and all you're going to do is leech his potential in life. The things he's been able to achieve before you came along have been astounding. He's a hard worker, and it's served him well. That's how he's made it so far, not with me and his father's money. You don't make it to fourth rank if you're not ambitious, and that's exactly what Jacob is… was… until he brought you back with him. Now he's none of those things. All he's ever concerned with anymore is babysitting *you*… So… do you understand what I mean when I say if you love him, and you really want the best for him, then you will leave him?"

Everything she was saying hurt. It felt like she ripped my heart out and was sitting there threatening to stab it. But even with the pain of the words, I couldn't deny the message. I couldn't help but feel she was right. The voice didn't even have to speak to concur this time. I just knew it was true.

"O-okay," I said softly as I nodded my head.

"You will?" She asked like she was slightly surprised but pleased to hear it nonetheless.

"Y-yes," I said, trying to keep myself from tears. "Because I love him…"

"Good… See, that's a good girl… Sometimes we have to sacrifice what we want most for the ones we love." She said, looking more sincere now. "It might be hard, but I promise you, he'll move on…" Then she smiled like she was genuinely happy.

15

PAINFUL ASSUMPTIONS

"You're not very talkative tonight. What's wrong, baby?" Jake asked.

"There aren't enough bubbles," I said, referring to our bath, but that wasn't really my problem.

He sighed. "You're not a very good liar." He reached over and grabbed a large bottle then opened it. "But here," he said as he started to pour a good amount into the water, "now you can tell me the truth."

"Lane said I was a good liar." I began to swirl my arms around in the water to help create more bubbles.

He chuckled, "Oh yeah… What did you lie to him about?"

"I told him you said you saw Katherine. I thought he would tell me how it went since I didn't think you would," I said, then leaned back against his chest again.

"All right… well, if you wanted to know you could've just asked me." His voice was soft and earnest.

"Okay, well, how did it go then?" I asked, wondering if Lane had actually lied to me when he knew I lied to him.

"I saw her… She came over to say hi, but that's it. I was too preoccupied watching for you to return to really pay any attention to what she was saying. That's when I had Lane go check on you, since you left the room."

"Then he did lie to me," I scoffed. I knew I lied first but I couldn't help but be bothered that Lane would lie back.

"I'm sure he felt like he had a good reason. He's never liked Kat so I can see why he didn't want you to know she was there. He told me that's why he wanted to dance with you actually… He knew she hadn't seen you yet since you were out talking to E.J. and he wanted to show you off for me. I still let him have it for taking you away from the table, but I couldn't really be all that hard on him when he told me why."

"Well, how did she know I was with you and not him?" I asked, now confused.

"Because he made it clear when she walked over to the table. He told her, 'Jake's *girlfriend* will be right back, don't get comfortable. She's just out there talking to the *First Rank.*' He had the biggest smile on his face. He was seriously enjoying rubbing everything in her face too much so that's when I sent him away to watch for you. I didn't know what else he was about to say… and I don't really want all of our personal business gossiped about since Kat's known for talking to the other agent's wives."

"Oh," I mumbled. I wasn't as upset with Lane after that explanation.

Jake brought his hands up to my hair and started to get it wet with the water from the bath. "Now you want to tell me what's wrong? I was honest with you… So you can be honest with me."

I didn't respond. I wasn't sure what to say even though I knew exactly what my issue was, and I knew it was something I couldn't tell him about.

"Is it 'cause we haven't moved to Lane's yet?" He asked, probably sensing my hesitance. "I was going to have our stuff taken over there but you seemed like you had a good talk with mom last week so I didn't know if it was as urgent anymore."

"No… I don't care about that now," I said, closing my eyes. I knew he couldn't see me but I didn't want to cry either way just in case.

"Oh, ok... Your talk with her must have gone better than I thought then. That's good." He reached over and grabbed the bottle of shampoo, put a dab in his palm then rubbed his hands together before using them to massage it into my hair.

"You're too sweet," I said, feeling guilty for how kind he was being to me. I didn't feel like I deserved it.

He laughed, "I'm just taking care of my Mustang, baby, that's all."

The next morning I had intended to sleep until the sun rose, which to Jake was sleeping in. The sun hadn't fully come up though, when Jake actually woke me.

"Eva!" There was tension in his voice. He didn't sound happy, but I had no idea what I would have done while I was asleep that would have upset him, so I wasn't sure what his problem was. "Wake up, now!"

I opened my eyes not sure what to expect, but didn't like the way he sounded.

"Explain this!" He said coarsely, looking down at me from beside the bed. He was holding up a couple pieces of paper with an opened envelope.

"Uh... It's paper?" I said softly, not trying to be sarcastic but not clear on what he actually wanted me to tell him about it.

"You're joking, right?... Sit up, so I know you're paying attention." He sounded more than just mad, maybe a little scared, too.

I did what he asked and sat up while trying to get my eyes to open wide enough to pay attention like he wanted, even though it was hard to. "Why are you mad at me?" I asked, expecting him to deny it like he usually did and calm down.

"Do you even realize what you've done?" He wasn't calming down at all. It sounded like he might have been getting more upset.

"No, I don't… I don't know what you're talking about," I said as I finally cleared my eyes after rubbing them thoroughly.

"You went behind my back and got papers on yourself… with *my name* as the owner!" He said, raising his voice while still keeping the same tone. I couldn't remember him ever being that mad at me before.

I stopped to think about what he was accusing me of before replying. "No, I didn't," I said finally, looking up at him.

"Stop lying to me, Eva! I told you, you're not good at it." He threw the papers on the bed next to me and pinched the bridge of his nose probably trying not to unleash his full anger.

I didn't know what to say. I think I was shocked at what was happening. Not only was I still disoriented from waking up so abruptly, I was also confused at why he would have papers when I knew I didn't get them. I wasn't lying and didn't like that he didn't believe me.

"You don't even understand what this means… I told you not to, but you don't listen—"

"Jake…" I said, trying to get him to stop and pay attention to me. "I'm not lying. I didn't do it."

"You had to, Eva! They have your fingerprints. So unless someone came and took them from you while you were asleep… stop freaking lying." His voice was still raised and now the flush in his face appeared darker with the growing tension.

"I swear I didn't do it, please stop yelling at me… Jake, I swear I didn't." I was now upset along with him, but obviously for different reasons.

"You can't be here now…" He said, calming down a little. I didn't know if he believed me or not. "I called Lane. He's going to come pick you up and take you to his house until I decide what to do with you."

"What do you mean 'what to do with you'? Are you going to get rid of me?" I asked, trying not to cry but I couldn't help it as all the emotions suddenly became too strong, threatening to take over.

"What!? No, I'm not going to get rid of you… What the heck, Eva?" He said still sounding mad but confused by my question. "Your full name is in the Coldier system now… It's linked to my name and this address. You were safe with me when the Sicari didn't know where to look. Now, if they can track you, then you've given them the exact location to know where to come and find you."

He doesn't believe me. I didn't say anything else. I knew it wouldn't do any good trying to deny it again. I pulled my legs up and wrapped my arms around them, then leaned my face down to rest it on my knees so I could cry with a little privacy. I thought maybe he was cooling off after I didn't hear anything else for a minute until I heard the door open then slam. With that, I realized I was wrong.

I lifted my head to confirm he'd left, then once I saw that he had, I got up to get dressed so I would be ready when Lane got there. When I was done with that, I packed my bags, then sat on the couch with them beside me. I figured it was the best place to wait for Lane. I was too upset to think about much, other than how someone got my fingerprints.

I hoped when Lane finally arrived, he wouldn't be mad at me, too. I didn't think I could handle that much rejection all in the same day if everyone was upset with me all at the same time. After sitting there for a while and not knowing how much longer it'd take, I leaned over to rest against my bags and went back to sleep.

"Kaleah," I heard Lane's voice. I opened my eyes to see him standing above me, looking down at how I was lying on the couch. "How is that comfortable?"

I didn't answer him. I sat up, reached over and grabbed one of my bags to hand to him then took my other one as I stood up next to him.

"It's that bad, is it?" He said, seeing I didn't feel like talking.

I nodded as I began to walk toward the door.

"Okay… well, I can work with that," he said, then quickly moved past me to grab the door and hold it open. "Don't you want to say goodbye to Miles before we go?" he must have noticed I was headed straight for the exit without looking around.

"No… It might be hard, but he'll move on." I said finally, trying to remind myself what Jake's mom told me so it would be easier to leave.

"Um… I don't think I heard you right. Can you repeat that?" Lane was trying to move as quickly as I was going down the stairs.

"Where's the car?" I wanted to know which way to go once I reached the bottom.

"Out front… Kaleah… you sure you're not going to say goodbye," he said slowing down, "I can find him. He's around here somewhere."

I didn't respond. I just kept walking, figuring he'd get the idea soon enough. When I reached his car, I opened the trunk, threw my bag in the back, and walked around to the passenger side's back seat and got in, shutting the door behind me. It wasn't long before I heard him shut the trunk then get in to drive.

"Well, when he sees you're gone I guess Bethany can tell him she saw me pick you up." He looked at me through the rear-view mirror. "Why are you sitting back there? You sure you don't want to ride up here with me?"

"No," I murmured not really feeling like talking still, "I'm good."

"Okay…" He said as he put the car in drive to pull out, "What's going on? Why are you acting like this?" He must not have gotten the idea I didn't want to talk as he continued to ask me questions.

"Jake thinks I did something I didn't do," I said quietly as I looked out the window.

"What did you not do?" He asked, acting like he didn't already know.

"Why did you come pick me up? Didn't he tell you already?" I looked back at him.

He didn't respond for a moment, then did finally, "Yeah, I just wanted to get your side of it."

"He called me a liar and wouldn't believe me when I told him I didn't do it. Now he hates me."

"Um, that seems a bit harsh… No, really harsh, actually. Miles doesn't hate you, Kaleah… He might be a little upset but he'll get over it, especially when he finds out who did it since it wasn't you."

I wanted to tell him by that point it would be too late but I didn't say it. All I could think of was what Jake's mom had said—he'll get over it, he'll be fine… *It's best for him if I'm not around.* I closed my eyes, holding back tears as I let all the thoughts and everything she had said swirl in my mind, reminding me of what I needed to do.

"Leave him…"

"Kaleah?" Lane said, breaking me from my thoughts, not wanting to allow a lull in the conversation. "He loves you… I don't know what he said to you this morning but I'm sure if it was harsh, he was probably just upset and he didn't really mean it."

Lane was so kind, he probably couldn't help himself. I wanted to tell him I was going to miss him, but again I knew I couldn't say anything that would give away my intentions when we finally got back to his house. "Lane, do you think hell is real?"

"Um, that's an odd question. Let me think about it." He paused for a moment. "Yes," he said finally, then swallowed. "I would like to think it's reserved only for terrible people but who am I to judge what makes someone bad or not… Why do you ask?"

"That's the only thing that still scares me." I said, looking back out the window.

"You're scaring me right now, Kaleah."

"Why?"

"I've never seen this side of you… Has Miles?"

"Jake see's what he wants to see," I said solemnly still looking out the window. "I'm sorry…"

"For what?" He sounded puzzled.

"For being a burden!"

"Nothing… I just, I didn't know if you had to work today and had to take time off to come get me." I said, clarifying even though I really had meant it the way I heard the voice say it.

"Oh, no… today's my day off, you're fine," he sounded like he was trying to be upbeat although I suspected he was probably lying so I wouldn't feel worse.

"Okay…" I said, trying to drop the subject so we wouldn't have to keep talking. It worked. He didn't say anything else the rest of the way to his house.

After the elevator opened, he helped me take my bags to his guest room then asked me if I was hungry. I hadn't had anything to eat that morning so I said yes but I wasn't. I just wanted to give him an excuse to leave me alone. I think the idea of him getting to cook for me made him happy because he sounded a bit more chipper after that as he left the room and went into the kitchen.

I took everything out of my bags and placed it all neatly in a row on the dresser, still lost in my thoughts. I thought about what his mom had told me. I thought about what happened that morning and how mad he had been with me and how he didn't believe me. So many things I began to think about made me feel worse the more energy I gave the thoughts. They were beginning to take on a life of their own, swirling downward like tub water when you've pulled the plug, spiraling with everything quickly sinking deeper and darker.

It wasn't long before I had a plan and knew what I wanted to do. I realized his mom was right and if I loved him as much as I thought I did, then I only had one option…

I didn't hear Lane but knew where he was so I figured it wouldn't be hard to slip past him and go to the roof. I remembered how to get there from when Jake took me.

I walked out of our room and over to the elevator. Before I was able to push the button to call for it, Lane hollered to me from the kitchen. "Kaleah… I just checked my voicemail and Miles left a message. He must have called not long after we left."

I quickly went back to the doorway of our room so when I hollered back, he wouldn't suspect I had been anywhere else and get suspicious. "Okay?" I yelled back.

"He said he didn't know you left already, and he was on his way here to talk to you. He probably figured out who did it…" Lane sounded optimistic, but I was mentally past any point where sheer optimism would do me any good.

"Okay… good," I said, trying to sound more upbeat. When the conversation was over I went back to the elevator and pushed the button. I knew it would make a loud buzzing sound when the doors opened. I wouldn't have much time when I got on it to get the doors shut and go where I wanted before Lane heard and tried to come after me.

It made the sound just as I thought it would, so I quickly got in and pushed the button that would take me as far to the top as it would go. Then I pushed the button that would make the doors shut faster.

It wasn't as quick as I remembered thinking it was. Standing there hearing the buzzing and thinking about how much trouble I would be in if Lane caught me made me anxious. I pushed the door-close button again a few more times in succession, hoping it would go faster.

Then, as soon as the doors started to close I saw him shoot out of the kitchen and into the entryway. He saw me. Our eyes connected, but he didn't have a chance to say anything before they finally closed. Not that he needed to. The look in his eyes was enough that I felt guilty and ashamed. I hated what I was about to do, but didn't feel like I had a choice. I loved Jake. I loved him so much.

"This is the only way, Eva." I told myself so I would have enough courage to go through with it and not go back. "If you love him, you'll leave him…" I chanted it back to myself over and over. "It's the best for him… You're not good enough for him…"

The elevator doors opened to the top floor where I saw the same do-not-enter signs that I had when Jake had taken me up there. I passed through them just as I had with him and went up the last flight of stairs to the door. I paused as I laid my hand against it, knowing once I opened it what I had intended to do.

"Do it!"

I closed my eyes and took a deep breath, then pushed…

16

LEAVING WITH NO GOODBYE

The view wasn't the same as it had been the night I was up there with Jake. This time, it wasn't nearly as beautiful. I stood there staring out, thinking about what I was about to do. I walked close to the edge and looked down. I was immediately scared. Just standing next to it was hard, so I sat down. I needed to give myself time to feel convinced. I looked out across the city, gazing at all the buildings as I contemplated life, what it meant, and how it would feel to give it up.

I don't know how long I was sitting there when I finally decided, or thought I had, and stood back up again to look down.

"Jump!"

I didn't understand why I felt like I did. I knew the voice was in my head, not some external person speaking to me. Not only that, but I was beginning to hear it all the time after we got to New York. I don't know where it came from or why it was there, but it had gotten stronger, and I had no idea how to make it stop.

I should have stopped listening to it, but I couldn't. So often I felt like I had no choice but to listen. It was like something inside myself, trying to protect me from feeling pain, emotional pain. I wanted to fight it, but I felt powerless like I had no control, no choice but to relent to it, hoping if I obeyed it would stop the pain.

"Just jump, that way it will all be over!"

I couldn't help but question it this time as I looked down. I was high, very high… *Why am I this high?* I didn't want to listen to it or do what it said. *Why am I even here? Think about Jake.* I tried everything I could to change my mind. *What will this do to Jake?*

"You're replaceable."

It was right; I was nothing but a Gypsyin. Jake could surely find someone else just as easily as he'd found me. I didn't have a child with him yet. I didn't even know if I could anymore. Just like his mom had said, I wasn't good for him; he could do better. I didn't want my thoughts to go there, to agree with the voice, but I couldn't help it. They concurred with each other so well. They were giving me no choice. I had to do it. He couldn't love me. I was holding him back. I couldn't let him love me. I wasn't good for him, and it would be selfish of me to hold on… I couldn't hold on.

I looked down one more time, secretly stalling, rebelling against the voice, just hoping for more time to think. Maybe there was some way I was wrong. If I were, there would be no way back. I could only make the choice once. I needed to know if it was the right one. It was so far down. I hesitated… *What am I doing?*

I heard the roof's door open behind me. I froze for a moment, trying to think about what it meant. *Have I been caught? Will I have to tell whoever it is what I'm doing?*

"You should feel ashamed of yourself. You had your chance, and you didn't take it. Now you look stupid!"

Before I thought much further, I couldn't help but turn to see who it was. "Lane?"

"Kaleah, what are you doing up here?" He didn't sound mad. He asked calmly like he already knew the answer, as he gently shut the door behind him and cautiously walked closer to me.

I didn't respond. I was still frozen, and I knew I was caught. Now I felt horrible and ashamed just like the voice told me I should. I didn't want to answer him. I didn't want to admit anything to him. I didn't want him to tell Jake.

"It's okay, it doesn't matter why you're here… but… Miles is gonna be here soon. So… if you don't want him to read my note saying you ran away, then we should hurry and get back down there before he does."

"If he finds out I left you he's going to be really mad at me. I hate it when he's mad at me. "

He slowly moved closer as we talked, trying not to make any quick movements. He swallowed as he hesitated to respond. "No, he won't be mad. He'll just be happy I found you… Why don't you come here? You're too close to the edge. Just walk over to me, okay?"

"You're lying!" I couldn't help but call him out. I knew Jake would be upset with me.

"Kaleah… *please*… Can we talk about this on our way back?" He cautiously toed the ground like he wanted to come closer, but didn't feel comfortable near the edge like I had.

"I don't want to talk about it on the way back. I don't want him mad at me again. Please don't tell him. I don't want him to yell at me again like he did this morning."

"Kaleah… This morning was a misunderstanding. Give him time and he'll see it. Please… just get away from the edge. If you fall or if anything happens to you, and I didn't stop it… he'll kill me! Do you want that? You don't want him upset with me either, do you?"

I shook my head. He was right. I didn't want Jake mad at him, either.

"Good girl… Just come over here then, and we can put this all behind us, all right?"

I began to nod, agreeing to walk over to him when a thought popped into my head, stopping me. "Wait... How did you find me up here?"

The concern on his face was joined by something else, a tenderness... a vulnerability. He didn't respond at first, he just stood there thinking. When he spoke, there was a softness in his voice, revealing the depth of the emotions he was now feeling.

"I wondered with how you were acting in the car... You seemed sad, like... I could just tell. Kaleah, please come to me. If Miles gets here and finds out you left... he won't be angry like you're afraid of. He'll be devastated like his whole life just disappeared. I don't know why you want to do what you're doing up here, but... you can't. It would kill him. Are you listening, Kaleah? You'd kill him inside. He would never be the same."

"That's not what his mom said." I didn't intend to tell him that, but it came out nonetheless.

He looked down at my feet, probably judging how close I was to the edge, then slowly started walking closer, apparently feeling a little more confident the more we talked. "I know you don't know yourself all that well yet, Kaleah, but this isn't you. You're stronger than this... You can fight through whatever is in your head telling you that you have to do it."

I never told anyone about the voice, but what he had just said made it sound like he knew and understood. "I hear a voice..." I said, giving in, hoping since he understood maybe he could help me.

"Okay... tell me about it," he insisted as he inched his way closer to me.

"It started when Luca... after I lost the..." I looked down and away. I couldn't finish what I was saying; it hurt too much.

"Okay... it's okay... Kaleah, look at me, it's *okay*," he said softly, trying to reassure me. He'd gotten close enough; he finally stopped and reached out his hand, offering for me to take it.

I slowly lifted my arm to reach for him. As soon as I did, he quickly snatched my hand and pulled me toward him, wrapping his arms tightly around me, making sure I couldn't go back. Then he moved with me swiftly back over toward the door and as far away from the edge as possible. We stood there for a moment like that. I could feel his heartbeat pounding in his chest. He held me tight against him like he didn't want to let go then pulled back just a little to look down at me.

"Please, don't ever do anything like this again," he said, keeping his arms firmly around me. "I'm terrified of heights... That's like the only thing that I'm really afraid of."

"I'm sorry." I said softly under my breath, looking up at him. I felt bad again and now I was ashamed of myself as well.

He looked at me for a moment without responding. The silence was unsettling yet peaceful at the same time. His eyes slowly drifted from mine down to my lips before he quickly blinked and pulled away. "Let's get back, maybe Miles hasn't found my note yet," he said, releasing one of his arms to open the door but keeping the other one tight around my waist so I couldn't easily escape him.

He didn't say anything else to me the rest of the way down the stairs or while we were in the elevator waiting to reach his floor. I think we were both anxious to see if Jake was there.

When the elevator reached Lane's floor, he pushed a series of keys on a number pad next to the floor buttons and, as the buzzer sounded, the doors opened.

Jake *was* there—standing with his arms crossed—waiting for us. His face held a mixture of anger and relief with his jaw clenched and an upturn to his brow. Without saying anything, before I even had a chance to step out, he quickly walked toward me and bent down to grab me and throw me over his shoulder.

"Jake!" I squealed, but only from the shock of what he was doing and fear of what he was about to do.

"Miles," Lane said before Jake was able to take me very far, "I need to talk to you first."

"You can talk to me later, Lane," Jake said as he started to carry me away, I presumed, toward our room.

"Miles, I'm serious." Lane said, following us down the hall.

"*Lane*, I'm serious... this is between me and her. Thank you for finding her but I'm dealing with it now." Jake snapped back as he walked into our room and shut the door behind him. Then he walked toward the bed and lowered himself, releasing me to fall onto it.

I didn't say anything. I knew he was mad.

"Eva..." he started with an angry tone and his stern face. "I don't even know what to say to you. Do you have any idea the danger you could have been in?"

He didn't get far when I heard Lane knocking on the door. "Miles!"

"Lane, go away! I won't tell you again," Jake ordered, sounding more than serious.

I heard the door open. I looked away from Jake and over to where Lane was now standing just inside the door. "Get your ass out here and talk to me like a brother, Jacob."

Holy shit, I've never seen Lane this serious...

Jake looked at him, then back at me, "Stay put!" He said as he pointed a finger at me then walked out with Lane and shut the door behind him.

I couldn't hear them wherever they went, but I figured it wasn't far. I moved up in the bed and pulled the cover down to crawl under it then pulled it back up and over my head. It wasn't long before I started to get hot, but I didn't care.

I thought about the voice, and what Jake's mom had said. I was upset that I had failed. I knew what I had needed to do, and I didn't do it. I started to cry as all the emotions began to boil up inside me. It wasn't long before I nodded off.

"Kaleah... Baby..." Jake whispered at the same time I felt him curling up under the cover with me.

"Hmm?" I didn't really feel like talking. I just wanted him to yell at me and get it over with so I could go back to sleep.

"I'm not mad at you anymore, I just need to talk to you." He sounded way calmer than he had before.

"K..."

"Can you tell me more about the voice?"

"No…" I was tired. I didn't want to talk.

"Kaleah, open your eyes and look at me. We need to talk, baby. I'm serious."

I opened my eyes to see him lying next to me, staring at my face.

"When did you start hearing voices?" He asked softly.

I didn't respond. I just stared at him. I didn't feel like I could talk even if he wanted me to.

He brought his hand to my head and started to caress my temple with his thumb. "I'm sorry I yelled at you this morning. I should have listened when you told me you didn't do it. I shouldn't have called you a liar and I shouldn't have walked out on you afterward either. I screwed up. I screwed up so terribly and I'm sorry. You can't just shut down and not talk to me about it, though. I need you to talk to me, baby."

"You don't need me," I said the first thing that came to my mind.

"What? Why would you say that?" He paused then continued, "When my mom spoke to you alone, what did she say?"

"She asked me if I loved you. I said I did." I stopped to look away from him as I tried to keep myself from crying while thinking about what I needed to tell him, but knew I wouldn't be able to get it out. "I can't stay with you, Jake. I have to leave you…" My voice was clipped as tears welled in my eyes and started to stream down my face.

"That doesn't make any sense, Kaleah. Look at me."

I brought my eyes back to his like he asked then waited for him to continue.

"You're not leaving me. Not only does that make no sense, it's absurd." His voice was more stern again.

"I'm not good for you; I'm ruining your life." I couldn't say it without crying more.

"Kaleah Eva, you're going to tell me right now what my mother said to you," he growled as he started to sit up.

I swallowed. I didn't want to say it. I knew what I had to do—what was best for him and I wasn't going to let him talk me out of it. "It doesn't matter anymore. Now that I have papers, you said it yourself; you can't be around me."

"*Bullshit* I can't!" He was starting to get upset again but I couldn't tell if it was at me or not. "We can't be at that address anymore... I never said I couldn't be around you. It just complicates things, but in no way does it mean we can't be together. It's the opposite. Now I have to watch you closer since they might know where to find you."

"Don't you see, Jake... that's the problem. You're spending your entire life doing nothing but babysitting me. You have better things to do, like... you had a career, ambition, a—"

"I had nothing!" He interjected emphatically, "I had absolutely nothing without you! Don't you get it? My life is you and I don't care what anyone, especially my mother, says about it! *You're* what makes me happy. That's what I want and the only thing I want—you!"

"Well, I don't care what you want," I raised my voice to match his, "I'm not good enough for you... You'll find someone else and get over me. I'm leaving you because it's what's best for you." I sat up and pulled the covers back to get out of bed.

"I don't know what you think you're doing, but you're not going anywhere," he said like he was dead serious and would tackle me again before he'd let me walk out.

"You can't stop me," I said as I began to make my way to the edge of the bed and stand up.

"*Bullshit* I can't! You're my Gypsyin now, remember?" His eyes continued to watch me, his body ready to pounce if I took a step too close to the door.

"I thought you weren't willing to own me?"

"I'll do whatever I have to do to keep you with me," he said, standing up out of the bed as well. "You had your choice six months ago to leave me, but you stayed. It's not my fault if you don't remember it! Then three months ago when you erased yourself, the last words you said to me were that I could have you as my Kaleah. Then last week you committed yourself to me again. You said you'd marry me. So no, I don't really care what you think you want right now. You don't get to decide what you want to do when you've even admitted you're listening to someone else's lies inside your head."

"Jake," I started to argue with him again as I began to walk around the bed.

"No!" He raised his voice, "No, Eva… You leave someone if they hit you, or beat you, or starve you, or abuse you…" he was getting more worked up the more he went on, "but you don't leave just because they love you and you don't think they should."

I just stood there staring at him, listening to him. He was so upset but it was with passion this time, not rage.

His shoulders slumped as he ran his hand over his face. "If you don't love me back, then you can leave," he lowered his voice now to almost a whisper like he was trying not to cry as he sat back down on the bed. "I won't stop you… But you're wrong, I won't get over it. I won't find anyone else and I'll never be the same again. If you're willing to have that on your conscience, then go."

I just stood there, still watching him. He was willing to let me go even though it would kill him to do so, just because he didn't want to refuse me my choice. At that moment, I realized, that's what sacrificial love looks like not what I thought I was doing.

I walked around the bed and over to him, then kneeled down between his knees, placing my head in his lap. "She told me if I loved you then I should leave you, but because I love you I want to choose you. I don't want to leave you." I felt a release as soon as I said it. It was like everything in me, down to my core, my soul, wanted it too—except the voice.

He leaned forward and embraced my head, resting his cheek next to mine. He sucked in a breath like he was breaking a sob. "Baby, forgive me… I've tried to protect you from everything except the one thing you asked me to. I'm sorry I didn't listen when you told me she was saying things that hurt you. And I'm sorry I didn't take it seriously when you asked me to move."

"I forgive you," I said softly as I closed my eyes and brought my arms up to hug his back.

"I'm sorry I didn't believe you about the papers either. I shouldn't have assumed you disobeyed when I asked you not to get them. After I yelled at you and walked out, I regretted it. The more I thought about it, the more I realized it wasn't really something you even knew how to do. But you were already gone when I went back into our room to apologize."

I didn't say anything, I just rubbed my hand up his back so he knew I was listening.

"Promise me you won't try to hurt yourself again," he said, pulling back and placing his hand under my chin, lifting my face to look at him.

I blinked a couple of times, thinking about what he was asking of me. "Okay," I said softly, looking up into his eyes.

"No, Kaleah… really promise me, because I know you won't make promises you can't keep."

"I promise…" I said really trying to mean it.

"Good, because you know what that would do to me if I found out you killed yourself?" He asked as he put his hands under my arms to pull me up to sit with him.

"No, what?"

"It'd break me in a way I could never be put back together."

"Okay… I promise then…" I knew it wasn't that simple, but if it made him feel better, I was willing to say the words, truly hoping if it ever came to it again, I could keep my promise.

He smiled. "That's my girl," then leaned in to kiss my forehead.

17
WRONG WOMAN

"When did you say Chelsey was visiting?" I heard Lane ask Jake. They probably didn't know I was listening to their conversation. I had been reading in the study but thought I would see what they were doing. Apparently, I was a good sneaker because I had worked my way up to standing just outside the door of Lane's workout room without them knowing I was there.

"Friday," Jake said, answering Lane's question. "I haven't seen her since I went to Nashville. She was griping at me just like Mom did before I left, telling me I shouldn't go… I was gonna ruin my life…" Jake stopped and sighed.

"You gonna take Kaleah to meet her?" Lane's voice wasn't as loud now, but it sounded more strained like he was lifting something heavy.

"She can't go back to my parent's house. It's not safe there for her anymore… So no, probably not. Besides, I don't think Chelsey would be all that nice to her since she's just a mini version of Mom and you see how that went." Jake's voice sounded normal but I could hear him breathing harder than usual.

"True… Well, if you'd like, Kaleah can stay here with me if you wanna go see Chelsey on Friday. I don't have to work again until Sunday."

I didn't know who Chelsey was but from what they were saying she sounded like a member of the family.

"Or," Lane continued with another idea, "you can invite her to come see you here if you want, I don't mind. It's been a while since I've seen her." He paused at the same time I heard metal clanging together. "Actually, now that I think about it, the last time was right after you and Kat split. Chelsey wasn't really all that happy with you."

"Yeah, her and Kat were pretty good friends…"

I took a step closer to the door to hear better but instead I heard the floor creak a little under the pressure of my foot.

"Kaleah?" Jake asked suddenly.

"Uh, yeah?" I walked into the room where they were and acted like I had heard nothing. "I was just seeing what you guys were doing." I said, smiling as I looked at Jake so he wouldn't be suspicious.

Lane didn't say anything, he just continued lifting a bar with metal weights at each end. Jake grinned. "How much did you hear?"

I rolled my eyes up, trying not to look at him. "What… um?"

"You really aren't very sneaky," he said, as he started to laugh. "I knew you were out there five minutes ago."

I returned my eyes to him, then glanced over at Lane as he let the weights down and sat up. He was grinning now just like Jake. "Fine!" I said, seeing I had walked into something that would make me the target for them to tease. "Who's Chelsey?"

"My sister," Jake said nonchalantly as he bent down to pick up his shirt off the floor then used it to wipe the sweat off his face.

"You never told me you had a sister." I said, trying not to get distracted by either him or Lane flaunting their bare muscular chests. I could tell it wasn't working and my eyes were drawn to them so I let my eyes roll up to the ceiling again while I waited for his response.

"Wow, Kaleah, are you blushing?" Lane asked before Jake had a chance to respond to me.

"Shut up, Lane," I said finally looking back at him so he knew I wasn't scared to.

Jake spoke up, drawing my eyes back over to him. "I did tell you, baby, but it must have been before you were erased last time. I'm sorry I didn't think to tell you again."

"Okay," I said softly, so he knew I wasn't upset about it. "I'm gonna go make myself something to eat. Either of you want anything?" I asked, looking straight at Jake and not letting my eyes divert to Lane since it felt weird looking at him without a shirt on.

"I'm good, I'll make myself something when I'm done in here," Lane said quickly as he lay back down under the bar.

"I'm fine for right now too," Jake said, looking at me, still grinning. I figured he saw how uncomfortable I was and thought it was funny. "You gonna be all right in there alone?"

I knew why he was asking. It'd been a couple of weeks since my roof incident but he didn't seem to be forgetting it very quickly. "Yes, I feel fine right now. I'm not gonna try to escape. Is that what you want to know?"

He wiped his face again with his shirt. "I'm not scared you're gonna escape again, baby. I just wanna make sure you're safe... not hearing any voices or anything, that's all."

"No, not right now... I'm fine."

He smiled, "Good, call for us if you need anything, k?"

"Okay," I said, smiling back at him, then I turned and walked out toward the kitchen.

I looked through the fridge, trying to decide what I was in the mood for when I thought I heard something from the other room. I closed the door expecting to hear one of the guys walking in, but didn't see anything when I heard the noise again. It was a low clicking sound, then after a few seconds I heard a voice but this time it wasn't the one in my head.

"Henry, I'm here to see Jacob." It was a woman's voice. I recognized it was coming from the elevator's speaker. I stood there for a second, wondering if I should go get one of them. The more I thought about it the more I figured it was probably Chelsey, since Lane mentioned her coming to his house to see Jake instead of him going to his mom's. I began to panic the longer I stood there thinking about what to do. I didn't want it to take me too long if I went to get Jake and then Chelsey could be gone when we got back. I didn't figure he'd be pleased if that happened.

I looked over at the button that was against the wall right inside the kitchen. I'd seen Lane use it before when Jake was in the elevator asking to come in. I didn't hesitate any longer. I reached over and hit it, then walked around, ready to greet her.

As the doors opened, I could see a woman just as I had expected but what I wasn't expecting was her appearance. She didn't look anything like Jake; quite the opposite, actually. She was thin and short with straight shoulder-length blonde hair. Her eyes didn't match his either. They weren't almond shaped and her facial features were different. Initially, I wouldn't have thought it was his sister if I hadn't seen her bright red lipstick. That looked like the same color his mom wore when I first met her. After seeing that, I thought surely it was Chelsey, since he said she was a miniature version of Liz.

"Hi!" I said, trying to sound chipper so we could get off to a good start.

She looked confused at why I was the only one standing there greeting her, "Uh, hi... Where is Jacob?"

"He'll be out here soon," I lied. I didn't want to tell her right away. I wanted her to have to talk to me first before he got to see her. "He's just getting cleaned up from a workout. Here, come take a seat..." I turned and started to walk toward the living room, expecting her to follow me.

"Do you even know who I am?" she asked, walking behind me just as I hoped she would.

"Oh, yeah... the guys were just talking about you." I took a seat on the couch and motioned for her to take a seat across from me. "My name is Kaleah," I said, trying to smile as much as I could.

"I know who you are... but this isn't what I was expecting at all." She didn't even try to match my pleasantries, she just kept looking at me, confused.

"Oh, uh… did Liz tell you about me?" I started to realize why she probably wasn't as excited to meet me as I was with her.

"Why are you still here?" She asked, keeping a sour face. "Liz said you were leaving Jacob."

"Uh…" I wasn't sure I liked her at that point anymore. "Well, she was wrong." I didn't really know how to answer her but since it wasn't any of her business, I was going to be vague.

"I thought you promised her, since you knew you weren't right for him." The way she said it sounded just like she was mimicking what Liz had said to me. After a second of letting what she said sink in though, I finally caught something else she had said that I didn't catch the first time… *She called her Liz…* I couldn't help but wonder who called their mom by their first name.

"How do you pronounce your name?" I asked, diverting from the previous subject until I could figure out who I was actually sitting across from.

Her face looked even less pleasant than it had when she realized I changed the subject. "Jacob calls me Kat, but it's Katherine."

I made sure not to let any of the shock and surprise I felt within me show on my face. I kept it stone-cold just as I saw Jake did when he didn't want to show his feelings. "Right, that's what I thought… Cat… cute." I didn't know what else to say. I just let it come out as I tried to collect my thoughts, trying to come up with what else I wanted to say to her.

"So, why aren't you leaving him? You told Liz you would." She didn't waste any time jumping right back into the previous subject.

"Because I love him… Is that why you're here, because you still do too and you want him back?" Her face stiffened when she heard the question like she was shocked that I would be so upfront with her.

"How could you love him? You haven't even been with him very long. I'm sure you don't even know him very well. It's obvious you're just with him for his money and rank. Even Liz sees it," she said, sounding extremely defensive.

No, she didn't… "I bet I know him better than you do." I was bluffing. I really didn't know which of us might have known him better but it didn't matter, I wasn't about to give up my spot to that twat.

"Okay, then, what was his favorite sport in school?" I didn't know why that's what she thought was a good one to throw at me first but it was a good one nonetheless. *Dammit,* I thought to myself, I didn't know. I probably did before I erased myself but I didn't know now.

"Football," I said, totally guessing. She looked irritated and didn't deny it. That made me figure I was right. *One point for Eva!*

"That was easy... What work did he do before he became an agent?" She rapid-fired off another question.

I actually remembered that one from when he told me everything when we first came to New York. "He worked for his father at their investment firm." I said, then grinned like I knew I won another one.

She rolled her eyes. "Fine..." Then she paused, probably trying to come up with something harder. "What got him promoted to his rank as a Track and Capture Agent?"

I couldn't bluff knowing that one and it wasn't something I could guess at either. I hesitated, trying to think about what to tell her.

Seeing I was taking too long, she went ahead and answered her own question for me. "He was top in his squad for catching *Gypsyins.* He brought more of them in than anyone else in the agency... hundreds his first year. He was a natural." She smirked as soon as she was done saying it. She knew she had me on one of them.

I was shaken. *Holy Shit...* "Get out!" I shouted as I stood up.

"No," she scowled, acting indignant as she leaned even further into the couch in defiance. "I came here to see Jacob, and that's what I am going to do." She raised her voice as she said it.

"Jacob doesn't want to see you!" I said, raising my voice to match hers as I pointed toward the elevator.

"Kat?" Jake's voice came from behind me. Her eyes quickly shifted away from me and over to him. "What are you doing here?" He asked.

I turned to look. He was standing there still without his shirt on, eyebrows raised with his mouth gaped, looking rather surprised that she was standing in front of me.

"Your mom told me you were here, and you wanted to see me. She said you'd broken it off with… *her.*" She gave me a dirty look, then gestured toward me as if appalled.

"Eva?" Jake looked at me, then at her then over to the elevator like he was trying to figure out what had happened and how she was there. Before he said anything else, Lane walked in behind him. He was fully dressed though, and looked like he'd showered.

"Wooohh… What the hell?" Lane said as soon as he realized I wasn't the only one standing in his living room.

Jake started to walk over to us. I turned to glare at her while I grinned. He was going to kick her out, and I was happy to see it. "Eva, go to our room, please. I'll be there in a minute."

"What?" I said suddenly, turning back to look at him in confusion. That's not what I was expecting at all. "No… I won't go to our room." I said, trying to take the shock on my face and make it serious so he knew I wasn't going to listen.

He looked at me like he half expected my response then sighed. "Fine… Kat, come with me," he said looking at her, then glanced over at Lane, giving him a look that apparently he would understand as an order.

"What? I can't hear what you're going to talk to her about?" I scoffed. I wasn't happy. I sat down on the couch and crossed my arms. Lane quickly came over and sat down across from me as Kat walked over to the elevator with Jake.

"It's okay," Lane said, trying to console me. "Now, if he tries to give you any shit about opening the doors for her, you don't have to take it."

I couldn't help but crack a smile at the idea. "You're right… I didn't even think about him being upset that I opened the doors for her. When I buzzed her in, it was because I thought she was Chelsey."

"Ah," he said, leaning back against the couch. "Well, I wouldn't worry about him talking to her," he looked over at them after he said it. "He'd be an idiot if he picked her over you," he smiled, then looked back at me. "And you don't wanna be with an idiot, I'm sure."

I nodded, then looked back again at her and Jake standing there talking. I couldn't hear what they were saying but I could see Jake didn't look all that comfortable and she looked too comfortable, which I didn't like one bit.

"Jake said you don't like her?" I said it in a way to invite Lane to tell me why as I looked back at him.

"Nope… I don't," he said as he ran his hand through his hair making a mist of water fly off in all directions.

"But you like me? What's different between us?" I asked.

He grinned, studying me before he answered. "Oh, don't get me started… She would have been like a Stepford wife from hell. You're like the cute girl next door."

I looked at him a bit puzzled. I didn't understand his reference.

"Okay," he must have seen my confusion, so he continued to clarify. "She's like a sheep that thinks she's a wolf. She'll blindly obey but only 'cause she's ignorant as hell and doesn't have an original thought in her head. She also thinks she's God's gift to the world. I don't think she has a humble bone in her body. You… ah, how do I say it nicely… You can be hard to babysit, I'll be honest, but it's fun. You're fun… The adventure that's in you… that *is* you, makes Miles happy, honestly happier than I've ever seen him. You're also the coolest girl I've ever met and you act like you don't even know it."

"Oh, okay," that was a good answer that I wasn't really expecting but it made me feel better after hearing it. I looked back over at her and Jake as they continued to talk. It wasn't long before she placed her hand on his arm while she spoke. Her face was brighter than it had been when she was speaking with me. Jake didn't move it, he just let her stand there touching him. "Am I just supposed to sit here, watch this and pretend that it doesn't bother me?" I asked without looking back at Lane.

"Nope! I think you should give him shit for it. If I were you, I would go to your room and slam the door." I looked over at him as he paused. "Okay, well, if you slam it just try to do it in a way that you're not actually breaking anything. You guys cost me enough staying here as it is. Like last month, my housekeeper charged me extra for having to clean syrup off the sheets…" He furrowed his brow a little, then smiled like he wasn't really mad.

I chuckled as I thought about what he was saying. "That was his fault," I said, then straightened my face. "Okay, I'm gonna do it now." I looked at him, then winked before I walked off loudly, stomping each of my feet as I went toward our room and slammed the door.

"Kaleah, baby, unlock the door," Jake demanded at the same time I saw the knob wiggle.

"No…" I yelled back to him, "Lane said I didn't have to!"

"Lane said you didn't have t—, Lane!" The knob stopped wiggling as I heard Jake's voice get softer like he went to find Lane to yell at him.

After a few minutes, they both came back, and I heard Lane's voice now, "All right… All right… Kaleah… Miles said I have to tell you I didn't mean it and you should open the door for him." He didn't sound enthusiastic whatsoever.

"Nope…" I yelled back to them. "You tell Miles he can go sit on the couch and wait for me to be done sitting here."

"She said you can go sit on the couch and wai—"

"Stop, Lane, you're not funny. You can stop smiling like that, too. I don't appreciate you causing me more grief than Kat already has."

"Kaleah," Lane spoke to me again, "he's walking off now… I think he's going to the… nope… Okay, he's going to the kitchen. Are you hungry? I can bring you some food if you want to make him wait it out longer…"

"Lane!" Jake yelled at him again, then I heard Lane, still outside my door, start to laugh.

"Don't worry about it, Lane," I yelled back to him. "I don't wanna get you in trouble. I'll just come out when I'm ready."

"Pizza it is!" He said loudly, then I heard him walk off.

18

MUSTACHE MAN

"Kaleah, baby, can we talk now?" Jake wiggled the knob then came in when he realized it wasn't locked anymore.

"How did your private chat with Kat go?" I asked sarcastically.

"I didn't come in here to fight with you, Eva," Jake said, standing there, still shirtless, now holding a plate with pizza on it that Lane intended for me.

"Then don't fight with me. Just give me my pizza and leave." It was obvious the conversation wasn't starting well.

"You're so stubborn sometimes." He set the plate down out of reach across from me on the bed.

"Whatever… I hope your talk with her was productive. I'm sure she liked looking at you from a foot away without your shirt on." I said as I crawled across the bed to get the pizza.

"Is that why you're mad? Sorry, I didn't know it would bother you. I still need a shower. I'm all sweaty."

"Naw, it didn't bother me at all," I was being sarcastic again. "Let me just stand there talking to Marcus topless and see if it bothers you."

Jake didn't say anything. He just watched as I got the pizza then crawled back to my side. "Eva..." He said finally, "You remember Marcus?" He asked like he'd seen a ghost.

"I had a dream..." I looked away from him as I continued, "It gave me enough of an idea that we were together. I didn't figure I'd ask you about him though... you don't like to tell me about that kind of stuff in my past. I guess I understand. You're probably afraid I might go running back to him." I took a bite of pizza then set the rest back down on the plate.

He didn't say anything at first, he just let out a deep breath then sat down at the end of the mattress on his side. "Look at me, baby," he said, then stretched himself across the bed as he reached out for me.

Oh no, I thought. By the way he was acting, I shouldn't have brought Marcus up. "Was I cheating on him with you?" I asked finally seeing how his mood changed.

"No, baby," he moved closer and took a hold of my hand. "I don't think you'd ever do that to someone you love... He was killed before you ever met me." He said it softly like he expected it would be hard for me to hear.

"What?" It was hard but since I didn't really remember him well, I could tell it was something that wouldn't take me long to get over. "By who?"

He hesitated, probably to think about the best way to answer. "A Sicari..." he said finally.

"Oh, okay." I pulled my hand back to take another bite of pizza. "You being sweet right now though, doesn't mean I'm not still mad that you told me to go to my room like a child so you could talk to your ex where I couldn't hear you." I looked back up at him intentionally not smiling.

He looked away as he brought his hand up to scratch his eyebrow.

"And don't think you laying there without your shirt on is going to do anything either."

He laughed and looked back at me after I said it but he made his face serious again as he responded, "I didn't ask to talk to her privately for her, it was for you."

"Have you ever thought you might be too protective?" I said after clearing my throat.

"Nope... never," he smiled.

"What would she say that you think would hurt my feelings so bad that I couldn't hear it? You realized I talked to her for a good ten minutes before you ever came in the room, right?" I asked.

I got the idea he didn't realize that when he furrowed his brows like it shocked him, "No... I didn't know that. And I wasn't afraid she would say something to hurt your feelings. I was afraid she'd say something to *provoke* you... Then you would attack her and being a Gypsyin with papers, if you did, she could have you taken away from me."

"Oh, well, that makes sense," I said, taking another bite of pizza.

"You were yelling at her when I walked in though, so she must have already said something that bothered you..." He said as he reached over, picked up my pizza and took a bite then put it back down.

"Well, you tell me what you talked to her about for so long first and then if I am satisfied you're not holding anything back, I might tell you what she said that made me so mad."

He smiled, "You're ornery, but fine... What do you want to know?"

"Everything..." I smiled innocently back, acknowledging he was right. I was being ornery, and he was going to have to deal with it.

"Okay..." he said as he rolled to his back on the bed, "She said she missed me and wanted me back. I explained that I didn't love her and didn't miss her and that wasn't going to happen. She said that Mom told her you agreed to break up with me... I said yeah, you did, but Mom was manipulating you and I didn't want you to leave, so you didn't. She tried to tell me the same crap that Mom told you about you not being good enough for me. I told her you were more than good enough for me, and we were engaged and going to get married. She wasn't all that happy when she heard that..." He stopped.

"Was that it?" I asked.

"No... then she threatened me..." He said quietly like he was recounting within himself how she said it.

"Okay?" I said, wanting him to go on.

"She told me she wouldn't stop until she found a way to break us up… Honestly, I think she's just desperate. She wasted four years trying everything she could to be my wife. She lost four years of her prime, and now she can't find anyone else that can give her what she wants—prestige, money… favor. That's why she hates you so much… She sees we genuinely love each other and you're getting ready to live out what she's always dreamed of… And you didn't have to do anything to work for it, except love me back."

"Okay…" I didn't know how to respond. "What do you mean she tried everything?" I didn't understand.

"She lies, manipulates… she wants what she wants, and it's not my love, it's the position of being my wife. I didn't see it all until after we split up and I moved to Nashville. She's toxic, and I didn't even realize it until I had been away from her for a while. After I had a chance to finally breathe, it was easy to see everything. She doesn't want *me*… I don't know if she really ever did." He paused to sit up again and look at me. "Now, are you satisfied?"

I nodded. "Sure… She told me something you probably never wanted me to know, though."

His face instantly looked worried. "All right… uh, I'm not sure what that would be but okay…" He said, hesitant to hear what it was.

"Why don't you tell me how you were promoted to being a TC agent?" I said, suggesting he give me his side first before I tell him her side.

"Oh…" His face didn't really change, he still looked worried. "Okay…" He took a deep breath then continued, "Before I knew better, I was one of the agents that went out and captured Gypsyins," he said as he looked away from me like he was ashamed. "I was trained that they were the enemy… and my job was to go and seize as many of the enemy as I could. I was good at it, so good they promoted me. They made it my full-time job, but once I became a TC Agent, I didn't just capture random Gypsyins anymore. After that, I was the agent they sent out to capture the spies, assassins, double agents… the—"

"Me?" I interrupted him once I realized where he was heading.

He didn't answer me, he just looked at me like a deer in the headlights.

"If that's the case, why were you sent to capture me?"

"Eva... it's not that simple. You had a letter that said you were something that you weren't."

"Okay..." I said willing to let go of that one but I wanted him to address the other part of it that was bothering me. "But you were the agent who brought Gypsyins in to be slaves?"

"That's not... no... ugh... I don't want you to think that." I could tell he was beginning to panic about where I was taking it. "I never knew what they were doing with them, that was before they... Oh god, Eva, it's not like that. I did what I was ordered to do, and as soon as I was suspicious that they weren't treating them right, I left. That's when I went to Nashville. I didn't want anything to do with it anymore, so I left."

"How can you say *no* when it sounds like that's exactly what you did?"

"Do you want me to be the bad guy? Will that make you feel better?" He asked, getting frustrated.

"No, I'm just trying to understand, and I want the truth, not the watered down 'Kaleah-safe' version like what you usually give me."

"Eva, I'm not perfect! I was young, ignorant... I did things that I'm not proud of and I'm sorry. If I knew a way to atone for my sins, I'd do it. I'm not trying to make excuses. It was wrong. People should never be slaves... No one should ever have the right to own another human being! Period. But you have to believe me when I say I didn't know what I was doing... I'd never have become an agent if I knew that was what I'd end up being a part of." It clearly bothered him. I could see he was getting emotional the longer we talked about it. It wasn't all that often I saw him become emotional, either.

"Do you think that's why you fell in love with me?" I said softly as the thought popped into my head. "When you saw I was a Gypsyin, do you think you were trying to redeem yourself by saving me?"

He stared at me blankly for a moment after I asked it. "That's a good question," he said, then looked away like he was thinking about it. "I don't know… Will the way I answer that change how you feel about me?"

"What, are you worried I won't love you if you have flaws?" I asked feeling intrigued. I never saw this side of him. He was vulnerable. For the first time that I could remember, I was seeing a side to him that was genuinely scared that I wouldn't love him back.

"Maybe…" He said as he looked away again.

"Jake, I don't love you because I think you're perfect. I know you aren't. But I don't want you to love me just because you see me as a weak helpless Gypsyin that needs to be saved either."

"I don't!" He said vehemently, "I mean, I'll admit maybe that's what I initially saw and was drawn to, but that's not the case now at all, 'cause that's not what you are, baby. You're not weak or helpless at all. I've never met a woman stronger than you. I'm not talking just kick a man's ass strong either, which you are by the way… I mean emotionally strong. You don't even know all the shit you've been through in your life but when you did, you were something else. You're a warrior! That's why I love you, not because you have weaknesses but because you have perseverance and strength to overcome them—every time."

I sighed, then took another bite of my pizza. "You just can't help yourself, can you?" I asked.

"What?" He acted like he didn't know what I was talking about.

"Laying there all hot and sexy without your shirt, saying sweet things about me… I know what you're trying to do." I tilted my head and looked at him from the corner of my eye.

He laughed, "Is it working?" He asked as he took his hand and slowly ran it down his abs.

"Maybe… I just got one more question for ya."

"Okay?" He said, "Shoot."

"What's your favorite… um everything?"

"What?" He sounded confused by the question, although I thought it was pretty clear.

"Kat said she knew you better than me and then she started to quiz me and I didn't like it when I couldn't answer all her questions correctly. So I need to know more about you and I figured all your favorite stuff would be a good start."

He nodded silently as I explained it to him, "Ah, all right… Well, hm… My favorite food is steak… Dessert is ah, apple pie. My favorite sport is football. Well, it used to be when people still played it, anyway. My favorite person is you…" He smiled and looked at me then continued. "My favorite color is blue… like the color of the ocean where it meets the shore, like in the Caribbean, you know, that blue."

"Have you been there? The Caribbean?" I couldn't help but ask.

"No, I always wanted to go, but now the closest we'll probably ever get to it is if we go to Florida." He reached over and rubbed my leg as he said it.

"We can go there?" I thought the extent of our future was strictly New York.

"Yeah… I don't see why not. Would you like that? We can go for our honeymoon after the wedding."

"Uh, yeah!" I said excitedly. "This is the first time you've really talked about the wedding… Have you thought about it more? Do you know how we can do it?"

"Well, I have some ideas…"

"Okay… then tell them to me!" I insisted.

"I don't think that's the best idea. I don't want to get your hopes up if they don't pan out. How about I tell you more when I really figure out what we're doing?" He moved closer as he continued to rub my leg. "Besides you said you only had one more question, and I already answered it so…"

"Okay, just one more." I figured I knew what he wanted and thought he likely wouldn't deny me.

He let out a loud sigh, then smiled. "What, baby?"

"So if I see Kat again, you're telling me I can't kick her ass?"

He started laughing. "That's exactly what I'm telling you."

"Ah, man!" I said as I threw myself back against my pillow.

It didn't take him any time at all to finish moving himself up to lie next to me. "Sorry, baby, I'm sure you'd enjoy it but we just can't chance it," he paused to chuckle again. "However… if you really are itching to spar with someone I'd love to see you up against Lane, that'd be fun to watch!" He sounded overly enthusiastic like he was proud and ecstatic that he thought of it.

"You're right, that's a great idea!" I rolled to my side to sit up and get out of the bed.

"Woe, woe… Where do you think you're going?" He quickly reached out and wrapped his hands around my waist to pull me backward toward him.

"To go fight with Lane like you said I should," I said, pulling against his hands as I tried to stand up. I knew what he wanted and thought I would play with him a little to see how hard he'd try to get it.

"Wait… we had plans, remember one question… then two… now this! No, you can't do that to me," he said like he was playing as well, but still not about to let me go.

"But I wanna fight…" I said again, trying to throw all my weight into standing.

"Then wrestle with *me*." I could hear him behind me. It sounded like he would have laughed if he wasn't putting all his energy into stopping me.

"Nope… you said Lane," I pulled harder one more time, making his fingers slip, releasing me.

"Nooooo," he whined as I quickly took a few steps away from the bed so he couldn't grab me again.

I turned around and grinned at him as I slowly walked backward toward the door.

"Fine…" he acted like he wasn't going to chase me, "If I'm gonna miss out on some lovin', then you better kick his ass real good to make it worth it." He said as he sat up and smiled really big. "'Cause he deserves it after the shit he pulled earlier."

"I'll sneak up on him," I said, grinning. I felt quite mischievous at that moment and was happy to have the all-clear from Jake.

"Wait, I wanna watch," he shot up out of the bed.

I opened the door and turned around to whisper. "Where would he be?"

"Study…" Jake whispered back. "Don't sneak up on him if he's standing. I don't want him to hurt you."

I got the idea he didn't really have as much faith in my fighting as he had in Lane's responsiveness. "Yeah, okay… whatever." I whispered again under my breath as I started to head toward the study quietly.

I noticed the door was open as I got closer, which I was thankful for since I figured he would hear if I tried to open it and that would be a dead give-away. I sneaked closer to it as quietly as I could and peeked in. It was perfect; he was sitting with his back to us looking down; I assumed reading.

I slowly walked up behind him and then quickly, before he knew I was there, wrapped my arms around his neck in a position that would put him to sleep. I surprised him just as I had wanted, but he didn't react the way I thought he would.

As soon as he felt my arms, he stood up, twisted and bent forward, flinging me over his shoulder onto the ground in front of him.

"Kaleah! What the hel—"

I didn't let him finish before I quickly rolled to my side and hit the back of his knees with my leg, making them bend forward with him falling against the floor next to me.

"Seriously, Kaleah?" He said after he hit, then slowly began to roll away from me.

"Jake told me to," I said quickly as I turned to roll with him, then wrapped my arm around his neck again and held it with my other hand behind his head. He didn't wiggle at all or squirm trying to get out of it, though; he just lay there, giving up. "Aww come on, Lane… Play along!" I said. I could hear Jake standing behind us, laughing.

"I don't want to hurt you," Lane said, still just laying there after I loosened up my grip. I got the idea he wasn't having as much fun as I was. "Psych," he said, then before I realized what he was doing he took a hold of my arm and rolled over, quickly flipping me again to land flat on the floor beneath him.

He looked down at me like he'd won and he did, but something about the way he was looking at me triggered something in my mind. I instantly had multiple flashes of the mustache man rapid-fire through my thoughts. I saw him holding me down, doing things to me that I didn't want done.

"Kaleah?" Lane said, suddenly concerned. "Did I hurt you?" He quickly released my arm and moved to the side.

Jake moved swiftly into position over me, looking down, now concerned as well. "Baby, you all right? What happened? What's wrong?" He asked no longer laughing but now looking serious.

I couldn't help but cry as my eyes started to water without my permission.

"Eva, baby, tell me what's wrong," Jake's voice got more stern as his eyes went from mine down my body, scanning me for the problem.

"Dude, I'm sorry. I was trying to be easy with her." I could hear Lane from the side.

"I'm fine." I said finally, trying to fight back more tears.

Jake's eyes shot back up to mine. "You're lying," he said like he could see right through me.

"Well, I'm not hurt so..." I wiped the tears away from my eyes then tried to sit up but he pushed me back.

"Then why are you crying?" He asked, leaving his hand on my shoulder in case I tried again. "Just lay here for a minute until we figure out what's wrong. If you hurt your back, I don't want you to move. Are you afraid I'll be mad at Lane?"

"It was an accident, Kaleah, he knows I didn't mean to hurt you." Lane chimed in, still thinking he broke me somehow.

"I'm not hurt!" I said again, looking at one then the other, "I just don't wanna talk about it... Jake let me up."

He moved his hand from my shoulder, then grabbed a hold of mine to help me sit. "Okay," he said, relenting.

Neither of them said anything else. They just sat there looking at me puzzled.

I could feel my body want to cry again and I knew I wouldn't be able to stop it so I pulled my legs up to rest my head against my knees. "I saw mustache man," I gave in and mumbled it loud enough so Jake could hear me.

"Oh… baby…" He wrapped his arms around me and lay his head against my shoulder. "It's okay, I got you… if you need to cry that's fine, let it out. I'm right here," he said softly, then lifted his head a little. "Lane…" he started to address him.

"I'll go make her some tea, that'll help. She likes tea." Lane said like he already thought about what he should do before Jake had the chance to tell him otherwise.

Jake didn't say anything else. I just felt him move his head like he nodded to agree.

19
INTERVENTION

If it hadn't been rainy out, Jake said he would have taken me to the park. He referred to it as 'the' park like I was supposed to know what he meant by it but I really didn't. Going there would have been nice, but the sounds of the rain were soothing enough. I didn't mind sitting all curled up on the couch with him. Lane didn't have a TV, not that there would have been anything on it to watch anyway, so our main pass times were eating, cuddling, reading, talking or being intimate. Most of the time we were able to get all of those fit into a day quite nicely too, especially when Lane was at work.

We would talk about our future and what we both wanted it to look like. We'd discuss our past, as much as Jake felt comfortable to, anyway. Then we'd cuddle some more before getting hungry so Jake, most of the time, would go fix us both food. We'd eat then sit down to cuddle again. If we didn't fall asleep generally, the whole process would start over and be repeated. I didn't know what life was supposed to look like or what would have been normal, but whatever we were doing was precisely the life I felt like I wanted.

"Did you enjoy seeing your sister?" I had waited a couple of days to bring it up, since when he first got back from his mother's, he didn't seem happy with how it went.

"No," he said, tightening his grip at my waist. "The only thing I got from seeing her was realizing why I haven't wanted to see her. It's been over a year... I wasn't excited about going but I didn't know why until after we talked."

"Really? It was that bad? Why didn't you say anything about it on Friday when you got back?" I asked, surprised.

"It was actually worse than that but I didn't want to say anything to you 'cause I knew if it bothered me as much as it did, then it'd really bother you."

I moved my head from his shoulder to his lap so I could look up at him while we talked. "You can talk to me about it, baby... If it bothered you I wanna know, maybe I can make you feel better." I knew it was a long shot, but I was hoping I could get him to eventually believe he could open up more and not be so afraid to tell me things.

"It was a mess. I don't think talking abut it will fix anything, but I can try." He said, looking down at me as he stroked my hair. "Kat was there... Chelsey, Mom and Kat..." he looked away as he went on. "It was a set-up, like they freakin' planned it."

"Whaaat?" I said, drawling out the word, now really surprised, hoping he would go on and not hold anything back.

"Do you know what an intervention is?" He asked, looking back at me.

"Um, yeah," the term wasn't as readily available in my mind's dictionary as others but it sounded familiar enough that I felt like I knew what it meant. "Like when everyone talks to a family member to help them with an addiction... like drugs or something?"

"Exactly," he said as he brought his other hand up, placing it under my shirt to gently rub my stomach. "It was like they decided to all gang up on me, like they were having a freakin' intervention but it was for my Eva habit, not drugs."

"Oh my gosh... Are you serious?" I found myself getting more surprised the longer he went on.

"I wish I weren't." He looked back down and smiled but I could tell it wasn't easy for him. "It doesn't matter what they said though, baby... I told them I'm not leaving you and you're not leaving me!"

"You're not gonna tell me what they said?" It felt like we'd just gotten to the climax in the story and him not going on was a huge letdown.

"I don't think that would be a good idea," he said as he continued to stroke my hair.

"Okay…" I gave up. I knew it didn't matter what I said. I wouldn't be able to convince him. "Well, at least they don't know I'm a Gypsyin," I chuckled a little after I said it, "that could be bad."

He didn't respond. He'd been looking away and kept his eyes there like he was thinking.

"They don't know… right?" I asked, seeing he was still silent. I wondered if I was wrong and that was why.

"They shouldn't…" he finally looked back at me, "but, Kaleah, baby, I still don't know who got you those papers."

"Okay… well, let's talk about it. Maybe we can figure it out." I reached my hand up to rub his face. He'd shaved it clean that morning and didn't have his usual stubble. I enjoyed how soft it was. "Who could have found out that I'm a Gypsyin?"

"That's not our biggest problem. What bothers me is how they got your fingerprints."

"Okay… well, let's think about that. Hmm… Who could have gotten 'em?" I looked off into the distance, trying to think really hard.

"It could have been anyone. They could have taken them from a glass you drank out of. Who knows?"

As soon as he said it, I instantly thought of his father and how he insisted that I drink. "I think I know who!" I said suddenly. It made so much sense.

He started to respond when we heard the clicking sound of the elevator. I felt his whole body tense up as he looked over at it. "Lane's not supposed to be off work until tonight."

"Well, maybe he got off early," I said, trying to reassure him it probably wasn't a problem.

"No, it doesn't work like that," he said, gently lifting me out of his lap so he could stand. "Stay here."

"Okay?" The way he was acting was beginning to make me nervous even though I really hadn't expected there to be an issue.

"TC Agent Miles, it's MP Agents Snider and Gains. Please open the door." A man's voice came through the elevator speaker.

"Jake?" I said, no longer feeling like it wasn't an issue.

"It's all right, baby, I don't have a choice. I have to let them in. You'll be fine. I rank higher," he said as he went into the kitchen.

I heard the buzzing sound when the doors opened. I couldn't see them all that well but just like the voice from the speaker said, it was two men both in black uniforms similar to what Jake always wore.

"What is this about?" Jake walked right up to them, apparently not frightened or nervous at all.

"I'm sorry, Sir. We wouldn't be bothering you on a Sunday afternoon but we've had a complaint that we have to check out before we can be cleared."

"Of course, what and by whom?" Jake asked. He didn't have a shirt on, but still stood there, exuding all the authority of a commanding officer.

"A woman by the name of Katherine Burgess… She reported that you were harboring a Gypsyin without owner papers." The man said it and then looked over straight at me.

Jake didn't say anything at first, he just nodded. I could tell by the look on his face he was holding back a deep rage inside himself, but knew better than to let it be displayed in front of the agents that were just doing their job. "She *has* papers…" He said finally, very calm like.

"Okay, well we are going to need those when we take her in to verify." The agent that was talking acted like he felt extremely uneasy. He wasn't doing a very good job of standing still.

Neither of the men were as tall or muscular as Jake. That alone might have made them feel uncomfortable around him even if they did both have guns holstered at their sides.

"I'll show them to you. That'll be enough. You won't be taking her in." Jake said, ordering them without actually saying, 'that's an order.'

The agent talking made a gesture like he would allow Jake to move away to get the papers. Jake nodded, then before walking off to our room looked over at me. I couldn't distinguish by his look if he was trying to tell me it'd all be okay and I could relax or if he was actually just as concerned as I was.

As soon as Jake walked away, the second agent that hadn't talked yet made eye contact with me and started to walk over to where I was sitting in the living room.

"Ma'am, I need to see your arm please," he said it respectfully. I knew it wouldn't help Jake's position any if I tried to fight him, so I did as he asked and pulled up my sleeve to show him my arm. When he saw I didn't have a tag and I was a Gypsyin, just as he suspected, he moved closer. "Stand up," he ordered.

"Wait… Jake said you didn't need to take me. He's getting my papers!" I said, beginning to argue with him.

I could tell that wasn't the best thing to do, and he didn't take a Gypsyin defying him all that well. "Stand up, now!" He said lowering his tone and raising his voice.

"No!" I knew better but I couldn't help but rebel.

He didn't ask me again, he just reached down and grabbed a hold of my arm and pulled it toward him, twisting it in a way that would force me to stand or suffer the painful consequences of rebelling.

"You can't do this. Jake said you couldn't take me," I said as I began to wiggle and squirm. Then I felt him tighten something cold around my wrist, so I squirmed more so he couldn't get my other wrist to continue.

"Agent Miles," I heard the other agent near the elevator. "You need to get your Gypsyin under control."

I looked over to see Jake walking back into the room. When he heard what the other agent told him, he immediately looked over at me and saw the agent behind me trying to grab my arm. "Let her go, now!" Jake ordered as he swiftly moved over toward us.

"Miles!" The agent still standing by the elevator drew his gun and pointed it at him. "You know your rank can't change our orders when there's been a complaint."

Jake hadn't made it to me. He stopped suddenly and turned about halfway when he heard the other agent yell to stop him.

"We're taking her in one way or another so if you don't want your property damaged when you get her back, you better tell her to hold still." The agent behind me said, now speaking to Jake.

"Eva, sweetie…" Jake turned back toward me. "Stop!" I could tell it was hard for him to comply. He looked like he wanted to turn and attack the man closest to him but I knew he couldn't and why he was telling me to stop.

Everything in me, while I still had a free hand, wanted to turn around and beat the man, but I knew the best thing for Jake was to listen. "Okay…" I said, finally relaxing and dropping my other arm. The agent didn't waste anytime grabbing it and securing it tightly with the other side of the cuffs. "Owe," I complained. I must have made him angrier than I thought with how tight he made them and how much rougher he was being with me, since I hadn't complied.

"Now lower your gun, MP," Jake said, addressing the other man. "What unit are you taking her to? I'll follow."

"Pillar 14," the man said as he brought his gun back down and re-holstered it. "But I'm sorry; you know how we process them. You can't be there."

The man who cuffed me had taken a hold of my arm and was now pushing me in front of him to walk over toward the first agent next to the elevator.

"Eva," Jake looked at me as we slowly walked closer to him, "you're going to be okay, hear me?"

I nodded, trying not to cry as I was pushed past him.

"When I get her back, if I find out anyone has mistreated her, both of you will be on the strictest disciplinary action of your lives!" Jake warned, looking up at the first man.

He nodded like he heard and reached his hand out to take the papers from Jake. "Sir, we'll do the best we can."

"She better not fight me any more then," the other agent said under his breath behind me, likely low enough Jake couldn't hear him.

"Wait… I need to get dressed and I need my shoes," I said after a second, when I realized I wasn't dressed appropriately enough to leave the apartment. I wasn't wearing more than a thin nightgown that barely came down past my thighs.

"This is good enough," one of the men said but I couldn't hear which.

I looked up at Jake. I could tell he was trying to think about how to remedy the situation as well. He probably knew as soon as he walked away to get any clothes for me, the two men would take me away and it wouldn't do him any good. "You're not taking her out in the rain like that… I don't care what your orders are, if I don't get my Gypsyin back in the same health as she was in when you detained her, that's in violation to code 12 of the Gypsyin fair use law. She could get pneumonia wearing that in this weather." Jake spoke up like he knew he had to allow them to take me but he wasn't about to allow anything else.

"Fine!" the first agent said, sounding reluctant but willing to agree because he didn't want to argue about the laws. Maybe he didn't know them as well as Jake or maybe he knew Jake was right and he didn't want to risk the disciplinary action Jake had threatened.

Once he had agreed, Jake quickly turned to go toward our room.

I heard the one who cuffed me begin to whisper. "You know we don't have to listen to him. Right, Snider? I don't see why we can't just take her like she is."

"Because he ranks high enough to discipline our commander's commander, let alone what he could do to us… So, why don't you just keep your mouth shut and let me handle it?"

It wasn't long before Jake returned with my shoes and a jacket. He took my shoes, kneeled down and slipped them both onto my feet then stood up and looked at me. He pulled my jacket open like he was about to help me put it on until he remembered my hands had been cuffed. "Un-cuff her!" He ordered as he looked at the agent behind me.

"I can't do th—"

"Now!" Jake ordered again, not giving in to the agent's refusal. "You can put them back after I get her jacket on."

The agent didn't say anything else, then I felt him release the cuffs from one of my wrists then the other. As soon as I was free of them, I pulled my arms to my front and instantly reached up to rub the wrist that hurt worse.

"You son of a bitch!" Jake clenched his jaw and his face suddenly turned three shades of red as his eyes went from my wrists over to the agent behind me. "You've already bruised her. She's not far from bleeding!"

I looked down to see what he was talking about when I heard the first agent jump in when he saw Jake was upset. "Miles, it was an accident," he said as he turned his head to glare at the agent behind me. "She's small and fair. You know it'd be easy to do, especially when she was fighting with him... I'll re-cuff her myself." He said, trying to loosen the tension that was now between Jake and the asshole agent.

Jake relaxed a little, then looked back at me as he started to hold up my jacket again. "If they do anything to you that isn't appropriate, you let me know tomorrow when I come get you, okay?"

"Tomorrow?" I didn't understand what they needed to do that would take so long.

"It's okay," he said as he helped me put my jacket on and button it up. "The process shouldn't take longer than that. They have to follow protocol. They aren't allowed to do anything to you except confirm the prints on the paperwork are yours, though. If they touch you anywhere else, you tell me when I get you tomorrow, hear me?" He said it but started to look at Agent Asshole half-way through, like it was more of a warning for him than anything else.

"Okay..." I said softly.

He looked back at me, "You'll be okay, sweetie, don't be afraid. It's okay."

I nodded. I didn't know how much I was allowed to say where they could hear us so I didn't tell him I loved him and didn't expect him to tell me back for the same reason.

"Turn around now please," the first agent said, looking at me as he took the cuffs from Agent Asshole. I did what he asked and put my hands behind my back so it wouldn't be as hard for him, hoping he wouldn't tighten them as much if I cooperated.

After he finished putting them on me, he grabbed me by the arm like the other guy had then pushed me over to the elevator.

No one else said anything as we stood there waiting but when I turned to look at Jake one last time I noticed he already had a shirt on and was now putting on his uniform jacket. I assumed he must have picked them up when he went to our room to grab my stuff.

He mouthed something to me when he saw me looking at him but I couldn't tell what it was so he held up his hand, making the letter L. I was about to make some sort of look or gesture back letting him know I didn't understand when I heard the clicking, quickly followed by the buzzing sound. Before I looked away, I mouthed 'I love you' to him as well as I could, then turned to walk into the elevator with both agents.

20

COUNTERFEIT

"You're gonna cooperate and start answering my questions or your owner, Mr. Miles, won't be getting his property back when he thinks he will!" Agent Asshole was upset that I hadn't felt very talkative when he decided to start the processing paperwork. Neither he nor Agent Suck-up could help but argue with each other the entire way from Lane's. Apparently neither of them wanted to process me but knew someone had to do it so after a thorough game of rock, paper, scissors like four-year-olds, they decided it would be Agent Asshole's privilege.

"When did Agent Miles acquire you?" He continued with his questions.

"A few weeks ago," I didn't know most of the answers to what he was asking, but knew he wouldn't accept that if I said it so I figured I might as well make shit up.

"Oh, so you *can* talk… you little…" He sighed, stopping himself from calling me names but I could tell he still wanted to badly. "Good, now answer my last one. *Where* did he acquire you? Your papers don't have a GPF number."

"Look, AA, I don't even know what a GPF is, so you're gonna have to figure out that one on your own."

"What the—?" He scowled. "My name is Agent Gains, not AA… The GPF is your Gypsyin processing facility. Which one did you go through?"

"Oh… that… Well, why didn't you just ask?" It was hard, but I thought I was doing well, keeping myself from grinning as I continued to toy with him. I was actually starting to enjoy myself. "It's number 5493062978… 4"

"That doesn't even sound right, there aren't that many num—"

"You're right, I'm sorry…" I interrupted him. "Sometimes I get those wrong with all the other numbers I keep in my head. How many are there supposed to be again?"

He looked at me puzzled, then answered like he really was an idiot and didn't realize I was totally screwing with him. "Three!" He huffed.

"Ohhhh that number, right, right… right… Yeah, that's 123." That time it was harder not to smirk, but I caught myself early before I thought he saw it so I was still good.

"Ugh, okay," he said, sighing again as he slowly wrote down what I was telling him. It was obvious he was as thrilled about having to process me as I was having to be processed. "Now… State your full name just as it is on the paperwork."

"Why? You that lazy that you can't just read it?"

By his expression it was clear he did *not* like me calling him names. He immediately looked up from the papers and glared at me like he was hoping I would do it again probably so he had an excuse to use excessive force with me like he did with the cuffs. "One more time, Gypsyin, and I'll throw you back into the processing facility. See how easy it'd be for Mr. Miles to find you then!" He said it rather hatefully but I got the idea. "Now state your name!"

"Fine," I said as I thought about what name had been on there, "Ugh… it's Eva… Kaleah… no, wait… Jordan Kaleah," I couldn't remember. There were so many names floating through my head. I probably could have remembered if I wasn't under so much pressure to get it right. "Okay, wait, I know it…" I said as I was about to proceed with another guess before he stopped me.

"You don't know your name?" He said flatly, not enthused whatsoever.

"Well, why don't you get erased, have five different people tell you who you are and who you're supposed to be and then try to remember your name… plus the freaking GPF number? How 'bout that!"

He didn't argue with me, he just looked back down at his paper and went on, "Okay, hmm," he was mumbling, talking to himself, "I assume you've been sterilized, check… Uh, you just said you were erased, check…"

He didn't have a chance to ask me anything else before we heard a knock at the door and he turned to see who it was.

The door opened, and to my surprise it was Lane who walked in. I was about to greet him with excitement but then stopped myself when I noticed he hadn't made any facial expressions toward me like he knew me.

"It's Gains, right?" Lane didn't even look at me, he just went straight to addressing Agent Asshole, "I'm here to take the Gypsyin to have the prints verified."

"What? Where's Snider? He was supposed to do that."

"Yeah, well, Anderson brought me in 'cause he said you guys were short and needed help with processing. I don't know where Snider is. My job isn't to babysit other agents. You can ask him what he's been doing the next time you see him!" Lane spoke like a superior but I didn't know if he was or not.

AA hesitated for a second, then shook his head like he didn't care and motioned to me. "Fine, take her. But I'll warn you, you've got your hands full. She's a feisty li'l shit if I ever saw one. The agent that owns her is a high rank too. So if you decide to mess around with her just make sure that it can't come back on you."

Lane nodded as he looked over at me, still keeping his face like he didn't want me to act like I recognized him. "Sure thing," he said, looking back at AA. "Have you already done anything? I mean, I don't want no sloppy seconds."

I wanted to laugh when I heard him say it but I didn't. Lane probably didn't know it but he was a great actor, so good that I was almost convinced.

"No, dude!" AA scoffed at even the suggestion. "I'm serious! If you're gonna touch her like that, you better not get caught... This guy'll own your house, man!"

Lane chuckled as he looked back at me and started to walk closer. "He probably already does," he mumbled, then winked at me. "Stand up!" His voice suddenly morphed into a stern, forceful one.

Play along, I thought to myself. I was trying really hard not to grin, but it was difficult the more I thought about how much fun I could have giving Lane a hard time.

I did what he said, but very slowly.

"Let's go, Gypsyin, I don't have all freakin' day. Turn around!" He ordered me again, so I did what he said. Then I felt the same cold metal touch my wrist as Lane spoke again, but this time not to me. "If you're so worried about her owner, who the hell cuffed her last?" He sounded pissed.

"Yeah, that was me," AA said unapologetically. "She wasn't cooperating so... you know, shit happens."

"Ha... It does, doesn't it?" Lane said sarcastically. "You piece of f'in shit." He whispered under his breath.

"Which scanning room are you taking her to?" AA asked as Lane finished cuffing me.

"Four, you got the key?" Lane asked as he spun me around and pushed me forward toward the door.

"Yep, here." AA pulled his desk drawer open, then picked a small ring of keys out and handed them to Lane. "I'm serious too, man... If you're gonna do anything crazy with her just make sure you plan on erasing her again afterward. Me and Snider are the ones with our names on the file... I don't want that shit coming back on us, got it!"

"Yeah, don't worry about me, dude," he said reaching down again, "I'll take real good care of her, you'll see." The way he said it sounded like he was being sarcastic but I knew better. AA handed him the paperwork from the desk. Then Lane opened the door and pushed me out into the hall.

"Don't talk to me until we get in the room," he whispered after the door shut behind us.

I listened and didn't say anything. We walked past a few more offices and quite a few more agents when finally we arrived at a large solid white door with the number four on it and the words 'scanning room' next to it. Lane took the set of keys in one hand, still holding my arm with the other, and put them into the lock and turned them, unlocking the door. After we walked inside, he shut the door behind us.

"Lane?" I said, hearing the door click like it re-locked itself.

"Eva..." he was still standing behind me so I couldn't see his face but he said it oddly.

"What are we doing?" I asked, wondering what he was planning and how he even knew I was here.

"You wanna be erased again?" He asked still sounding off somehow, not like himself at all.

"What?" I didn't understand.

"You heard me!" He said as he let go of my arm and began to un-cuff me.

"You're scaring me, Lane. I don't understand why you're acting like this."

He didn't say anything. He just finished taking the cuffs off and turned me to look at him. As soon as I saw his face, I couldn't miss the huge grin he was wearing. "Gotcha!" He said, then began to laugh.

"You son-of-a... Jake's aunt..." I leaned in to hug him, then when he wasn't expecting it, I pulled back and hit him really hard in his gut.

"Owwwe, Kaleah!" He bent forward a little and held his stomach. "Okay... I probably deserved that... even if I did just save your life!"

I laughed, "Oh, Lane, I love you... even if you are a turd." I said, trying to help him stand straight again. "Thanks for coming to get me."

His smile quickly subsided as I said it. "Right... about that," he frowned. "I can't take you away. You will still have to wait for Jake to come and get you in the morning. All I can do is make sure the process goes smoothly until then and make sure no one *messes* with you."

"Oh," I'm sure he could see the disappointment on my face. "Okay... I was hoping you could take me home, but I understand."

"I'm sorry. I know that's not what you wanted to hear." He said, pulling me back in for another hug. "But you'll be okay. I'll make sure of it." He held me for a moment, trying to reassure me.

"How did you know I was here?" I asked, stepping back again to look at him.

"Jake knew where I was working today so he came to get me. He was really upset. I had to talk him down from going and ringing Kat's neck." He said, then looked down and turned toward the machine behind him. "I'm gonna put your prints in the machine and verify them like what we're supposed to do in here. But when we're done, I don't have to take you back for a while so we can talk more then. Why don't you take a seat?" He said as he pointed toward a little black chair in the corner with a metal bar over it, likely where they re-cuffed the Gypsyins.

"Okay," I said, looking at the machine. I couldn't really tell how it was supposed to work, but I trusted him so I didn't figure it would hurt or anything. It was sitting on a table and extended from one side of the room to the other. There were two large glass surfaces. One had a lid on a hinge that looked like it would cover it and the other had nothing over it.

"I know he said he didn't, but have Gains, Snider or anyone else done anything to you that you want to tell me about." He didn't turn around, he just kept pushing buttons and moving right then left, doing something else with the machine as he asked.

I didn't respond right away. I was thinking about the whole trip over from his house to there and what all they did and said that I might need to report. Agent Gains was such an asshole that I wondered what I could say to get him in trouble without making stuff up.

He turned to look at me. "They didn't, right?" His face looked concerned that it would take me so long to answer. "'Cause if they did —" I could tell he was getting angry. "Kaleah, tell me if they did!"

"No… no," I finally answered, trying to help him calm back down. "They didn't… other than my wrists, but Jake saw that. He couldn't do anything but he knows."

He relaxed as he took a deep breath in then nodded slightly. "Ok, good!" He said then turned back toward the machine. "Miles ranks so high he has to be careful what he does. He has farther to fall… But not me, I have nothing to lose, I'd kill 'em. You mean a lot to me, Kaleah. I want you to know that." He said as he continued to fiddle with the machine more.

"You're sweet, Lane." I said as I continued to watch him, "If I had a sister, I'd want her to be with you."

He chuckled still looking away, "If you had a sister, I'd want to be with her." He said softly, then paused, "but you don't, right?"

I laughed then I stopped to actually think about what he was asking… "I don't know," I felt a bit unsettled at the idea of not really having any clue about that part of my past.

"Don't worry about it." He said, finally turning toward me, "Come here now, it's ready."

He took the papers and placed them on the glass surface with the lid then closed it and motioned for me to stand in front of the other glass surface.

"Will it hurt?" I asked, seeing the machine looked so ominous.

"No, it won't do anything but scan. You'll be fine. Here," he said, taking a hold of my hand, "lay all your fingers flat against the plate. Your other hand too."

I reached up with my other one and made it mirror the first just like he said.

"Great, you look good. Now stand there just like that," he moved over to the end away from me to push a button.

The machine started making a loud vibrating noise, and I saw a bright, blinding light shine up through the glass. "Owe," I said, closing my eyes and trying to look away without moving my hands.

"Oh, yeah, sorry about that," he chuckled. "I forgot to tell you not to look at it."

"Thanks," I said sarcastically still keeping my eyes closed.

"Well, I haven't been in this unit for a few years now so it's easy to forget stuff. You understand," he said as he began to laugh again harder.

"You're funny, loser." I couldn't help but laugh with him. "At least

I forget things for a better reason than being old." I said, trying to get back at him.

"Hey now… I'm not that old. Besides, I'm younger than Miles and you don't seem to have a problem with him."

"I like older men. What can I say?" I shrugged, then grinned, still keeping my eyes shut.

"It's done. You can sit back down now if you want." He said as he placed his hand on my back, letting me know I could open my eyes again.

"Oh, okay." I turned to find the seat, which was still a bit hard to do since all I could see was a large blackish-blue cloud in the center of my vision.

"It shouldn't take long. The machine will tell me they match and you'll be good to go… It looked like you were really enjoying Agent Gains' company."

"Bull… shit… you mean Agent Asshole?" I asked, grinning even though I knew he wasn't looking.

"Ha… good one, yeah, I can see that." He moved over and took the papers back out of the machine then he folded them before he put them in his back pocket. "When I take you back in there, you have to behave yourself though, all right? Don't give that idiot a reason to use force with you again."

"Are you going to leave me alone with him?" I asked, wondering if that was where he was trying to take the conversation.

"I might have to, but I'll try my best not to. We'll see how it goes. Don't worry, I plan on staying close either way until Miles comes to get you tomorrow."

"Oh, ok… so you won't let them hurt me?"

"Not a chance," he said still looking at the machine. Then before he said anything else I could see his posture change. "Kaleah…" he said like there was a problem, "Do you know who took your prints?"

"Um, I don't. Why? Is there a problem?" I answered, but then continued, hoping more information might be helpful to him. "Jake and I were actually just talking about it right before the agents came in to take me. I hadn't had a chance to tell him but I thought it might've been Jake's dad since he offered me a drink in his study… I thought maybe he got them from the glass."

He turned to look at me as he listened. "Ugh, okay, well… shit…" His whole body was suddenly tense as he brought his hands up to scrub his face.

"What's wrong?"

"Neither of your hand prints match… It says they're unidentified, so they're not already in the system." His voice was tight with concern, as his eyes darted around like he was trying to think about what to do about it.

"Okay? Lane, you have to tell me more. I don't understand what that means and why it's a problem."

"Has Miles ever told you what happens if the prints don't match?" He steadied himself against the machine as he asked it.

"Uh… he might have. I don't remember. One time I asked him what would happen if you had the wrong prints. Like if he used another Gypsyin's prints for my paperwork and he said they'd hang me or something like that so I tossed the idea and didn't think about it again."

He swallowed before he continued. I could tell he felt uneasy and was verging on panic. "If they don't match, it's illegal. When you're processed at a legit GPF, they put your prints in a machine like this one. It doesn't get them wrong, you know? So… when I put them in to verify, they should all match identically. When they don't, the machine see's it and flashes an error code saying your papers are counterfeit. If they were verified, it would have printed off a page that I put in your report that tells them that you're all clear. Without that paper, Miles can't pick you up."

Counterfeit? "Uh," I couldn't make my mouth say what I was thinking, which was '*oh shit, oh shit, oh shit. What the hell does that mean?*'

"Yeah… it's a problem." He looked away as he scratched his head.

"Okay… What do we do then?" I hoped he had a great idea, since I was obviously clueless.

"I don't know… call Miles?" He was beginning to look pale.

"Lane? Are you all right?" I asked, seeing it was really bothering him.

"Shit, Kaleah, this is so serious... I don't even know how Miles does it. Every time stuff like this happens with you, he always acts so calm, like—" He stopped suddenly, looking at me as if he just realized something then slightly shook his head. "Never mind," he said, letting his face soften. "I see how... He does what he's gotta do 'cause he loves you. I've never understood that until now." He stood up with new determination and began to walk toward the door. "Here," he said as he tossed the cuffs to me. "Put these on around the bar in case someone else comes in. I'm gonna go call him. I'll be right back."

"Promise?" I asked now feeling a bit concerned that someone else might come in.

He hesitated, then smiled as he began to open the door. "Yes, I'll be back, I promise!"

21

SERUM ROOM

"He's not coming back… He doesn't really care about you!"

I hated that I was still hearing the voice. I tried everything I could to ignore it when I heard it. Sometimes it would work but sometimes I just couldn't fight it. It would win and take my mind to a hopeless and lonely place even when I didn't want it to. I sat there for what felt like forever, though it probably was no more than ten minutes when I heard someone put a key into the knob to unlock it then open the door.

"Hey… okay, we gotta go!" Lane swung the door open then shut it behind him. He seemed agitated, almost frantic, so I couldn't help but wonder what Jake had told him to do.

"Okay?" I didn't want to ask too many questions in case it might confuse him and make him forget important details about his plan of action.

"This is so screwed up… Ah, shit…" He was half talking to me and half to himself. He pulled the set of keys out as he walked over to me and started to fumble through them. I think he was looking for the one for his cuffs.

His hands were shaking. I couldn't move mine since I'd re-cuffed myself so I moved one of my legs over to touch his calf with my ankle, "Lane, it'll be okay, just calm down. Slow down a little and it'll be easier."

He looked up at me, then nodded as he closed his eyes and took a deep breath. He looked back down at the keys, and like magic he reached for the exact one he needed. "Here, we should hurry," he said as he used it to unlock the cuffs. His hands weren't shaking as badly now but there was still an urgency in his voice.

"What did Jake say?" I thought it might be a good time to ask finally.

"He was upset because he wants to come help you, but he can't. This is my unit though, so they won't suspect anything if I'm walking around with you."

"But he told you what to do to fix it, right?" I brought my hands up to rub my wrists again when the cuffs fell off.

"Uh, yeah well… it's ahh…"

"Spit it out, Lane!" I could see he didn't want to tell me.

"I have to take you to the room with the serum. It has another machine in it that I need to use." He said finally as he went over to the machine in the room we were in and quickly pushed a series of buttons.

"The serum room?" I asked as I stood up, thinking about what that meant and why he didn't want to tell me. "What is the… oh my god… no… no no no…" It finally hit me what he was referring to.

"Kaleah, don't worry. I'm not going to erase you. That's why I didn't tell you. Just calm down." He said quickly, then after pushing a couple more buttons the lights on the machine blinked a couple of times then went out as he turned around. "You'll be fine… let's go." He said as he started to walk over toward the door, then look at me with his hand on the knob. "Oh crap," he looked down at my wrists. "Ugh…" He swept his hand through his hair, clearly getting frustrated again.

I knew what the problem was, so I quickly turned around and put my hands behind my back.

"Thank you," he said from behind me as I felt him take the cuffs and move swiftly to put them back on. "Great, now let's go!" He took a hold of my arm, turned me toward the door, and opened it, then pushed me out into the hall.

We started walking back past where Agent Asshole's office was when I saw him spot us through his window and stand.

"Shit, Kaleah... when we walk by start acting belligerent if he opens the door and expects us to go back in. Tell him I did things to you if you have to, all right?" Lane whispered, "He needs to suspect that's why I'm taking you to the other room, so I can erase you."

"Okay," I said, keeping my eyes on AA as we walked closer to his door.

Just as Lane suspected, he opened it and stood there, waiting for us. "I'm guessing that went smoothly?" He asked like he didn't actually care and didn't want to be there, but was just doing his job.

"Help me, please..." I didn't hesitate. I was going to say more, but Lane interrupted me.

"I gotta take her to be erased," he started to laugh. "The key is on the same set you gave me, right?" He asked AA.

"Please, don't let him take me, please!" I said, looking at AA as well, trying to make it sound realistic.

He smiled, approving of what he thought Lane was about to do to me. "Ha... yeah, buddy, same set!" he said then grinned at me as we continued to walk by.

"Perfect," Lane said then pushed me harder like he couldn't wait to get there.

We walked past a few more offices until we turned down a long hall that looked empty except for one single door at the end.

"You're not gonna fight me anymore now, you hear me, Gypsyin!" Lane said again loudly as he pushed me toward it.

"You're enjoying this too much," I whispered over my shoulder.

"I never get to do this kinda stuff. Now I see why Miles has so much fun with you." He whispered back, sounding rather upbeat considering the circumstances.

I wanted to laugh at what he said but I knew better. When we made it to the end of the hall, he used the key to open the door, then push me inside and shut it behind us. I stood there and looked around. If the last room was ominous, this one was downright terrifying. It not only had a similar machine but bigger, it also had a table with restraints on both sides and a wall of cabinets that looked to be full of medical stuff.

"Lane?" I hissed.

"Kaleah, trust me… all right? I'm not going to actually erase you. Miles told me what I had to do… So just listen to what I tell you and you'll be fine… I'll get the paper I need, you'll leave here acting like I erased you and he'll pick you up first thing tomorrow morning."

"Eh, fine," I said, trying to make myself breathe, so I didn't pass out. All I could think about was what torture had happened in that room before to other poor Gypsyins.

After Lane removed my cuffs again, he walked around in front of me and stood there like he wanted me to listen to him, "Kaleah…"

"Lane…" I stared back, widening my eyes.

He swallowed hard. "You need to get on the table and let me strap you down, all right?"

I was stunned, speechless.

"All right?"

"The hell I will!" I said emphatically. I couldn't believe he would expect me to be ok with that. "Why?"

"Oh god, Kaleah…" He palmed his forehead in frustration. "Miles said you'd probably try to argue with me… There's more than one key to this room. If someone else comes in and sees you just sitting, watching me fiddle with the machine, don't you think it might look suspicious? Or if someone comes in and sees you laying there like I'm gonna erase you—"

"Fine!" I got the idea without him having to finish. "I don't like it though."

"I'm sure you don't, believe me, this is almost just as uncomfortable for me as it is for you," he said sincerely, holding out his hand, motioning toward the table. "I won't make the restraints tight, don't worry."

I walked over to the table, bounced to hoist myself up to sit on it, then lay down. "And Jake told you to do this?" I asked, confirming he knew about it and was okay.

"Yes..." he sighed. I could tell he wanted to get a move on it but I was slowing him down with my hesitance.

"Fine," I said, positioning my hands near the restraints so it would be easier for him to put them on me.

"Thank you!" He started at my left hand then moved to my other hand to buckle it before he went to buckle the ones at my feet. "None of them are too tight, right?" He asked after he finished the last one.

"No," I said, feeling awkward and extremely vulnerable.

"I know this is hard for you. I'm sorry... I'm gonna try to hurry," he said as he turned toward the machine behind him. "This will take me a minute. I have to calibrate it. Just close your eyes and take a nap. You like naps." He said with a nervous laugh.

"No... I'd rather talk." I continued watching him. "Tell me what you're doing and how it all works."

"Uh, all right." he was looking at a little monitor in the center of the machine. "This machine is similar to the ones at the GPFs. It can print out new papers once the Gypsyin has been erased. So it's like I can start all over again with you," he said as he moved to one side to lift a lever then back. "It takes a minute but once I get all the information put in, I will get you back up and bring you over here to put all your prints in."

"Okay," that didn't sound so bad after all.

"Do you want to go with the same name?" He asked, looking at the monitor again as he started to type something.

"I have a choice?" I thought that was pretty neat.

"Ah, well... since your last prints didn't match, and they were linked in the system with the name on the papers... yeah you might want to change your name."

"Um, okay... How about Elliceva?" I remembered Jake telling me that name meant something to me when we first met so I thought it might be a good one to use.

"Ah, okay..." he sounded skeptical. "That's kind of a weird name, but if that's what you want, I'll do it. I don't guess anyone has to actually call you that so… whatever," he shrugged and went on typing and mumbling to himself. "Address is my house… Uh, I'm sure you don't know your birth date so I'll just guess a year… How old do you feel?"

I thought it was funny he would ask, since I had no idea. "I don't know, seventeen?" I laughed.

He turned to look at me. "Nice try," he said as he chuckled. "I'm thinking maybe—"

"How old are you?" I interrupted him.

"I'm twenty-four," he said as he cocked his head and continued to examine me with his eyes, "you don't look like you're as old as me, though… I think you're probably closer to twenty or twenty-one. Yeah, let's go with that," he said, then turned back to the machine to type it in. "Okay… you've got brown hair… green eyes, and yes, you've been erased…" He stopped to laugh. "I'm not lying at least, since it doesn't ask when." He chuckled again. "All right… How much do you think you weigh?"

"I don't know… how much do you weigh?" I thought I could use him for reference.

He turned to give me an odd look. "Way more than you!" He turned back, "Ugh, I'm just gonna say 125 pounds… Okay, your height… uh, I'm thinking five-foot-seven… Now, what ethnicity are you? Hmm…" He turned around again to look at me. "You're about as white as they get." He turned back like he figured it out.

"What does that mean?" I felt a little offended by the way he said it.

"It doesn't mean anything, you're just white, so the only category on here for that is Caucasian… I mean unless you're feeling exotic. I guess I could change it for you…" He laughed.

"You're so funny," I said sarcastically.

"I know…" He sounded like he actually took it as a compliment. He didn't say anything else after that for another few minutes as he continued to type and move from one end of the machine to the other. Then, without any warning, the door opened, and a man dressed in a white uniform, not black, walked in.

After Lane immediately turned to see who it was, about to freak out again, he stopped, took a deep breath and acted normal. "Hey, Doc. What'cha doin'?"

The man was older and had a thick gray beard. Even though I had an idea who he was from the way Lane addressed him, instead of being more scared, I thought there was something comforting about the way he looked.

"Agent Gains said you might be in need of assistance with the injection." He looked over at me as he said it.

"Oh, um… nope, nope… I'm good but thanks… She's actually already been erased. You're a smidge too late." He laughed nervously. "I just beat you to the punch, doc. Like literally just beat yo—"

I cleared my throat nonchalantly, hoping he'd get the idea he was rambling.

The doctor nodded awkwardly. "Oh, well… would you mind if I saw the injection site then so I can sign off that it was done properly?"

"Of course… um," Lane hesitated as he looked over at me. "Actually, to be honest with ya, Doc, she was fightin' me so bad when I did it, I can't remember where I injected her… I gave her a small enough dose that she didn't go to sleep with it but I mean, either way, it's in her now so she's harmless." He shrugged, nervously talking quickly again. "If you want to undress her and inspect her for it, be my guest. I'm just gonna be over here working on the paperwork."

I glared at Lane after he said it, wondering what the hell he was thinking.

"Oh well, no, I trust ya. She looks good and healthy. I'll just put in the report that it went well, and you only used a small dose." The doctor said, then patted my foot a few times as he gave me a sympathetic look.

"Okay, well, thanks for coming to check on me," Lane said then looked back at me only then seeing my angry expression. I'm sure he was quite eager for him to leave.

"Okay…" The doctor slowly turned around and walked out, shutting the door behind him.

"You're dead meat, mister," I said in a low voice after I heard the lock click.

Lane grinned, "I didn't know what else to say. It was that, or let you really get erased. Which would you prefer?"

I didn't say anything else. I just looked at him with a scowl.

"Good talk…" He smiled again then turned back to the machine.

He wasn't there long when again we heard a knock at the door like someone else wanted to visit. "Oh my gosh!" he said as he turned around again. "No one's ever this needy until I'm doing things I shouldn't be doing…" he said under his breath as he slowly walked toward the door, opening it. "What do you want?" He asked the person who was standing there, irritated that he was being interrupting again.

"I'm just here to check on the Gypsyin." The man's voice sounded familiar. I think it was the second agent—Snider.

"She's fine! Look, all erased, happy, docile… I'm just finishing up the paperwork," Lane said, getting grumpy.

The man stepped in and looked at me. It *was* Agent Snider. I realized if I had just been erased though, then I shouldn't recognize him so I didn't act like I'd seen him before.

"Ah, shit…" He groaned, eyeing me.

"What?" Lane sounded slightly concerned.

"Didn't Agent Gains warn you about her owner? He's gonna be ticked if he gets her back and she's been erased again," Snider groaned, acting like he actually cared. At that moment, I realized how much of an asshole Agent Asshole actually was, since he never acted like it was all that much of a bad idea.

"Gains was the one who told me I could do it!" Lane pipped up, sounding rather defensive.

"Ugh, well, we all know he's an idiot. I wish you'd have waited for me." Snider said.

"Well, shit… What are you gonna do now?" Lane continued to poke at him, "I mean, I know it's not my name on her file, so…" he shrugged, "there're no repercussions here."

"Dammit!" Snider grumbled, sounding rather annoyed. "I don't know what there is to do…" He said like he was trying really hard to think of a solution.

"Was he pretty upset when you took her? Maybe if you didn't make her wait in the holding cell overnight and just gave her back after I'm done with the paperwork, he might not press charges..." Lane started to grin after he said it, then quickly bit his lip, stopping himself.

"Ugh, you might be right... Dammit, that idiot, you wouldn't believe the trouble he's got me in the last two months." Snider scratched his head.

"Oh yeah? I didn't realize Gains was that new." Lane continued.

"He's not!" Snider said suddenly. "He just doesn't give a shit anymore. His paperwork has been a mess. He's been overly forceful with the incoming Gypsyins... Ugh..." He groaned again.

"You know what..." Lane went on like he had a great idea, "If charges are filed, I'll make sure that they go under his name not yours... And if you think it'd help, once I get all the paperwork done, I will hand deliver her back to the owner myself. That way, if he *is* upset, I'll handle it so you don't have to."

"Aww, man, that sounds great." Snider relaxed a little, apparently relieved.

"Great! Well, I just gotta finish the paperwork. I'll bring it to you to sign off on it, then I can return her." Lane sounded like he was holding himself back from openly expressing his excitement.

"That's good... yeah, that's good..." Snider said, looking down, speaking to himself. Then he looked up at me again, "If she's done up here I can help you take her off the table."

"Uh," Lane hesitated, probably not sure if he should say yes or no, "Naw, I got it... but thanks. I'll bring her in there when we're done."

"All right," Snider said, then walked out, closing the door behind him.

"Shoo, I think I'm brilliant," Lane didn't waste any time praising himself as he turned around and went back to the machine. I knew he couldn't see it but I rolled my eyes. He typed in a few more things, then turned to walk back over to me. "Miles is going to be so happy when I bring you home today," he said as he started to loosen up the things holding my wrists.

"Oh, so you don't think he'll be mad that you got me erased

again?" I asked nonchalantly. I thought I'd mess with him since it wouldn't be hard for me to act erased when I got back to Jake.

"What?" He'd stopped loosening the ones at my feet and looked up at me, concern and confusion written all over his face.

I grinned, knowing he'd get the joke soon enough.

"Ugh," he said finally, relaxing, "don't play like that..." He finished at my feet then walked around to the front of me, "Here, let me help you down."

"I'm sorry," I said, not realizing it would bother him so much.

He placed his hands under my arms and helped me to the floor. "I know you're playing... I just... I hate it when Miles is upset with me, you know? So the last thing I wanna do is screw you up somehow before I take you back," he said as he led me over to the machine. "Here, place both your hands on it like you did last time."

"I really am sorry," I said as I did what he asked. "I didn't mean to take the joking too far... but with that stunt you pulled in the scanning room you kinda had it coming. You had me scared to death."

"I know..." He smiled. "Close your eyes this time."

It didn't take long to complete the same process as what we did in the last room, except this time the machine didn't flash any error signals, it just printed out new papers saying exactly what he told it to. After he got them, he looked over them quickly to verify they said what he wanted, then he folded them like the last ones and put them in his back pocket. He didn't cuff me again. He said it wasn't needed since everyone at that point knew that he erased me. So they wouldn't be suspicious anymore if I was walking around without them.

He took me down the hall and straight to Snider's office, totally skipping past Agent Asshole. Once we were in there, Snider seemed more than happy to sign whatever documents he needed to sign to send me on my way. He acted like the threat that Jake sent him off with had been more than helpful in keeping him in line. After we were done there, everything else seemed to go just as smoothly for Lane. No one else asked him any more questions and no one else tried to stop him when he walked outside with me, free as I had been the day we came to the city.

22

RELUCTANT REUNION

I didn't know what to expect when the elevator doors opened. Jake didn't know I was going to be back so soon so I thought it would be nice to surprise him. Lane agreed to go in quietly with me so I could do just that.

I tippy-toed in and looked around. I didn't see him anywhere.

"Go check your room," Lane whispered, "but if I see him first, I'm totally gonna toy with him."

"Don't give him a heart attack, Lane!" I whispered back then turned toward the hall that led to our room. I slowly slipped in close to the door then peeked around to see if he was in there but he wasn't. *Aww, dammit,* I thought. That would have been the perfect place to surprise him. I turned around and went the other way. As I thought about where he would be, suddenly I heard him talking like Lane found him first.

"What are you doing here? I told you to stay with her, Lane!" I slowly walked closer to the voice. Jake didn't sound happy to see Lane whatsoever.

"I'm sorry, man," Lane sounded like he was trying to talk fast. "Don't worry, I got her to the serum room. I got her some new papers, now she's just resting."

"*Resting?*" The voices were coming from the exercise room. I heard a loud clang of metal after Jake said it like he'd thrown something down. "Where the hell would she be resting and why are you here?"

"Calm down, man. I told you, she's fine… I mean there were a couple of times it was a close call but—" Lane didn't finish before Jake interrupted him.

"Henry, I swear to god, if you don't get your ass back down there and watch over her, I'm gonna kick it into next week!" Jake must have been upset; I'd never heard him call Lane by his first name before.

"Jake, baby," I said, finally peeking around the door. "Don't hurt him… He did well. I'm back!" I didn't want to give Lane enough time to hang himself or irritate Jake so much that he was beyond consoling.

"Kaleah?" His head snapped over to look at me with his jaw stuck open, genuinely surprised. "Oh my god, baby," he said as he pushed Lane out of the way with one hand and started toward me, "Come here!" I stepped inside the door as he made it to me and hugged me tightly. "Oh, baby…" Jake's voice cracked, clearly relieved to see me. "You're okay right, nothing bad happened to you?"

"I'm fine," I said, leaning away just enough to look at him, "except… well… Lane did threaten to erase me," I said with a mischievous grin as I looked over at Lane.

"That was a joke, Kaleah!" Lane quickly defended himself. "Miles… I was just joking!" He actually sounded a bit concerned.

"Don't worry about it though, baby," I said, looking back at Jake. "I socked him good in the gut so he knew not to do it again." I said with a huge grin, rather proud of myself.

Jake smiled back, "That's my girl," then pulled me in again to continue the hug. "Lane, I'm trusting you got everything done the right way… I don't have to be concerned that you brought her back so soon, right? We're not gonna have agents knocking on the door looking for her, thinking she's escaped… *Right?*" Jake asked loud enough for Lane to hear him, but hadn't released the hug to actually turn around and look at him yet.

Lane hesitated, probably trying to mess with him again, then Jake finally let go of me and turned to look at him. "Yeah, Bro, we're all good." Lane said, sitting down on one of his workout benches, "I did just what you told me to. I took her to the serum room, strapped her down, used the machine to get the paperwork I needed, then—"

Jake quickly turned to look at me and talk over Lane as he continued, "Sorry about the restraints part, baby," he said, then smiled and looked back at Lane.

"*Then...*" Lane said it in a way he knew he had been interrupted but was going on, "The doc came in and I thought, 'oh, shit,' but it was all good. I just told him if he wanted to find where I injected the serum he'd have to strip her down and check." Lane looked up at Jake and grinned before he tried to continue. "Then—"

"You're joking again, right?" Jake interrupted, not sounding pleased.

"No, he really said that!" I added not really caring if that time it got Lane in trouble.

"What the hell, Lane?" Jake said. The look on his face was like he was dumbfounded.

Lane laughed, "Well... I thought it was pretty brilliant myself... The doc's so old he doesn't have time for that, so I wasn't worried about it."

"Or he's so old, he'd make time for it!" Jake still sounded perplexed at Lane's decision-making, "What the hell were you gonna do if he took you up on it... stand there and watch?"

Lane hesitated, then smiled like he felt guilty, "Well it's not like I haven't seen her scantily dressed before. I mean, you two aren't all that discrete around here, ya know?"

"Whatever..." Jake gave up, probably seeing that Lane had a point, "Go on..."

"Okay, well then, after that, Snider decided to intrude. He was just concerned that he thought I'd erased her, though. He was pretty upset, like he wasn't too far from the shittin' himself kind of upset," Lane laughed. "You really scared him with whatever you said when they took her. He was so concerned you'd be pissed that she'd been erased on his watch, that it wasn't hard for me to convince him to bring her home to you early, like as a peace offering."

"Ah, ok, so that's how you did it, huh?" Jake asked.

"Yep… 'Cause I'm the man!" Lane was obviously very pleased with himself.

I was half expecting Jake's response to be him disagreeing since Lane had to call him to actually know what to do, but that's not what he said at all. "You really are, man! You got her back to me safe and sound and that's what matters. I appreciate it, Lane. I owe you, brother." Jake sounded like he was trying to be thankful without getting too emotional. "That's why you're my brother, man. I love you and I know you got my back when I need ya."

The rest of the day went as expected. Lane stayed and worked out, probably trying to release all the built-up tension of the last 24 hours while Jake took me to our room to get a quick shower then some cuddle time. He told me he was beyond upset that Katherine would do something so vile and intentionally try to have me taken from him. He hadn't decided yet how he was going to handle it or what he wanted to do. However, he knew he had to be careful since she was devious and could potentially have other plans that might be worse.

I asked if he thought she really knew that I was a Gypsyin since I didn't see any way that she would have and he said he wasn't sure. Though, he suspected she was just trying any tactics she could think of and hoping something would work and that time she just got lucky.

We talked about the machine, and how it didn't recognize my hand prints. It was obvious the papers were counterfeit at that point but we still didn't know who would have ordered them. Jake acted like he suspected who but didn't want to say, probably not until we had more evidence to back up his suspicion. He said he was going to look into it more and get to the bottom of it. Either way, knowing I had legitimate papers now, thanks to Lane, gave me a sense of relief that nothing like that should ever happen again and I was safe.

The talking we'd been doing quickly died down after we got out of the shower. I was tired, but I got the idea Jake had other plans and needed to reconnect. Even if we hadn't been apart for all that long, I could tell the stress of me being taken like I was had been hard on him and he needed more than just talking to help him de-stress. Most of the time he didn't show his emotions like other men, but there was one place where he would let himself go and allow himself to be vulnerable and that's when we made love.

"You know you're the best thing that's ever happened to me, right?" I didn't know if he was asking me that because he was just coming off of an amazing high or just what but it was sweet.

"Better than chocolate syrup on a sundae?" I was enjoying my own afterglow and didn't mind the reconnecting one bit.

"Better than the chocolate chips in a chocolate chip cookie," he said, trying to up the ante.

"Nooo," I said then gigged before rolling toward him to throw my leg over his stomach. "That's too much!"

"I meant every word." He brought his arm down and wrapped it around my back, pulling me tighter against him. "I don't want to wait to marry you, Eva…" He said softly.

"Then don't…" I smiled. I didn't know what that meant or how he could change anything but I didn't think it would hurt to spur him on in that direction.

"What do we need? Do we need a priest? Do you need a white dress? Flowers? How nice do you want it? Do you want it to be like the wedding we went to? Because—"

"No," I stopped him, "I don't need anything except knowing that it's legal… Well, a pretty white dress wouldn't hurt either."

He leaned over and kissed me on my temple, "You say the words, baby, and I'll get it… If you want an elephant, I'll invite a circus!"

"You're enough, Jake! I just wanna be yours, that's all." I said softly.

"All right… then I'll go tomorrow, first thing in the morning and talk to my dad. He'll know what to do, and how to do it."

"Can he make me a Coldier?" I asked a bit excited at the idea.

"Ha," he slightly chuckled. "Oh, baby, I wish he could... Money can buy a lot but that's not something that can be purchased."

"Oh, ok..." I said, trying to hide the disappointment in my voice.

"You're so cute, I just love you!" He said squeezing me again.

"I love you too, baby, more than you know!" I tried to squeeze him back with my leg.

The morning came early. I woke up to the smell of bacon being cooked, but figured Jake had already left when I looked over and didn't see him. He'd made his side of the bed all nice and tidy and tucked in like he usually did. I'm sure he would have given me a kiss goodbye as well if he hadn't been concerned about waking me up.

I didn't know how long it would take him to talk to his dad or when he would return so when I got up to get dressed I thought harder about what I wanted to wear. I wanted to look good for him when he got back, more like a bride, so I picked out one of my favorite white linen shirts and threw it on with the shortest jean shorts I could find. I figured they'd be perfect since I knew I had to cover my arms but not my long legs.

I took my ring off as I walked over to the mirror and set it down next to the sink; I didn't want to snag my hair with it. It was so pretty. Just looking at it made me think of Jake and how much I missed him already. As I picked up the brush to gather my hair into a ponytail, I let myself daydream. I couldn't help but imagine what our future would be like. I thought about what our house would look like, how many babies we would have. I got excited the more I thought about it all.

As I was finishing up my hair, I heard a loud noise from outside the room. I stopped for a second and looked away, trying to think about what it sounded like while waiting to see if I heard it again, but I didn't. The longer I thought about it the more I was concerned with what it could have been. *Did Lane drop something in the kitchen?* I walked over to my door and opened it.

"Lane? Was that you?" I yelled.

"Kal... ahh," I heard him. I couldn't tell what was wrong, but there was something definitely wrong.

I quickly left my room and went the direction I thought I heard him, "Lane? Are you all right?"

"No... stop," he yelled again. This time, I could hear his voice was coming from the living room.

"Lane, I'm coming, hang on." I didn't know why he told me to stop but I wasn't about to listen, not when he sounded like he needed me. As I got closer, I saw him. He was sitting on the floor, leaning backward, holding his leg. "Lane!" I came in from one of the entrances at the side of the room.

He looked over, shocked to see me, "No... Kaleah, go back," he said then looked back toward the elevator.

"What? No!" I said as I got closer. Then I quickly got on the floor next to him to look at what had happened, and what was wrong with his leg.

"Eva..." He looked at me with terror in his eyes, then back toward the elevator again, "Stop... just stop..."

I wasn't listening. I wasn't paying any attention to anything except his leg, what I thought happened, and what I could do to help fix it.

"Elliceva!" A man's deep throaty voice spoke from behind me, in the direction Lane had been looking when he wasn't talking to me.

I froze with my back to the voice still looking down at Lane's leg, "Lane..." I whispered, looking at his bloody leg, now terrified by who I knew was the likely culprit. "I think you've been shot... I don't want to turn around."

No sooner had I said it than the voice spoke again, "Eva... I'm here to get you."

I couldn't help but feel angry at the voice. "You shot Lane!" I screamed as I finally turned around to see who it was.

I was almost as shocked when I saw him as I was knowing he was even there to begin with. I didn't know who the man was, but there was something familiar about him. It was like I'd seen him before but I didn't know from where. "If I wanted to kill him, he would be dead." The man spoke matter-of-factly like he was used to getting straight to the point.

"Well, who the hell are you, and why are you even here? I don't need *gotten*!" I yelled it at him. I was upset that he had shot Lane and I didn't know what else to do but use my words.

"Eva… you're not this man's property. They've erased your memory so you don't recognize me but I'm here to take you back. I can reverse it; you can know who you were again."

"What? You're wrong… and you can go to hell before I go anywhere with you." I said, trying to stay focused and not let him confuse me.

"Ugh…" The man rolled his eyes while his shoulders slumped in frustration.

"Kaleah…" Lane whispered, "Run to my room and lock the door. If he follows you, I'll try to get up and call Miles."

I didn't turn to look at him; I didn't want the guy pointing the gun at us to know Lane gave me instructions. I put my hand on his calf and squeezed it a little so he knew I'd heard him.

I was about to stand up and run when the man spoke again. "Marcus never was able to bridle that mouth of yours…" At that moment, with those words, a memory of the man from one of my dreams popped into my head. This man standing here was the man who had tried to punch me. He was the one who I'd told I wasn't a cow and then he didn't pick me. I sat there thinking about what it meant and what I was supposed to do.

"Show me your arm!" I said, trying to buy time. I knew if he were to take me, I needed him to leave Lane with enough information to tell Jake so he would know how to find me again.

The man tilted his head and looked at me, trying to figure me out. "All right…" he said finally. Then he rolled his sleeve up and there they were—three small deep red circles all lined up in a row.

"Holy shit!" Lane gasped, "You're a… you're a Sicari…"

"I am!" the man said proudly, "and so is she!"

23

MORE THAN JUST A GYPSYIN

"What? Like hell she is!" Lane growled, not happy that the man would accuse me of something so atrocious.

"Look, I don't know why you're here, but I don't need saved. I know I'm not property. I'm choosing to stay here. This is where I wanna be," I said, speaking to the man.

I felt Lane as he reached over and took a hold of my hand. "You'll have to kill me before I'm gonna let you just walk out of here with her," he said. I could tell by the way his voice broke though, he was in a lot of pain.

"All right then," the man held up his gun higher to point it toward us again.

"Wait! No!" I moved over in front of Lane as best as I could without sitting in his lap. I believed the man actually would have shot him again if he felt like he needed to.

"You're still loyal… nice to see some things don't change," the man said, slightly lowering his gun so it wouldn't still be pointing at me. "But, Elliceva, Hun, I'm taking you out of here with him dead or alive, so if you don't want him in a casket tomorrow, you need to get up and walk over to me. Do I make myself clear?"

"Why the hell would I go with you? I don't even know who you are?" I said still sitting in front of Lane just in case he decided to be brave again and get himself really shot up.

"That really breaks my heart…" The man said it like he half meant it but was also being sarcastic. "Why, you're one of the best young Sicari I've seen straight out of the academy… This isn't the kind of life you were made for. You're a fighter, Eva!" He genuinely sounded troubled by who he saw I was now.

"That still doesn't tell me who you are…" At that point I didn't know what else to do but stall and either hope Jake returned in time or try to talk the man out of taking me.

"You're right, I apologize… My name is Reagan. That's all I can tell you right now until I reverse your memory wipe, then you won't need me to tell you anything. You'll know enough at that point, everything in fact." Despite him already shooting Lane, he was acting very polite, almost too polite. I wondered if it was a ploy to persuade me to freely go with him.

"Kaleah, don't listen to him, Jake wouldn't lie to you." Lane whispered.

"I know," I said quietly back so he alone could hear me, then I spoke louder to talk to Reagan again. "I appreciate you trying to save me since we apparently have a past together but I'm happy here… so you can leave now."

"Eva, you don't understand… I can't do that… You need to come with me. I don't have a choice. This was my mission." Reagan said now relaxing more and lowering his gun even further.

"Your mission? To come and get *me*? Who the hell wants *me* enough that they'd send you to—"

He didn't let me finish before he interrupted. "You don't even know how special you are, do you?"

I didn't say anything at first. I just looked at him, perplexed by what he was telling me. *Don't let him bullshit you with fancy talk, Kaleah,* I thought to myself. "No…" I said finally, "So you're not like an ex of mine?" It was the first thing I'd thought to ask.

"Ha… You really don't remember anything…" He sounded

amazed again at my lack of memory, although I thought we'd already covered that subject thoroughly.

"No, Reagan, I don't know shit!" I got the idea he wasn't about to shoot me so I could speak to him however I wanted.

"Kaleah…" Lane whispered again.

I turned away from Reagan to look at him. "Oh my god, Lane," I said, looking down at his leg. I had no idea what I was looking at but it looked like a lot of blood that was all over the floor under him.

"Kaleah… Don't leave… you can't go with him… please…" He begged, his eyes full of pain and grief. "I can't lose you…"

"Reagan, look what you've done. He's gonna bleed to death!" I yelled so he could hear me from behind, "I'm not going anywhere with you if he dies!"

"Oh, Eva," I could hear Reagan closer to me, "you've always been so dramatic… It's only his leg, and I missed the artery. It could be way worse. He'll be fine. We need to go now though, so come on, get up!"

"You can't, Kaleah…" Lane said again sounding desperate as he tightened his grip on my hand.

"Okay…" I mouthed so he could see it. "Reagan, I need to stop the bleeding!" I shouted, my eyes still focused on Lanes.

"Ugh, Eva… I swear," Reagan sounded like he was getting tired of the exchange.

I turned back around to address him. "Look, if you know me as well as you say you do, then you know that I don't go anywhere I don't wanna go, not without a fight, so tell me what to do! I'm not gonna let him sit here and die."

"Fine… Will you come with me if I let you help him?" Reagan asked, then squinted his eyes, trying to catch if I lied.

"Kaleah, no!" Lane moaned. I turned back to look at him. "Please, you can't," he said like he hadn't really thought about the impossibility of what he was asking of me.

"Tell me, Reagan, tell me how!" I said, looking down at Lane's leg.

"Kaleah…" Lane pleaded, fear and disappointment written all over his face.

"I have to, Lane…" I said as I started to tear up. "I'm so sorry." I knew he was trying to be brave for me but it wasn't his decision, it was mine, and I wasn't going to let him die just for Reagan to eventually take me away, anyway. I continued to whisper to him "I'm sorry. Tell Jake how much I love him, will you? I love you too. That's why I have to do this." I didn't let him argue with me after I said it. I turned around and looked at Reagan again, waiting for him to show me what to do.

"Here." Reagan had already removed his belt and was now reaching down to hand it to me. "Take this and cinch it as tight as you can around the top of his leg." I reached to grab it but he held on as he looked at me in the eyes. "If you take this, you'll go without a fight, clear?"

Somewhere in the back of my head said, '*do what you have to do, you can always fight him later to get back,*' so I nodded. "Clear…" I said, agreeing to his terms.

I took the belt and turned back toward Lane who had now shifted to laying on his back. "Lane…" I tried to keep talking to him as I arranged the belt under his leg. "I'm sorry, Lane!"

"Kaleah… You're not a Sicari, he's lying to you…" He said trying to lift his head to look at me.

"Just lay still." I pushed his torso down with my hand as I continued with the belt. "It doesn't matter what I believe, I'll come back, all right? He can't keep me forever." I said it loud enough for Lane to hear, which was probably loud enough for Reagan to hear as well but I didn't care.

"That looks good," Reagan said behind me. "Now, let's get going."

"No, it's not enough!" I was still trying to do whatever I could to stall, even though I didn't expect it to really help any. "I need to call for someone to come help him. When we leave, he could still bleed out." It was honest, but I knew I had ulterior motives so I said it hoping to sound convincing.

"Ugh… dammit, Eva! You were never this soft before. Do you even realize how hard it was for me to get into this city? Getting you back out is gonna take time too. Time that we're quickly running out of." Reagan started to complain but I could see through it and knew he'd let me have whatever I asked for just so I didn't make it hard on him when we had to leave.

"Lane…" I said totally ignoring Reagan's rant, "What's Duke's number?" I knew Reagan wouldn't know who I was talking about so I didn't have to worry about being so open about it in front of him.

"Kaleah… you can't…" He said again still trying to convince me my life was worth more than his.

"Dammit, Lane! Please…" Feeling emotional, my voice cracked at the high pitch. I really didn't want anything to happen to him. "Give me his number. Jake will come for you and you're gonna be fine… Okay, I promise!"

He started rambling the numbers off. As soon as I heard them, I ran over to where he kept the phone in his kitchen. It wasn't long before Reagan was right behind me. He reached down and pressed his hand against the phone so I couldn't pick it up. "Eva… I'll allow it, but the moment you're done with the call, we're leaving. Don't try anything! If you think you're gonna pull one over on me and have someone come and save you, I'll shoot 'em and I'll go back in there and shoot Lane too, hear me?"

Shit, I thought still keeping a straight face, acting like he didn't just foil my plan. "Okay… fine," I said, agreeing. "Lane," I yelled back out, "say the number again."

As he repeated it, I pushed each of the numbers on the dial pad, then waited for it to ring through. I looked up to see Reagan standing in the doorway monitoring Lane while still staying close enough to stop me from doing anything that would keep him from taking me.

"Hello?" an older man's voice answered. It sounded like Jake's father.

"I need to speak with Jake. It's urgent." I said, beginning to feel frantic. I wasn't sure what the hell I was going to tell him that would help him save both me and Lane at the same time.

"Kaleah?" Jake asked like his dad handed the phone straight to him. "What's wrong, baby? Are you all right?"

"Lane's been shot… He's bleeding a lot. He needs help!"

"What? By who… Are *you* all right?"

"Jake," I had to pause so I wouldn't cry and waste time speaking with him, "I'm sorry, baby, I'm so sorry. I love you! He needs your help. Please hurry!"

"Eva, I—" I didn't get to finish hearing what Jake was going to say when Reagan walked over and pushed the click-y thing on the phone to end the call.

"Times up, let's go!" He said not sounding the slightest apologetic.

"You're an asshole." I didn't know how he would take it but I didn't care. I said the first thing that came to me.

He smiled, "That's the Eva I know, see you're still in there." He said as he took a hold of my arm. "You're going to come with me willingly like you promised." He tugged it toward him as he took me over to the elevator. "'Cause Eva doesn't break promises."

"Oh, we're taking the elevator?" I said, looking at him with surprise. I didn't know why I said it or why he shouldn't use it but I thought if I had a chance to confuse him, I was going to take it.

"Nice try," he said as he leaned in to push the button to call for it.

I turned around to look at Lane again. "Can I at least say goodbye? I love him," I said, looking at Reagan. He didn't know it was a sister's love, but I was still trying to do what I could to stall. At the same time, I really did want to say goodbye.

"Fine, but you'll owe me one when you get your memory back," he said. "You have until the elevator is here."

I tried not to act too excited even though that's exactly how I felt. I was also pretty surprised he trusted me so much. I looked around quickly as I walked back in toward Lane; I was wondering where his gun was. I didn't see it and I knew I was running out of time so I scrapped the last ditch effort idea and figured I would just use it to say goodbye like I agreed to.

"Lane…" I kneeled down on the floor beside him.

He opened his eyes and looked up at me. "Kaleah, you're so stubborn… Thank you…"

"I'm sorry. I couldn't let Jake loose you… I don't want to lose you either!" I tried to say it quickly since I didn't know when the elevator would ding and Reagan would pull me away again.

"I love you," he said it softly, looking up at me with his bright blue eyes. "I meant it when I said I'd die for you, Kaleah…"

My eyes began to water as I sat there listening to him. I reached down and grabbed a hold of his hand. "I know…" I could barely get any more words out. "But I'd *leave* for you… So that's what I gotta do… okay?"

He nodded, his eyes beginning to water as well. "We'll find you, I promise!"

"Okay…" I said, trying to force myself to smile through the tears when I heard the clicking of the elevator.

"Elliceva!" Reagan shouted, knowing it would be enough to remind me of our deal.

"I love you too, Lane, goodbye…" I said, staring down into his eyes, then leaned in and kissed him on the cheek. I released his hand and got up to walk back toward Reagan.

He'd walked into the elevator and was standing there waiting for me.

"I don't know if I liked you before but I really don't like you right now," I said, scowling as I stepped onto it with him.

"Oh, you'll love me again," he said sarcastically as he leaned over and pushed the button to take us to the bottom floor.

"Where are we going?" I wanted to try to get as much information out of him as I could just in case I had an opportunity to use it against him.

"The Praetorium," apparently he wasn't a man of many words.

"What's that?" I asked. Jake hadn't educated me very well on the ways of the Sicari so I felt pretty clueless.

"Are you serious?" Reagan said, shocked. "You can't be a Sicari and not know what the Praetorium is."

The way he said it made me think. I wondered if I actually believed him or not. *How can I be a Sicari if I didn't have a tag?* I also wondered if Jake knew that's what I was or if he'd be upset when Lane told him. The more I thought about it all the more confused I felt. "I can't be what you say I am, I'm just a Gypsyin," I said, pulling up my sleeve to show him.

"Ha…" He must have thought that was funny for a reason I wasn't aware of. "You're so naïve, it's cute… But don't worry, I have what you need to fix it."

The elevator buzzed, and the doors opened to the garage under the building. As we walked out, I was hoping to see someone there and that I could yell out that I was in trouble but as I looked around; it didn't do me any good. We were alone.

"What do you mean you have the stuff to fix it?" I asked still keeping an eye open in case I saw someone.

"Both the Coldiers and the Sicari have a memory erasing serum…" He said as he guided me over toward a black jeep. "The serums aren't the same. Ours isn't used for long-term memory wipes like they use theirs for. Ours was only created for field ops. We use it to temporarily put someone out… make them cooperative, you get it. Then when we take them in, we give them the antidote so they'll talk… Honestly, it makes interrogation so much easier." He opened the door and motioned for me to get in.

"But how do you know which serum I took? Your antidote won't work if it's the Coldiers," I asked as he shut the door behind me then walked around the front of the vehicle to get into his side.

"That's a great question…" He said as he leaned over and began to rummage through a bag in the back seat. "How do you think I found you?"

I didn't know how to respond. "Uh, I don't know." His was a good question too.

"Let me explain something… You don't need a tag on your arm, you had the rare privilege of getting a tag in your head… I know it sounds crazy, just hear me out," he continued talking while still messing with whatever he was doing in the back seat.

"The tag in your head sends the Praetorium a signal telling us where you're at, it's a tracker essentially… Well, if you got the Coldiers' serum running through you, it blocks that tracker…" He finally turned back around in his seat and relaxed as he continued to talk to me.

"When your tracker came back online, I used it to trace you. I just needed your address… And what would ya know; it popped up in the system last night right there next to your name. I for sure thought shit, if you were in the system, then they'd probably erased you again with their serum. But nope, your tracker didn't go out… So then today I go up there looking for ya. You can't remember me, but your tracker is still on… Boom, everything clicked. You were erased last with our serum." He smiled as he finished.

"Okay, I guess that makes sense…" I was still trying to digest it all when he began again.

"So, believe it or not that's a great thing. It makes no sense whatsoever but I don't care. I needed to find you and get you back… You got some info up in that little head of yours that is pretty valuable and we need it. And now I know when I give you the antidote you'll remember everything again. It's perfect!"

As soon as he said it, I remembered what Jake had told me about the Sicari thinking I knew something and that's why they were coming for me. "So you just want me for the intel?" I asked, hoping he'd be honest with me.

He smiled, "Oh no, I don't want you to get the wrong idea… You're of way more value to us than the intel. But don't worry, as soon as you get your memory back, you'll want to give it to us. That was your job."

I sat there trying to think about everything he was telling me and make it make sense in my head when, all of a sudden, I saw him move quickly. At the same time, I felt a sharp stabbing pain in my leg.

"Owe, what the hell?" I yelled. He was so fast I thought I knew what he'd just done, but it was a blur.

"Don't worry, it's just a li'l more serum for you… It'll make you feel nice and peaceful. That way, we can make it back without any trouble."

"You son of a bitch!" I wanted to reach over and strangle him but I could tell I was already getting dizzy and feeling like I was going to pass out.

"Oh, Eva… you know when we first met I couldn't stand your mouth, but now… I've missed you, I really have!" He reached over and pulled a lever on my seat to lay it all the way back, "Here, you'll be fine. Just take a little… long… nap. We'll be there before you know it."

Jake and Kaleah's love story continues with book four of the ERASEHER series - Weaving Whispered Secrets. CLICK HERE to download now.

A note from Sara…

"The main thing I want my readers to get from my books is that no matter how broken and flawed you are, you are still worthy of unconditional love and no matter how weak you feel, there is still strength inside you." - Sara Nichol Quincy

ABOUT THE AUTHOR

SARA NICHOL QUINCY is a website designer and novelist born and raised in Indiana. She's a mother, wife, and entrepreneur. The ERASEHER Series reflects her passion for writing romances that are sexy, twisty and edgy. Add in a little dystopian suspense and a touch of crazy and you have yourself an epic love story that only she can tell.

To read more of her personal story and see what other books are in the works, you can visit her website at:

SaraNicholQuincy.com

There you can subscribe to get new release updates and exclusive offers!

Plus… only subscribers get:
- Launch date perks (1st week sales get 20% off!)
- Cover reveals before launch date!
- Exclusive Bonus Chapters that aren't available
   anywhere else!
- FREE books! (When available)

- ARC Reader offers for new book series and much more…

Got a question or comment about her work? She'd love to hear from you. Reach her anytime at **Sara@SaraNicholQuincy.Com**

Thank you again for taking your time to read Hearing Hidden Voices. Please consider leaving an honest review. It would help immensely!

facebook.com/saranicholquincy

twitter.com/SaraNQuincy

instagram.com/saranicholquincy

tiktok.com/@saranicholquincy